DOLLAR BILL

A novel By JOY

This is a work of fiction. It is not meant to depict, portray or represent any particular real persons. All the characters, incidents, and dialogues are the products of the author's imagination and are not to be constructed as real. Any resemblance to actual events or persons, living or dead, is purely coincidental.

Published by Triple Crown Publications
P.O. Box 7212
Columbus, OH 43205

Library of Congress Control Number: 2003110361
ISBN 0-9702472-9-X

Content Editor: Clifford Benton (Audacity Literary)
Grammer Editor: Angela Reese (Angela812@msn.com)
Cover Model: Vincent M. Ward (www.vincentmward.com)
Photographer: Al Johnson (magichands2K@yahoo.com)
Graphics Design: www.ApolloPixel.com
Consulting: Vickie M. Stringer & Shannon Holmes
"The Gift" on page 167 used courtesy of Shelby M. Giles

Printed in the United States of America

This book is dedicated to my Uncle John Allen Davis Of Columbus, Ohio (R.I.P. 2003)

Damn, I'm missin' you

AKNOWLEDGEMENTS

My grandparents, Mr. and Mrs. Oliver Edwards, who believed in me and supported me without question.

Daddy, what can I say???? I'm daddy's little girl. Thanks for telling me how proud you are of me EVERY TIME we talk

Vickie and the TCP family, who is responsible for my first book deal and those other ones too ;-) There are no words strong enough and a mere "thank you" would be an insult.

My PR firm, Down to Earth Public Relations (Earth Jallow). We did it! All those years of working for me on the strength of belief instead of the almighty $ finally paid off.

Nick Ross, my son and daughters-MY EVERYTHING. Thank you for allowing me to do me and get the dang on thing done! I love y'all...live-breathe-and would die 4 y'all.

And although you had no idea you were inspiring me, Cheryl. Just know that you have inspired at least one person in life, me, and you didn't even know it. Imagine how many others you have inspired. Keep doing you (and keep writing those raps…what happened?). It's never too late to get into the game. Look at me………..)

For Trini of Chi/Gary, thanks for being my road map

Uncle Billy, Thanks for your insight and terminology

Thanks, Sissy, Angie and Uncle Johnny for always offering me your extra ends towards those printing orders in my self-publishing days.

Thanks, mom, for everything

Terri Deal, my hair stylist, Thanks for repairing my hair after months of my pulling it out trying to meet writing deadlines

Table of Contents

"I once asked God for the world. It was placed upon my shoulders. I suppose that means it is mine."

- The Author

Chapter 1

Popped Cherry

"Where the fuck are my boys?" Dollar thought to himself as he held Cartel and his two partners at gunpoint. The four of them, each with their own degree of fear, stood terrified in the middle of Woody's Garage. Way down under in that place called hell, Satan and his advocates were probably taking bets on whose heart was beating the fastest. Niggaz are always loyal at entertaining the devil and his advocates. This situation was no exception.

Dollar nervously handled the black semi automatic as he aimed it at the three men.

"I swear, not one of you bitches better move," Dollar said to the men. Not taking for granted whether or not Dollar's word was bond, the men obeyed as beads of sweat expelled from their foreheads and could be heard hitting the cement ground of the garage like water droplets from a leaky faucet in the middle of the night.

"I bet your punk ass don't even know how to fire that gun," Tone, Cartel's big mouth, big Jay-Z lip having partner, snickered. Although scared as hell, he had to test Dollar. He had to find out if Dollar was pussy in dick's clothing.

"You can probably hardly handle your own dick when you piss, let alone a gun."

Before Tone's chuckle could completely spill from his mouth, a bullet escaped the barrel of Dollar's gun and whirled pass Tone's dome. Dollar just had to fire off a warning shot to let them muthafuckas know that he meant business. The bullet soared through the air, piercing the red can of paint that was sitting on a work shelf behind where the three men were standing. The red paint from the can oozed on the floor in sync with the trail of piss that was now running down Tone's leg. Tone felt the slight breeze the bullet produced as it whizzed by him. It was as if the kiss of death had been blown at him.

"Now what, you bitch ass hoe?" Dollar said, surprising his own self that he could handle a gun. When he packed the piece, he never had any intention on actually using it.

A smile crept across Dollar's full lips, the smile that was a cross between a grin and a pout. The right corner of his mouth would slant upward and the left slanted downward. This was his "I'm that nigga" smile.

Not wanting to get too confident, Dollar kept at a couple of arm lengths in distance from the men. He had seen enough action movies to know that the closer he was to the perspective victims without pulling the trigger, the more chance he had in lodging the bullet in his own skull. The slightest flinch made by any of the three dead men standing ignited a reflex causing Dollar to simultaneously point the gun at each one of them. Back and forth from one to the next the gun steered.

The steamy stream of sweat occupying Dollar's hand made it a challenge to keep a firm grip on the gun. It soon became the weight of a cannon. Dollar was squeezing his hand so tight around the handle that his nails punctured through the flesh of the pit of his palm. The stinging from the sweat hitting the open cuts made Dollar feel as though he was holding a fistful of bumblebees.

Underneath Dollar's baggy Levi blue jeans, his long legs had a faint tremble.

"*If these niggaz bum rush me, I'm fuckin' dead,*" Dollar thought. "*I might can hit one or two, but all three*?" Dollar was starting to scare his damn self with all of the negative thoughts he allowed to constipate his mind.

Dollar couldn't help but wonder if Cartel and his dudes could smell the fear rising from up out of his pores. If not smell it, he wondered if they could see it rising like the vapor from a hot apple pie fresh out of the oven. Dollar had on his game mask over top of his timid face, but he still couldn't help but wonder if they could sense that he was just a pup at this robbin' niggaz shit. He stood before these unlawful tycoons a virgin to the game, like a pussy that had never been fucked.

"Where the fuck are my boys?" might as well have been tattooed on Dollar's forehead. He gazed over at the door a thousand times hoping to see them burst through. Through Dollar's actions, Cartel and his partners expected the company of some uninvited guest real soon. Not soon enough for Dollar though.

"You expecting someone?" Cartel finally found the balls to speak through his thick mustache. He sensed that Dollar was a rookie and one false move, or word for that matter, might compel his index finger to become trigger-happy. At the same time, from past experience, Cartel felt that if he pet the young pup on his head a few times, he could find a way to gain his trust and turn the tables.

"Where are your friends when you really need them?" Cartel said in a friendly tone, twitching his nose as if it was itching.

"Shut the fuck up!" Dollar replied. He couldn't focus on the door and conversation. He wasn't, yet, multi-taskful.

"Young blood," Cartel said pushing his luck. "I been where you at now, literally. I know what it's like to want to have shit with limited options of getting it. But, yo, you're making a mistake here. I'm not the enemy. I can help you. The little shit you might yank off of us tonight ain't nothing compared to what I can make happen for you."

Dollar appeared to be comprehending Cartel's words.

Cartel slowly eased his hands down until he had a straight shot of his freshly manicured nails. "All I wanted to do was help you get where I'm at. I still can help you. Like I said, young blood, I been there, so I can't hold this against you. I won't hold this against you. We can do this shit. We can do it together."

Slowly Cartel's hands dropped just below his chin. His partners prayed he could continue stroking Dollar long enough to go for his piece. All the while Dollar was fixated on where his own partners could be.

"Maybe they can't find the garage?" Dollar thought. *"Maybe they bullshitting around or arguing or something. I know they didn't bitch out. Naw, them niggaz just lost."*

It was very possible that Dollar's partners were lost. Woody's Garage sat way back in an alley off of Cleveland Avenue in Columbus, Ohio near a housing project notoriously known as Windsor Terrace. The black and orange *Sorry We're Closed* sign was a permanent fixture on the building's entrance door. The garage was regularly closed to unsolicited guest but always welcomed those with an appointment. Cartel, who ran a shiesty hustle out of the Garage, had penned in Dollar to meet with him that night. Dollar had driven in from Indiana in order for Cartel to make good on a transaction in the matter of a stolen vehicle.

Cartel was the mastermind behind a car theft ring. Not so much a master mind as a man who managed to induce some young and dumb thugs into doing his dirty work. For less than a 20% cut of the street market value, these wanna be Dons would heist whichever vehicle was Cartel's flavor of the month. The other 80% must have gone towards what is known as administrative fees. Little niggaz didn't care though. A quick grand for their misdeed satisfied their adolescent appetites for life's material wants. If they weren't lazy and put in work every week, a quick grand averaged out to $52,000 a year. How the fuck they never managed to make a come up out of the hood was beyond insane. Dollar was determined to get up out of the ghetto and he planned on taking his brother and his mother with him.

Standing there with his gun aimed, Dollar knew the move he had made on Cartel was foul, but a nigga had to do what a nigga had to do. He was sick of the grimy ass lifestyle him and his mother and brother were living on the streets of ghetto ass Gary, Indiana. He had to do something. He had to make this move.

"*Yeah, this shit that's going down right here is for my peeps,*" Dollar tried to convince himself. As he stood there in Woody's garage, nervous as fuck, thoughts of growing up in Gary, Indiana spun webs in his head. He didn't want to struggle financially anymore, or see his mother struggle anymore for that matter. Dollar thought about having watched his mother leave their one bedroom apartment for work at six o'clock in the morning and not return until after ten o'clock at night. At one point or another, she had managed to work for every fast food chain in America, as well as a few hole in the wall neighborhood restaurants, just to keep a leaky cracked roof over Dollar's and his younger brother's, Klein, heads. On most occasions she would work at two and three joints at a time. Once she got herself fired from Burger King because she kept referring to the kid's meal as a Happy Meal.

In spite of all the long work hours, Dollar's mother made sure that she did everything she could to see to it that he and his brother did well in school. It didn't matter how late she got in at night; going over homework was a must. Seeing their mother work so hard was probably what kept the two latchkeys kids out of trouble the duration of their youth. The last thing they wanted their mother to have to worry about was two bad ass boys. She already had to tolerate the white man's franchise all day long.

When Dollar was about ten years old, one night his mother didn't come home from work as expected. They couldn't afford a phone in their household so it's not like she could have called to give a reason behind her tardiness. Dollar was too afraid to go out and use the corner store pay phone to call the police. He feared the boys in blue might take him and his brother away and put his mother in jail for leaving them alone at night in the apartment.

It was after midnight when their mother's sister, Aunti Charlene, came knocking on the apartment door. Dollar scooted the footstool over to the door to make sure that the voice declaring it was that of his Aunti Charlene's, actually was.

Dollar unlocked the door and his Aunti Charlene barged in like Ms. Sophia from the movie "The Color Purple."

"Where's my mama?" Dollar asked his Aunti Charlene almost with tears in his eyes. Like a dog can sense a bad storm coming, children can sense when something's wrong. Aunti Charlene stared into Dollar's sad brown eyes.

"Don't question me as soon as I walk in the God damned door, boy," Aunti Charlene said. "You and your brother just get y'all's shit and let's go...and don't be cryin' and carryin' on and such either."

Aunti Charlene ordered the boys to gather some clothes and their toothbrushes because they would be staying with her for a couple of nights. Aunti Charlene had always been a stern, no-nonsense woman, but she had never cursed the boys before. Something bad had happened, something bad enough to put fear in Aunti Charlene's heart and a dirty tongue in her mouth.

Dollar would soon learn that his mother had an accident while running after the city bus and had been taken to the hospital by ambulance. Their Aunti Charlene comforted the boy's worries by assuring them that it wasn't a serious injury and that their mother had probably only sprang her ankle.

Apparently, Dollar's mother had been a little late leaving her first job. As she headed down the street to the bus stop to catch the bus to her second gig, with only one more block to hike, she could hear the roar of the bus trailing up behind her. While running to the bus stop the edge of her shoe skid on a small pebble. She skipped a step, losing her balance, and came down with all of her weight on her right leg. She could hear a crack and felt a horrendous jolt of pain. She cried out in agony while she lay on the sidewalk unable to move. After an ambulance was called and it transported her to the hospital, she learned that she had broken her ankle and busted up her kneecap.

Dollar naturally became the caregiver for his mother and little brother. Aunti Charlene did her part too, but she couldn't be there for them 24/7. There were occasions when Dollar even had to help his mother use the bathroom or wash up. This is probably one of the reasons why Dollar never got overly excited about girls like some boys his age did. He, unfortunately, had been forced to learn the female anatomy through the caring of his mother. This took away any future thrills of trying to grab at little tender nubs, booties and stealing peeks at bald coochies.

Dollar never once complained about all of the duties and responsibilities he was buried in as a child. He thought that it would only be temporary and that everything would be back to normal once his mother fully recovered. Neither his mother, nor Dollar himself, ever dreamed in a million years that ultimately she would end up losing her entire right leg. Initially her toe had to be amputated and shortly thereafter so did her foot. Dollar was too young to grasp all of the details but he knew it had something to do with his mother neglecting a prior diagnosis of diabetes.

After the initial amputations, only a few months went by before Dollar's mother ended up losing her entire right leg. The government had the nerve to deny her social security two times before finally giving in to her claim. Aunti Charlene had convinced Dollar's mother to hire a lawyer, who in the end would receive a third of the retroactive benefits awarded. By then Dollar's mom could barely afford to keep toilet paper on the roll. Seeing his mother in such a helpless condition murdered Dollar's spirit.

Because their mother had worked so hard to earn that almighty dollar, Dollar and Klein thought that money was the answer to everything. Dollar and his brother did anything they could think up in an attempt to become instant millionaires. They had yard sales that consisted of their broken toys and old clothing. They even set up a lemonade stand. There was nothing more rigorous for Dollar and his brother than setting up a lemonade stand in the projects and trying to sell lemonade to people just as broke as they were. Everybody wanted a free cup, wanted to use food stamps to pay for a cup, or didn't have any money period. Dollar's heart was always bigger than his pocket so most of the time he ended up giving away free cups on IOU's. Perhaps if Dollar had gone down on the price of a cup of lemonade, he might have made some sells. One dollar was pretty steep for only a Dixie cup of lemonade.

Everything that Dollar and his brother attempted to sell, Dollar would price at one crispy dollar bill. Whether it was a cup of lemonade, a broken old toy or a painted rock, Dollar would hold the item up and yell, "Dollar, dollar. It's only one dollar bill, y'all." Which is how he got the nickname, Dollar. Pretty soon, everyone in the neighborhood ceased the use of his given name, Dareese Blake, and started calling him Dollar.

As Dollar and his little brother grew older, Dollar's brother decided that he would use his mind to gain riches instead of trying to get the bums in the neighborhood to come up off of a measly dollar. His mother had always hammered the importance of education in her boys, so Dollar's younger brother set his mind to acing school and earning a free college education. That is exactly what he would end up doing. His dream was to become a doctor some day, enabling him a plentiful income in order take care of his family.

To Dollar, college was four years that he didn't have time to fool around with. Completing high school had already taken up four years of his time. College meant four more years of being broke. He decided that, like his younger brother, he too would use his mind to gain wealth. He would use his mind to think up a way to get fast loot.

Growing up in the projects and watching his mother shuffle from gig to gig, Dollar learned at an early age that everybody has to have some hustle in them in order to conquer life. Be it legit or otherwise, everybody has to have a hustle. It's the only way to survive.

Dollar came to the conclusion that he would let the love of money put its mojo on mankind. He would let the bankers bank, the pimps pimp and the teachers teach. He would let the plumbers plumb, the thieves steal, the hoes fuck and the ballers ball. Then he'd catch them slippin' and rob all of 'em blind. This resolution is how Dollar would find himself with a firearm aimed at Cartel and his two partners.

Dollar had portrayed himself to Cartel to be this eighteen-year-old kid from Indiana who jacked cars on a regular. Dollar had never stolen a bike let alone an automobile. He convinced Cartel that he could present him with a white Benz with gold trimming and honey leather seats. He ran down his bogus resume of a life of car jacking and won Cartel's greedy ass over.

Cartel couldn't wait to brand Dollar as one of his little accomplices to the good life. He never saw this set up coming. He only saw dollar signs.

Dollar's reminiscing thoughts of growing up in Gary, Indiana was interrupted by Woody's Garage door suddenly flinging open off of its hinges. At the same time, this startling occurrence would finally bring about some relief to Dollar. Two persons dressed like Ninjas made their way through the doorway. It was Tommy and Ral. Dollar's backup had finally arrived. Cartel and his partner's hands were damn near touching the ceiling now. Stiff and hard their arms were...straight up in the air.

Without taking his eyes off of his targets, Dollar gritted through his teeth, "Where the fuck y'all been? Eleven o'clock p.m. muthafuckas...eleven o'clock p.m."

"Nigga, we here now and that's all that matters," Tommy replied while pulling out a 9MM with Ral close behind doing the same. They each stood next to Dollar like statutes with their leather glove covered hands gripping the guns pointed at the designated targets.

In the midst of their captor's brief spat, instead of taking their chances and attempting to gain control of the situation, Cartel and his partners decided to remain submissive. If Dollar had planned on killing them he would have done it by now. They had a better chance of staying alive if they just waited this thing out and did as they were told. Besides, they could tell these kids were new to the game. There was even a greater chance that they might be able to catch them slippin'.

"Strip," Ral yelled to Cartel and his partners as he walked towards them. The three of them looked at each other with their hands still in the air.

"Did you hear my boy?" Tommy asked. "Strip. Take your muthafuckin' clothes off. What y'all niggaz waiting on, for us to throw y'all some dollar bills or some shit? Take all your clothes off and put them in a pile in front of you. Start by removing those pieces y'all carrying...one at time. And don't try no funny shit either."

The three men slowly removed the guns they were carrying from either their back hip or calf holster. Thank God

Dollar hadn't slipped up and given them a chance to go for their shit. Time and circumstance was on his side after all.

The men laid their guns on the ground as Ral stood behind them with his gun to their backs.

"Now the clothes," Ral said.

"Oh, y'all some faggots, huh?" Tone said as the men began to peel their clothes off slowly.

"Duck that hoe right there," Dollar said to Tommy. "He talks too fuckin' much. As a matter of fact, duck all three of 'em."

"Quack, quack," Tommy said obediently following Dollar's orders.

After a few minutes the three men stood butt ass naked displaying only their jewelry and a strip of duck tape across their mouths.

"Trick or treat, muthafuckas," Ral said as he walked in front of them carrying a brown paper bag he had removed from his jacket pocket and popped open. "Check all that shit in."

The men began to drop watches, necklaces and rings into the bag. They removed their diamond earrings and bracelets as well. That's what they get for trying to show off. Bling Blinging and ching chinging was one of the tactics Cartel used to lure his employees into his ring. He wanted to show them the things they could end up owning. The bling ching to the baby thugs was the dead raw fish being thrown to the killer whale to calm him into doing tricks. Dollar had studied Cartel and his crew's game like it was a textbook. He knew their steelo and was prepared to get paid off of their vanity.

Tommy went through every pocket of the pile of clothes on the floor. Some contained money clips filled with one hundred dollar bills. There were loose wads of money also. The clothes were thrown to Dollar after they had been successful raided by Tommy.

Dollar balled the clothes up under his armpit and headed towards the exit door. Tommy scooped up anything that slipped from Dollar's clutches.

"I want all of you to count 100 Mississippi's before you even consider moving. I mean your dicks better not even get hard and start to rise or you're dead," Ral shouted. "Start counting now!"

Dollar, Tommy and Ral looked around making sure they hadn't overlooked anything of value. Ral spotted what looked like a couple of cell phones laying on the worktable behind the men and fell behind Dollar and Tommy to go back and retrieve them.

Ral picked up the cell phones and as he skimmed over the worktable Cartel looked to make sure that Dollar and Tommy's backs were still towards them. They were pretty much walking out of the door at that point. Cartel knew that between him and his two dudes, they could be quick enough to overpower Ral, take his gun, and use him as a shield to escape. It was a risk, but it was one Cartel was willing to take. No way was he going to have his street reputation tainted by some 18-year-old punk. If Cartel allowed Dollar to get this one off, every little nigga Cartel had working for him would end up tryin' him and his crew. This was the last chance Cartel saw visible to eliminate future scenarios. Fuck it! It was worth the risk.

Cartel ran towards Ral in attack mode. His partners were right behind him. They had only gotten to 20 Mississippi, but this was their chance to beat Ral down for his gun, pump lead into Dollar and Tommy and get their money, jewelry, clothing and egos back.

Dollar had held the door for Tommy to come through and Tommy had done the same for Ral. When Tommy discovered that Ral wasn't there, Tommy looked just in time to see the three men dashing towards Ral. Not one of the parade of bullets Tommy let off without hitting Ral was unexplainable, but Cartel and his dudes dropped dead like flies.

"Whoa Wee...Hell yeah!" Ral shouted as he looked at the three bodies piled upon top of one another. "Didn't I tell y'all fools not to move until you got to 100 Mississippi? It pays to stay in school. You learn how to count and that shit would have kept your asses alive."

"Let's get the fuck out of here," Dollar shouted as he snatched the cell phones from Ral and threw them on the ground. "Who the fuck was you going to call, man? We got bodies on our shit now and for what, some fuckin' cell phones?"

"Fuck," Tommy yelled still in shock at the sight of the dead bodies, one still grasping for one more chance at life. Tommy began to wipe down the place with a shirt collected from one of the dead men, making sure that not a single smudge of evidence was left behind.

Tommy threw Dollar the car keys and all three of them ran out of the garage to the rental car that Dollar had some chick back home cop for them. They sped off leaving nothing but tire prints and three dead men full of bullet holes.

"That could have been my ass laying back there fuckin' 'round with you two late ass niggaz," Dollar said as he consistently looked in his rear view mirror for any sign of the police or someone following them. "I ought to fuck y'all up."

"Did you see that shit, man?" Ral asked still hype from the gunfire. "Tommy laid them son of a bitches out flat. Holy Shit. I could hear those caps poppin' they asses...Pop,pop,pop!"

"Tommy Gun to the rescue," Dollar said. "But I still ought to beat the both of y'all's asses for showing up late. Ral, you need to take your own advice about staying in school. You learn how to tell time."

"You need to quit talking to me like I'm some dude," Tommy, who was sitting in the passenger seat, said removing the baseball cap from her head, allowing her long jailhouse braids to fall down her back.

"Awe, you know you like one of the guys, Tommy, so quit trying to play all sensitive," Dollar said lightly punching her on her shoulder with his fist. "I consider you to be one of my boys."

Dollar loved teasing Tommy about being a tomboy. She tried to act like it didn't bother her as much as it did, but Dollar knew it did. Nonetheless, he still teased her. That's the only time Tommy ever looked like a girl was when she was defending her womanhood. All that neck snappin' was a given.

"Well, I got the goods to prove I'm all woman," Tommy said rolling her eyes and snappin' her neck out like an ostrich.

"Don't talk like that. I'm not trying to visualize you with a pussy," Ral yelled from the back seat as him and Dollar began to laugh.

"Both of you can go to hell. This pussy done saved y'all's life a many of times," Tommy replied. "Besides, I'd rather be a chick than a trailer park trash lookin' white boy."

Dollar continued laughing, but Ral's laughter faded quickly.

"Why you gotta make racial comments and shit?" Ral said, getting an attitude as he ran his fingers through his orangish red hair. "That's why I hate when a muthafucka save your life a couple of times. They think you always owe them something and that they can talk to you anyway they please. They be throwing it up in your face and shit."

"Quit acting like a bitch," Dollar said. "We got over $200,000 in cash and prizes and you back there crying."

Dollar always had to break up arguments between Tommy and Ral. He was the peacemaker of the trio. Besides that, Tommy and Ral were like family to him and he didn't want to see family beefin'.

"Man, I'm just saying," Ral added. "Why I gotta be trailer park trash just 'cause I'm white? I'm just saying that shit ain't cool."

"Well, don't just say shit. Tommy done had your back since she was whooping niggaz on the playground for your ass. You do owe her."

Tommy looked back at Ral and stuck her tongue out at him.

"Well," Ral said lightweight under his breath. "Just let a muthafucka die next time."

"You think I won't?" Tommy said. "Talkin' 'bout some count to 100 Mississippis...what kind of shit is that? White people, man, I swear."

Dollar couldn't help but laugh as the three jumped onto 70 West, the interstate that would take them from Columbus, Ohio, back home to Indiana. This was their first robbery and it looked like it would pay off well. It was the end of a life of have nots and the beginning of a life of having it all.

All Dollar wanted to do with his share was take it home to his mother. He was the epitome of a mama's boy. He felt just as proud to be in a position to give his moms some ends as a result of the Cartel stick-up as he would have been if he were turning over a hard earned paycheck to her.

Dollar hadn't thought of the lie he would tell his mother as to where the money had come from. If she knew what her son was doing, if the lack of will to live didn't kill her, the truth surely would. She had raised her boys to never put themselves in a position to encounter any sort of brush with the law.

Dollar had promised his mother that he would keep on a straight and narrow path. He had tried hard to be loyal to his words. His father had been anything but loyal to her and he never wanted to cause her that kind of pain again. Dollar's loyalty to his mother was fueled by his father's disloyalty to the family. Ironically, Dollar's loyalty to providing for his mother and brother would be the force behind him doing things that were against his mother's wishes.

Tommy and Ral, on the other hand, had engaged in some criminal activity before their task with Dollar, but nothing of this caliber. Tommy had a hustle flipping bank accounts. She would get people to give her their check books and ID. She would make spurious deposits into the accounts right before the weekend, then spend the entire weekend on a shopping spree writing one bad check after another. She would purchase jewelry, clothing, food and electronics. She would use Ral on the instances when the owner of the checks was a man.

If the owner of the checking account was light skinned Ral could get away with it by wearing a baseball cap. But being a white dude with red hair, it was hard for Ral to pass as a brotha. Nonetheless, he and Tommy would flip and split.

After all had been said and done Tommy would pay the owner of the account up to fifteen hundred dollars, depending on how much dirt she got away with over the weekend. Sometimes the collaborator would have special merchandise request and Tommy would just shop for them instead of giving them money. Come Monday morning the collaborator was to report their checkbook missing to their financial institution. By that time Tommy and Ral had damaged the account severely.

When Dollar came up with the idea for the three of them to start robbing people, Tommy and Ral were game. They were ready for a bigger and better hustle. Dollar, on the other hand, had just gotten his criminal cherry popped with the Cartel job. He had successfully robbed three occupational criminals. It wasn't in the plan to see them dead, but circumstance always determines the outcome.

No longer a pup, on that night, July 4, 1994, Dollar became a Dawg. He, Ral and Tommy had set the stage to become career hustlers. They had no intentions of stealing petty stuff or holding up liquor stores. Their hustle would be taking advantage of and profiting from other people's hustle. They would make a life for themselves by straight out robbin' muthafuckas.

Chapter 2

GOT MONEY?

The title of "stick-up kid" just didn't seem to fit the bill, the Dollar Bill. This eighteen-year-old *kid* stood six feet and four inches tall weighing 200 pounds. Dollar appeared to be anything but a kid. He looked more like a man with an innocent baby face. His smooth, baby soft, honeycomb complexion added to his innocent look. He had never worked out, but God decided to bless him with a nice little build. He wore his hair in a low fro, of which he picked 24/7 it seemed. There was a peculiar poise about Dollar, a mystery that the ladies loved and the fellas envied.

As far as haters, there were none, none who spoke their peace anyway. It would be hard to find one person in the hood to say something bad about Dollar. As far as the block was concerned, Dollar was that kid who would grow up to be something, like LeBron James or some shit. He wouldn't necessarily play ball, but everyone was sure he'd do something noteworthy.

People still pictured Dollar as that little kid in the neighborhood trying to make a dolla *the honest way*. He didn't fit the stereotypical dark skinned nappy-headed description of a brotha that most people inconspicuously feared when walking down the street. Dollar was proof that criminals came in all shades and personalities.

Dollar's suave and honest like appearance worked for him. It was most appealing to the ladies. Sometimes when Dollar strolled the Indiana University campus, the oncoming females prayed that Dollar's fine ass would approach them.

Little did they know that once he did approach them, after only a very few kind words of flattery, Dollar was snatching off their gold chains and running off down the street with it. This shit was funny to Dollar.

Once Dollar realized that he had gotten away with it, he would toss the chain to the ground. He never actually wanted the chain itself, he just wanted the confidence of knowing that he could get it. Dollar couldn't recall where he had heard about chain snatching, but it became his way of practicing being surreptitious and flattering.

While Dollar was practicing for a life of crime, his brother was practicing for a life of lore. His love for knowledge was just as intense as Dollar's love of money. Although the two had two different means of seeking riches, Dollar supported his brother's ambitions and made sure he showed his support with his actions.

"I'll give you $25 if you can tell me how many ways there are to make change for a dollar," Dollar said to his sixteen-year-old brother, Klein.

"293 ways," Klein responded as he swooped up the $25 from Dollar's hand.

This was Dollar's way of making his brother earn money from him. At first Dollar was going to deposit a lump sum of money into Klein's bank account. Their mother had seen to it that Klein started the account back when he got a paper route. But Dollar didn't ever want his brother to grow up thinking that anybody was just ever going to give him shit for nothing. So instead, every couple of days Dollar quizzed Klein of which he paid him $25 for every correct answer.

Without fail, Klein headed to the bank with the $25 in hand. It was $25 more towards his college tuition money. Up until he and Dollar started their very own ghetto rendition of Jeopardy, the balance of Klein's account was only $203.52.

After a couple of months his balance grew to the point that it could cover at least his first quarter at the community college.

This made Dollar feel good, and it kept Klein on his toes. He was already one of the brightest kids in his school. Dollar knew how important college was to Klein and wanted to do everything possible to see that it happened for him. Although Dollar graduated high school, he had no intentions of ever going to college. Klein still admired Dollar though, and in his eyes, his brother could do no wrong.

That's why it was important to Dollar that other than Tommy and Ral, no one was to have knowledge of his underlying demeanor. Dollar never wanted rumors about him skimming the streets and getting back to his family. That's why Dollar wouldn't even entertain the thought of fucking with anybody other than Tommy and Ral.

Tommy's evil ass never spoke to anybody so Dollar never had to worry about her runnin' her jaws. That's what Dollar loved about Tommy most. She was a mean ass bitch and always had been. She didn't allow new friends in her life. Even if she had, they wouldn't have been friends for long. Unless you knew Tommy from way back when, tolerating her attitude was impossible.

Back in school, chicks, and dudes too for that matter, couldn't look at Tommy funny without getting a beat down. She grew up fighting, mostly her mother's abusive boyfriends, so she was always on the defense. She hated the world and trusted no one, with the exception of Dollar and Ral.

Ral, on the other hand, was the Gary Indiana Crusader on foot. Because he pretty much lived on the streets, which he felt was better than staying at home with his junkie mother, he knew everything that went on in the streets. It's not like Gary is this huge town anyway. Most of the folks there commute to Chicago to work and play. But if an ant was fixin' to piss, Ral had already informed everyone before a drop ever hit the ground. He was good people though and not seen as a threat to anyone. Folks only paid attention to half of anything Ral said anyway. Ral was somewhat of a walking joke in Gary.

Ral, whose full name is Ralphie Kennedy, ever since grade school tried to pass himself off as one of the members of the prestigious and infamous Kennedy family. He pretended to be one of the family member's illegitimate kid or something. The shit was almost believable. This fool had studied everything about the Kennedy family from the great-great-great ancestors to the young bad ass cousins. Whenever Ral did come into some money or material shit, any one who would listen to him boast surely thought one of his rich relatives had sent it to him.

Ral was a year and a half older than Dollar and Tommy, who were the same age. Since his early youth, Ral had been in trouble with the law, nothing serious, but enough to have done a few months in the joint. Whenever they booked Ral, the arresting officer would always say, "Make sure y'all give this kid an extra blanket... he's related to John F. Kennedy." Of course everyone would burst out laughing, but underneath the laughter, a few were still curious as to Ral's bloodline.

The last time Ral was arrested it was for petty theft. He had just turned 18 so it was his first adult criminal offense. He had to do six months in the county. He ended up getting pinched because his loose lips bragged to some skank hoe how he was the one who had robbed a local electronics store of five DVD players in broad daylight simply by walking out of the store with them in his arms. When the owner posted a sign offering $1,000 in reward money, the slut dropped the dime on him.

During Ral's six months in jail he was raped. He learned the hard way about acquiring bragging rights. From then on, if he found a quarter on the ground he kept the shit to himself. He trusted no one, no one except Dollar and Tommy. They were the only ones who ever looked out for him and protected him. His own mother didn't even visit him when he got locked up and Dollar and Tommy were there for every visit. It was Dollar who did everything from yard work to cashing in aluminum cans to make sure that Ral had money on his books and soap to wash his ass. Dollar and Tommy were the only ones who ever wrote him a single letter. They were the only ones he ever told about being assaulted while in jail.

Dollar and Tommy ended up paying a visit to the chick who had dropped the dime on Ral. No one has seen her since. It was just unspoken that the three would never again discuss the girl or Ral being raped. This was the ultimate proof of loyalty in their friendship...or was it?

***

Since Dollar was the one responsible for setting shit up, he was the designated purse holder of the Cartel robbery and any other robbery him, Tommy and Ral were to engage in. Right after the stick-up, Dollar distributed $3,000 to each of them to tie them over until they could split the entire pot. First they each had to either take the valuables they got off of Cartel and his partners during the Columbus, Ohio robbery to the pawnshop or sell them on the street in Gary, Indiana. Once all the material items had been transformed into cash, the three were to congregate, cash in and split the remaining proceeds.

At Chase Middle School, where the three met, Dollar, Tommy and Ral would sit in the schoolyard and dream the same dream. With their dingy torn up clothing and holey tennis shoes, each of them would tell tales of how they would be thousadnaires (a thousand bucks was a lot of money to 12 and 13 year olds). Now, six years later, after the Cartel stick-up, the three walked away with $63,000 each. A dream so long ago had come to pass. They were now thousandnaires.

Words couldn't describe how proud it made Dollar feel to be able to pay the rent for his moms. For his mother's sake, though, Dollar pretended to be going to work everyday. He lied and told her that he had some construction gig laying asphalt. He would really be hanging out over Tommy's house all day or with some chick on the block that had noticed his new sophisticated demeanor. Dollar had to let his mother think he was out making legitimate money so that she would take the $500 a week he gave her. He went behind her back and paid off every debt she had so that the bill collectors would let her live in peace. He paid her utility bills down including the excessive balances that were accumulating in her PIPP accounts (accounts set up for customers below poverty level which allows them to only pay a small portion of their utility bill). She never seemed to pay close enough attention to the billing statements to even notice their depletion. Half the time she didn't even open the bills. She pitched them straight into the garbage knowing that she couldn't afford to pay them anyhow.

Dollar wasn't worried about filling his own pockets with his profit from the Cartel robbery. He was planning out stick-ups in neighboring cities and states that would give birth to his come up. He would get his, no doubt, but first things first. He had to look out for his family. Since Dollar had become the man of the house at the ripe age of three years old, he felt it was his duty to take care of his family.

Dollar was only three when his father abandoned them never to be heard from again. Word on the street was that he got into the pimpin' game and mastered it. Dollar's father had treated pimpin' like it was a franchise. He supposedly let one of his partners man his hoes in Indiana while he went to Detroit, Michigan to set up shop and eventually to Ohio. Over a period of time every hoe in the Midwest would want his name tattooed on their pussy.

The authority of having the power over another human beings body went to his head. He became one of the most crucial cats in the game. Bitches, and his so-called assistants, feared fucking up his money. Stories about Dollar's father and the pimp game were eventually over shadowed by success stories of the new entrepreneurial opportunity, slingin' crack.

Dollar figured that the hustle in him was the only thing he had inherited from that sorry excuse for a man known as his father. Dollar was determined to do for his family what his father didn't do. He would hustle, but only death or jail would keep him from taking care of his family.

Tommy, on the other hand, bought her a little house right outside the hood in order to get the hell away from her family. Her humble abode wasn't in the suburbs or anything but it wasn't suspicious either and that's all that mattered. Tommy didn't want anybody sniffing around trying to put the pieces together of her slight come up. She had to get a little job bar tending on weekends to prove she had an income in order to keep Uncle Sam out of her business. The house wasn't much, but it was better than the two-bedroom house she had been living in with her Mother, her mother's boyfriend, her pregnant sister and niece. It felt good to just be able to kick back in her own shit.

"Yo, T," Dollar, who was sitting on the couch in Tommy's living room, called to Tommy who was in the bedroom. "Let me cop another one of these sodas."

Dollar took the last swallow from the Coke can in his hand, pitched it in the trash and grabbed another one out of the fridge.

"Nigga, you ain't gon' come up over here drinking up all my shit all of the time," Tommy said entering the room with a brown paper bag in her hand.

"Must be that time of the month," Dollar joked popping open the Coke can.

"For real," Tommy continued. "You and Ral always coming up over here eating and drinking up my shit. Come over with some shit in hand next time. Replenish a muthafucka's kitchen."

Dollar ignored Tommy as he watched her dump out the contents of the brown paper bag. Dollar bills flooded the coffee table.

"Damn, T, have you spent any of your money?"

"Only what I've needed to spend," Tommy said licking her thumb right before she began thumbing through the money for a count.

"Let me guess," Tommy said. "You done tricked yours away like Ral, huh?"

"I'll beat my shit before I trick," Dollar said. "I had to take care of family matters. I ain't spending my shit on no hoes."

"Please, it's me, Tommy. I know all your business. Shawanda, Tish, Monique...all hoes. Don't none of them fuck for free and you with one or the other every other day of the week."

"I don't be fucking them tramps. I might let them sucky sucky, but that's it."

Tommy twisted her lips up and said, "Umm hmm, yeah right," as she continued counting her money.

"For real!" Dollar defended himself.

"So you ain't spending no money on them?" Tommy asked with an underlying self-concern.

"I mean shit, I done bought 'em some DQ or something, but I ain't never took one of them bitches out no where big or nothing like that."

Tommy began to laugh and replied, "I'm just fucking with you, Dollar. Calm down."

"So Ral trickin' tuff, huh?"

"Ral is trickin' his new money with every hoe that gets a whiff of it. Whatever portion of Ral's money that don't get stuck down some hoe's G-string, he puts in his arm."

"Word?" Dollar asked puzzled.

"Nigga, please. Where you been?"

"Why you ain't said nothing before now?" Dollar said, becoming serious.

"Shit, I thought you knew. Everybody know. If you pull your nose out from under them hoodrats' asses..."

Dollar stood up and began pacing across the living room floor.

"You're kidding right," Tommy laughed. "You really didn't know about Ral?"

"I ain't had time to baby-sit muthafuckas. I been making sure my family is taken care of and planning our next hit and shit."

"Relax," Tommy said. "Ral is a grown ass man. What he does is his business."

"No," Dollar snapped. "What that fool do is our business. We the same muthafucka. If he fucks up, then we fucked up. I can see his ass now wrapped up in some bomb ass pussy running his fuckin' mouth. Damn, T, you should have hollered at me on this."

"You know Ral like street candy. Quit acting brand new. You also know that the last thing Ral is ever gonna do is tell some trick his business."

Dollar and Tommy sat in silence.

"But that fool got a pretty nice hunk of change. That ain't safe for him if he fiendin' like that.."

Tommy looked at Dollar and sighed. She balled her money up and placed it back in the bag. She knew what had to be done. She went into her bedroom with the bag in hand and came back out with car keys in hand.

"You ready to go save that fool from the streets?" Tommy asked, as she shoved her braids up into a baseball cap.

"He ain't no good to the clique strung out," Dollar replied.

"Aiight," Tommy said. "Then let's go find this fool so I can get back to counting my shit."

Dollar and Tommy scoured the streets until they heard that Ral was over at a house party on 26th and Connecticut. Some cat named Chico was throwing a party at his mom's crib, which he did every time she worked graveyard shift. That's how he made his lunch money, a lunch that consisted of clothes, weed and hoes.

"Three dollars, niggaz," the lil' Martin Lawrence lookin' dude at the door said to Dollar and Tommy.

"I'm just looking for somebody," Dollar said. "I don't plan on staying."

"What the fuck we look like?" the little dude at the door said. "This ain't missing persons. I said three dollars."

Tommy sucked her lips and pulled out a ten-dollar bill and handed it to the dude. He took the ten and waved his hand as to give Tommy and Dollar permission to enter.

"Keep the change," Tommy said sarcastically.

"Thanks, my man," the dude replied to Tommy. She was used to being mistaken for a guy so she just proceeded through the door.

The male R&B group Jodeci's "Come and Talk to Me" remix was blasting through the speakers and niggaz was blazin' urb in every corner of the room. Tommy and Dollar shifted through the crowd of mostly high schoolers. It didn't take long for the two to find Ral. He was in the half bath in the basement sticking a needle in one arm while some chick, who looked to be a few years older than Ral, was sucking his dick.

"This shit right here is the muthafuckin' life," Ral said as he put the needle down on the sink and allowed his head to fall back. After only a few seconds he could barely keep his eyelids open. His mouth hung open as he began to moan at the almost immediate sensation of the high and the nut that erupted down the chick's throat.

"Now give me some, baby," The girl begged. "Now give me some blow, baby."

The girl wiped her mouth of any of Ral's cum that had managed to escape and removed the rubber band like object from around Ral's arm. She then placed it on her own arm. She picked up the needle from the sink that Ral had placed there and prepared the meal for her veins.

"Kick mud, hoe," Tommy said, as she and Dollar entered the unlocked door.

The girl was in a trance as she flushed her veins with poison. Just then Tommy and Dollar realized that Ral was sitting on the toilet with his limp dick hanging out of his pants.

"You want some too?" the girl said to Tommy.

"Hell naw! I don't fuck wit no drugs," Tommy replied.

"No, baby, I mean do you want some of this here?"

The girl pulled up her cheetah print mini tube dress, lifted her leg and allowed her nicely trimmed triangle to show. "You can get up in this hole for some blow. I do whatever you want me to...round the world, golden shower; you can even shit on me as long as you ain't got the runs. I'll fuck your friend too. It's good. You won't be sorry. Ask Ral here."

The girl winked at Tommy as she let the needle drop on the floor. She placed herself in a straddling position on top of Ral and began to laugh as if she was watching Richard Pryor's Live on Sunset Strip.

Beyond the point of disgust, Tommy grabbed the girl by her hair and yanked her from off of Ral. The girl began to scream and attempt to escape Tommy's clutch.

"Look here, Little Red Riding every dick in the Hood," If I ever see you around my boy again, you gon' be wearing your nipples as earrings. Pass it on to your other trick ass friends. Tommy turned the girl loose and flexed on her, daring her to try some shit. It wasn't that serious as far as the chick was concerned. She straightened up her dress and went on her way. She brushed by Dollar, but not without him getting a free feel of her fat ass.

"What the fuck you doing?" Dollar asked Ral.

"Nothing, now that you two cock blockers are here," Ral replied.

"I'm serious, man," Dollar said. "Is this what you doing with your loot? Is this what you call your muthafuckin' come up?"

"I was trying to get up and cum, but you two fools," Ral attempted to joke before Dollar grabbed him by his throat."

"You think I'm playing? You think this shit is a game?" Dollar shouted as Ral began to turn blue.

"Yo, D, let him go, man," Tommy said as Ral began his attempt to peel Dollar's fingers from around his neck.

"All those years of dreaming on the playground. We finally get some loot and this is what you do with it," Dollar said becoming emotional. "Man don't you want shit out of life? Or do you wanna end up like your mother?"

Suddenly Ral found the strength to escape Dollar's clutch. He tried his damnedest to take Dollar on but his little ass was no match. They tussled until Tommy managed to pull them apart.

"Don't ever talk at me about my mama!" Ral shouted.

"Will you two fuckin' stop," Tommy said. "You supposed to be boys. This is bullshit!"

Tommy's eyes weld up with tears. Her frozen spirit wouldn't allow her to cry in front of anyone. She angrily pushed Dollar and Ral and stormed out of the bathroom.

Ral and Dollar remained in the bathroom breathing heavily from the energy they had used up tussling with one another. Finally Dollar spoke.

"I'm sorry I talked about your moms, man," Dollar said, holding out his hand in apology.

"It's cool," Ral said, shaking his hand.

Dollar pulled Ral towards him and hugged him. "Let me know now if this is the life you want," Dollar said. "Tommy and I are putting our lives on the line to get out of the muthafuckin' projects. We don't want to have to leave you behind, man. But if this is where you want to be just say the word. If we know to expect this shit, then it won't be as disappointing."

"I want shit man," Ral said getting choked up. "I want out too. I want out too."

"Then the drugs, the hoes...man, you got to give it up," Dollar said.

"It ain't that easy, Dollar man," Ral said putting his head down.

"Shit ain't never been easy, but we've managed to overcome it, right?"

Ral nodded his head in the affirmative.

"Come on, let's go find, T," Dollar said.

Dollar and Ral found Tommy waiting outside for them in her car. Dollar got in the front seat and Ral got in the back seat. None of them spoke a single word. Dollar put his hand on Tommy's knee. She tried to ignore him, but no woman, not even Tommy could ignore Dollar's touch.

Tommy sighed and looked up into Dollar's radiant brown eyes. Still, no words were spoken. Their eyes said it all.

***

Just as easy as the money came, it was going. The three couldn't resist spoiling themselves with some named brand fancies such as shoes, clothing and jewels. Fubu, Gucci, Lugz and Figaros became necessities.

Before Dollar could start working on setting up their next job, the police were beginning to link the trio to the killings in Columbus. Eyewitnesses had reported seeing the rental car leaving the scene of the crime. The plates were traced back to Budget Car Rental where the vehicle had been borrowed.

A couple of detectives made their way to Indiana to question Bubbles, the girl who rented the car from Budget for Dollar. They shook her up so bad, threatening to charge her as an accessory and put her daughter in a foster home, that she gave them everything on Dollar except his blood type.

When the detectives arrived at Dollar's mother's apartment she told them that her son was at work. She told them that they would be wasting their time with any questions they might have had for him because her son was a good child and didn't even as much as hang out with the wrong crowd.

The detectives waited outside the apartment in an unmarked car until they spotted Dollar walking up the porch. Dollar never saw the detectives approaching him.

"Dareese," one of the detectives said to Dollar. "Are you Dareese Blake?"

"Yes, uhh, no, uhh," Dollar stuttered.

"Are you Mr. Dareese Ramelle Blake?" The second detective asked. "A.K.A. Dollar Bill."

"I'm Dollar," Dollar replied.

"We need you to come with us. We'd like to ask you a few questions regarding a robbery and triple homicide."

The detectives might as well have punched Dollar in the gut. A sharp pain darted through the pit of his belly. Dollar's head began to spin. He was dizzy to the point of fainting. There had to be some mistake. No way was this shit about Cartel and his boys. What did anybody care about some low life criminals? No this had to be about something else, some local shit. Yeah, it had to be.

"Will you come with us please?" the detective asked Dollar.

As Dollar's eyeballs floated about the sockets, for a split second he thought about running. Did he have the strength? Where would he run to? Where would he hide?

"Dareese, Dareese," Dollar's mother began to shout from their living room window.

"I can't run and let my mama see me get shot in the back or some shit," Dollar thought to himself.

By this time one of the detectives had sensed Dollar's temptation and pulled his gun out and placed it hard against Dollar's back.

"Go for it," the detective threatened Dollar. "Every time your mother comes outside do you really want her to see her son's blood stains in the cement until the rain washes it away? Go for it!"

"It's okay, mama," Dollar said. "It's nothing, ma. I'll be back in time for dinner."

"Dareese, baby, what's going on? Klein, Klein," Dollar's mother began to call to Klein who had been in the bedroom studying.

"What's wrong, mama?" Dollar could hear Klein asking. Shortly thereafter, Klein's head peeked through the window.

"Dollar, Dollar," Klein shouted.

"It's okay, man," Dollar replied. "You take care of ma. I'll be home shortly."

"Dollar, Dollar!" Klein continued to shout. "What's going on, man? Where they taking you? Please, Dollar. Please don't leave us...Please."

Dollar could hear Klein's voice cracking. It was breaking his heart. He wanted to break down right then and there, but he had to pull himself together.

"Who does the King of Diamonds represent?" Dollar said to Klein.

"What?" Klein asked as tears ran down his face.

"In a deck of playing cards, who does the King of Diamonds represent?"

"Man, I don't know."

"Yes, you do! Yes you do," Dollar insisted. "I got $25 for you when I get back. Who does the King of Diamonds represent?"

"Julius Caesar." Klein said as he began holding his mother to comfort her. "The King of Diamonds in a deck of playing cards represents Julius Caesar."

The detectives cuffed Dollar's hands behind his back and began to read him his rights. They pushed and shoved him over to their car. Dollar was scared, but he wasn't going to let it show. He sucked it up and allowed the detectives to throw him into the back of the car.

The engine started and Dollar wanted so bad to look back up at his mother and brother who were broken up as they watched him from their apartment window. The car rode off. Even though it could have very well been the last time Dollar ever saw his mother and little again, he didn't look back at them. He didn't look back.

***

Dollar spent a total of 14 hours and 13 minutes being interrogated by the detectives. They asked him the same questions over and over again, sometimes switching words around in an attempt to catch him in a lie. Dollar stuck to "yes" and "no" answers. He didn't offer anything extra which pissed the detectives off.

In the meantime, Dollar's fingerprints were being matched to those found on the cell phones in Woody's Garage. Once the detectives informed Dollar of this major piece of evidence, it was time for Dollar to start talking.

The detective suspected that Dollar hadn't pulled off the robbery and killings solo. No way did some young punk with no street respect take Cartel and two of his dudes down alone. The detectives wanted the names of Dollar's accomplices. If Dollar didn't tell, he would go down, taking all the heat alone, for a triple homicide. He would very well spend the rest of his life in jail. If Dollar did give up the name of the trigger man, he would go down as an accessory and walk away with a smack on the wrist as a first time offender...that was the deal.

Although Tommy was the one who actually pulled the trigger, Dollar still knew that Ral would go down hard as well. Unlike Dollar, Ral wasn't in a position to be making any type of deal for himself. He had several strikes on his record that would guarantee him time in the slammer.

To Dollar, it didn't make sense for all three of them to go down. Besides, he couldn't see himself snitching on his partners and he especially couldn't picture Tommy spending the rest of her life in prison. He knew, without a mustard seed of doubt, that if the shoe were on the other foot, both Tommy and Ral would do the same for him.

Dollar had learned quite a few things about hustling. No matter the nature of the hustle, every hustle has the same rules. One can only get down with people whom they have 100% trust in. The clique had to be willing to die for the hustle, do time for the hustle, and Dollar was willing to do just that.

Chapter 3

Murder was the case

Dollar couldn't look at his mother after initially seeing her as he entered the courtroom in his jailhouse garb. When he first set eyes on her she smiled at him. Her smile had always been a comfort to Dollar. Like the time he had a solo in the school Thanksgiving pageant. Dollar was so nervous as he stood on the stage, but when he looked out into the audience and saw his mother smiling at him, he knew that everything was going to be okay. Today, Dollar had a feeling that his mother's smile wasn't going to make everything okay.

Dollar's mother's smile quickly faded as tears began to fall from her eyes. Aunti Charlene sat next to her hugging and comforting her as she weeped endlessly. Dollar could see by the harsh look his Aunti Charlene was giving him that if by chance he did get set free, she was going to tear him a new hide no matter how big he was.

Dollar had to start thinking about things like sunshine and penny candy to keep from breaking down at the sight of his heartbroken mother. He had feared this day for the past few months that he had been in custody. Being charged with a triple homicide, bail wasn't an option for Dollar, so all he had was time in his jail cell to think about this day.

Dollar had failed his mother. He could only imagine the pain it was bringing to her. It was far worse than that "D" he got in Spanish when he was in the ninth grade. It didn't compare to the time he drank the last two cans of soda from the fridge and swore on Grandma Davis' grave that he hadn't done it. It was the type of failure that was an entire flight of steps up from telling a mother that her early teen child was about to become a parent.

If only it was as simple as Dollar impregnating some fast ass chick from the block. Being incarcerated is the ultimate reflection of bad parenting to any mother. Dollar knew the years of his mother working so hard, even to the point where she lost a leg, was now proven to be in vain.

Dollar's mind was instantly taken over by the vision of Tommy sitting in the front row behind the defense table. *"What is she doing here?"* Dollar thought to himself. Tommy could read his mind as she quickly stole a glance at Dollar's expression and put her head down in disobedience.

Dollar had made himself clear when he put the word out that Tommy and Ral were to lay low. Dollar had psyched himself up to take the fall alone. He had feared that Tommy's female characteristics would deliver her to the Franklin County Courthouse in Columbus, Ohio on the day he was to enter his plea.

Dollar stared Tommy down as he walked to his chair at the defense table. He knew she had to lift her head sooner or later and just as soon as she did Dollar's eyes would be pinned on her.

"Don't do it," Dollar lipped to Tommy while shaking his head in the negative. "Don't do it."

Just then the judge entered the courtroom.

"All rise," the bailiff ordered.

As the gallery stood up the judge entered the courtroom. In Dollar's eyes he appeared to be moving in slow motion. He was the Grim Reaper in the flesh. This robed man held Dollar's fate in the palm of his hand and on the tip of his gavel. He would dictate the outcome of the robbery gone bad. Dollar's life, if there was to be any more to his life, was in the judge's hands.

As the judge began to read aloud all the pleasantries of the case, Dollar's body became ice cold. The judge's lips were moving but Dollar couldn't hear a word he was saying. He was zoned.

"Dareese Ramelle Blake," the Judge addressed Dollar. "You have been charged with three counts of murder in the first degree. How do you plead?"

The courtroom filled with the sound of Dollar's heartbeat. The floor flooded with his pouring sweat. The time was now. If Dollar was going to vacate his commitment to the hustle then this would be his last chance.

"Your honor," Dollar gulped. "I plead...."

Just then Tommy stood up. Before she could say anything Dollar's mother began to cry out.

"My baby," Dollar's mother yelled. "I know my baby. He couldn't kill anybody. Please have mercy."

"Order!" the judge shouted. "Order in the courtroom."

Dollar turned to see his Aunti Charlene caressing his mother. Dollar wanted so badly to let his mother know that her labor was not in vain, that her first born son, although was capable of murder, was not a murderer.

"Is there a problem, young man?" the judge said to Tommy, who was still standing, mistaking her for a man. "And please remove your hat."

This was the moment of truth. If Tommy was going to save Dollar from spending the rest of his life in the penitentiary for a crime that she had committed, then she had to speak up now.

Tommy removed her ball cap, balled it up and stuffed it into the pocket of her oversized White Sox jacket. She and Dollar stared down one another like cowboys at a high noon shoot out. In this case, though, no matter who let off the first round and no matter who was left standing, there would be no victor.

Tommy took a deep breath and spoke, "No, your honor. There's no problem."

Tommy quickly walked down the aisle way to the exit door. The door closed slowly on its hinges until she could feel it hit her back. As Tommy stood there while her eyes welded with tears she heard Dollar's voice speak the words: "Guilty, your Honor," Dollar confirmed. "I plead guilty".

* * *

"Yo, Dollar Bill," Ed, the coolest CO (Correctional Officer) in the joint, shouted to Dollar. "She's back, man. What to do?"

"You know what to do," Dollar replied as he kept his face buried into this novel titled *Gangsta* by this kid named K'wan that was being passed around the joint. "I'm refusing the visit."

It had been five years since Dollar was sentenced to prison. It had been five years of his mother making attempts to visit him. Every month Aunti Charlene, against her better judgment, drove her to Ohio, where Dollar was doing his bid, in hopes that Dollar would change his mind and join her in the visiting room. Dollar wouldn't pour salt into her wound by allowing his mother to ever see him caged.

Dolar had written his mother a ten-page letter apologizing and explaining why he couldn't bare to see her. Dollar wrote to his mother that if anyone asked about her eldest boy that she was to say he was dead. The same message was passed along to his brother.

Dollar's brother stopped trying to visit him in jail a long time ago. He knew Dollar better than anybody did. When Dollar had made up his mind, there was no changing it.

Dollar wanted his mother and brother to continue life without the worry of him. He assured them that he could take care of himself and that they were to forget that he ever existed.

Although not having his big brother around hurt, Klein didn't sacrifice his education, something he had worked so hard towards. He had continued schooling, as a matter of fact, he graduated high school a year early. Klein missed the hell out of Dollar, but now he was all their mother had. He had to be strong and move on, just like when their father left them.

Being sentenced to prison forever, forever ever, forever ever, was hard for Dollar too. He couldn't conceive trying to go on; especially knowing the hurt that he was causing his loved ones. The day the gate that separated him from freedom closed behind him, is the day he considered both his mother and brother dead.

For some people locked up it was their loved ones on the outside that kept them going, but not Dollar. He had programmed himself to erase them from every seed of his soul. He had even gone as far as returning every single letter that anyone, including his mother and brother, had written him. Dollar waited for the month his mother would obey his wishes and cease her attempts to see him.

Dollar hadn't communicated with his mother in years. Years, decades or even centuries, though, could not have dissolved the deep seeded love and bond Dollar had with his mother. Although he didn't personally communicate with her, he did in spirit. He always spoke the words "Good morning, Ma" when he woke each morning. He always spoke the words "Good Night, Ma" upon each eve. But still, he refused her visits.

"So you plan on living the rest of your life not seeing your mamma?" Ed asked.

"This ain't living, man," Dollar replied with his back against the cell bars as his eyes scrolled the lines of *Gangsta*.

"I guess you got me on that one," Ed said, walking away allowing Dollar to continue reading his book.

Just like every other cat that gets jail time, Dollar spent his days pushing weights and reading. He didn't get into the Muslim loop, but had sat in on a couple of Jumans just to kill some time.

"A religious man in prison," Dollar thought. *"Yeah right. What I look like following the holy words of a criminal now claiming to be a changed man?"*

Dollar kept to himself. He didn't ride with any crew. He was the respected prison lone wolf. He didn't fuck with inmates and they didn't fuck with him. He didn't look their way and they didn't look his. This is how Dollar planned on serving his time.

In the beginning, though, Dollar wasn't nothin' but an 18-year-old fresh piece of meat, especially to the old heads. Niggaz placed bets on who was gonna get in his ass first and make him their bitch.

Wojo was the prison roughneck back then, before he was released. He was feared by most and challenged by few. Wojo was one of them pretty muthafuckas, half-white, half-black, good curly hair and gray eyes. He had tattoos all over him, every where from his neck to his hands.

Wojo loved boasting about all the pussy that fell onto his doorstep before he had gotten locked up. He enjoyed mostly bragging about the two bitches that sliced each other up over him.

Wojo had a nice size crew. Plenty of cats had his back, but his best friend was his dick.

With Wojo portraying himself as such a ladies' man, Dollar was shocked and caught off guard when Wojo and his crew set up shop in the showers to rape him.

Right before entering the showers that evening, Dollar had an ache deep in the pit of his stomach. Dollar had only been locked up a little under nine months. No one had tried him to date, but on this particular occasion, Dollar could sense some foul shit was up in the air and about to come down on him.

When Dollar entered the showers Wojo gave a look to the other inmates that immediately caused them to disburse. Before Dollar knew it, it was just Wojo, three of his crewmembers and himself in the showers.

Wojo watched Dollar shower as he stood across from him with a devilish look in his eyes. He lathered his private area and began to stroke his suds covered penis.

Dollar became uncomfortable and sick to his stomach at the site of a grown man stiffening up over him.

"Who da fuck you looking at, yo?" Dollar shouted. He thought about what his words would mean, but it was too late, they had already made their way through his lips. *"Fuck it,"* Dollar thought. *"These niggaz was gonna try me sooner or later. I might as well stand my ground now."*

"I'm looking at you, bitch," Wojo replied as him and his crew began to walk up on Dollar.

Dollar had to think quick. He couldn't run. There was no way he could have gotten around the four buff men. The only choice he had was to fight.

"You want a piece of me, little Nigga?" Wojo asked Dollar.

"Man, I think he do," one of Wojo's homies instigated. "If he didn't, his dick wouldn't be hard."

"My dick is hard because I'm thinking about how good it felt fucking your moms before I came here," was Dollar's come back.

Dollar knew the Mamma insult would get whatever it was that was about to happen to him started and over with. He braced himself as the four men rushed him hard. Blows punctured every part of Dollar's body. He fought back as best he could. The men had to have punched him over a hundred times before his naked lifeless body slid down the shower wall and onto the floor. He watched his blood be carried downstream through the drain by the falling shower water.

Like a new gang member, he had been initiated into the system with his first beat down. Wojo and his crew stood over Dollar asking him if he had had enough. When Dollar finally decided to nod in the positive Wojo reached his hand out to help Dollar up.

Before Dollar could even balance himself he was spun around and slammed against the shower wall. He felt Wojo's penis against his buttocks as the crewmembers each grabbed his limbs and nailed him to the shower wall. He stood their pinned against the wall like Jesus on the cross.

Dollar was helpless. He couldn't move. He couldn't scream. He had no idea what he was supposed to do in that situation.

"I'm bout to shoot these nuts up off in that ass," Wojo whispered into Dollar's ear as he positioned his penis to enter Dollar's anus. "When I get out of here this is what I'm gonna do to your mamma, you bitch as nigga."

"I'll kill you muthafucka," Dollar shouted to Wojo. "I swear to God if you stick your dick in me you gonna lose it. You gonna have to sleep with one eye open the rest of your bid. I swear if it's the last thing I do, I'll cut your fucking dick off, chop it up in little pieces and eat it over rice like fucking stir fry."

Before Dollar knew it, he had broken free of the men. With his eyes closed he stayed pressed against the wall. Eventually he heard the men's feet pounding the puddles of the shower floor growing further and further away.

After a few moments Dollar turned around to confirm that the men had in fact exited the showers. There was no one in sight, only a silhouette through the steam that Dollar couldn't make out. Dollar stood erect and mustered up enough strength to battle some more if he had to. Just as he positioned his dukes the image vanished and Dollar was alone in the showers.

Dollar knew that God must have been watching over him.

Ever since Dollar stood up to Wojo, he had appeared to have lightweight gained some true respect. If by chance his eyes did meet with another inmate's, they didn't mean mug him. They gave him the *what's up nod* and went on about their business.

Dollar might have had to exchange a few words with some new cat trying to be hard, but other than that, prison life for Dollar consisted of minimum drama.

But now, after five years of being locked up, Dollar couldn't understand why anyone would want to fuck with him. But low and behold, maybe because he felt intimidated by Dollar's solemn youth, some Old G had recently started eyeballing Dollar big time. Dollar knew it was only a matter of time before some shit would go down.

* * *

"So, little nigga," a deep Barry White like voice clouded over top of Dollar's head. Dollar knew it belonged to the Old G that had been eyeballing him. "I hear you got three bodies on you."

"And...." Dollar said as he sat against the bars of his cell reading the last page of *Gangsta.*

"Oh, so it's true?" the voice said. "I thought for sure your little punk ass was in here for stealing cigarettes or something."

"Ah ha," Dollar said. "The old man got jokes. Let me guess. You're in here because you pick pocketed the guest while you were working as a Walmart greeter."

Before Dollar could get his cackle out, a thick, muscular hand collected his throat through the cell bars. Dollar dropped the book and held his breath. He didn't fight or try to get away. He held his breath hoping his lungs were stronger than the Barry White impersonator's hand.

What seemed like forever passed before the hand released Dollar's throat. Dollar sat on the floor coughing and taking deep breaths, trying to get his breathing rhythm back.

"Don't you wonder why all these years you been sitting with your back against these bars and ain't nobody cut your fucking throat yet, boy?"

Dollar didn't respond. He was so mad he could have spit bullets. All he wanted to do was kick that muthafucka's ass. By the time Dollar stood up to face the assaulter he was gone. All Dollar could see was the silhouette of his body clearing the hall corner.

Dollar, even without seeing his face, knew it was the Old G, the old man known in the clank as Romeo. Dollar had never even looked Romeo's way and now all of a sudden he had beef. What the fuck was his problem?

* * *

As Dollar made his way to his grubbin' spot in the jail slop house he could feel a pair of eyes burning him. The old man was back on his trail. *"What is it with that old geezer,"* Dollar mumbled under his breath.

Dollar could barely enjoy his tasteless chow that consisted of meatloaf, peas and mashed potatoes. He chewed the same bite of meatloaf for five minutes as he watched Romeo out of the corner of his eyes. Dollar reached for his milk, with his eyes still glued on Romeo, and knocked it over.

"Fuck!" Dollar shouted as he scrambled to clean up the mess with napkins. He sopped up the milk and proceeded to continue eating. He took a bite of his mashed potatoes and prepared to stand watch against Romeo again. When he looked up Romeo was no longer sitting at the table he had been dining at. Dollar gulped down the bite of mashed potatoes and felt a presence behind him.

"You ain't scared that you might scoop up a razor blade in them mashed potatoes?" Romeo asked.

Dollar closed his eyes. He knew he had fucked up. He knew he had been caught slippin'. But like with Wojo, he was ready to stand his ground.

"Look, old man," Dollar said without looking away from his tray. "What's your beef? I ain't done shit to you, but if you want to throw them thangs then let's do it. It ain't gon' hurt my heart none to beat down an old man."

One could have heard a pin drop. Silence filled the air and Dollar braced himself for the first blow. Surprisingly, there was no blow. Dollar whirled his body around to face Romeo, but just as quickly as Romeo had appeared he had disappeared.

By this point Dollar was a basket case. He was watching his back tuff. He even discussed hiring some of Wojo's old crew to have his back. Dollar started asking around to find out what Romeo's story was or if there was word on why he was out to get him. Them niggaz was acting like hoes. Nobody supposedly knew anything. Just the mentioning of Romeo's name made half of them piss on themselves. The most information Dollar could dig up was that Romeo was in for life.

For the next couple of months Dollar slept with one eye open. He saw every muthafucka up in the joint as his enemy. Dollar laid on his cot while he started on his next book, *The Game*. No longer was his back against the bars.

Dollar molested every food item on his tray before sticking it into his mouth for fear a razor blade or any other deadly object might be embedded in it. He was always one of the first in and out of the showers. There was no way he was going to let the old man catch him slippin'. It was only a matter of time before the ultimate confrontation between Dollar and Romeo would erupt and Dollar could hear the clock ticking loud and clear.

One afternoon while Dollar was lifting weights Romeo entered the weight room. Dollar continued lifting as if everything was everything. Like zombies, dudes started surrounding Dollar. Romeo was no longer in his view as the inmates smothered Dollar with their shadows. Dollar continued lifting as if they weren't there. All the while he was scared shitless.

"Boy," Romeo said, "When you see trouble coming your way why do you remain in its path?"

Dollar placed the dumbbells on the rack and stood erect. Romeo looked at his fellow inmates and they immediately disbursed. Before Dollar knew it, it was just Romeo and himself alone in the room.

"How is it you've managed to survive in this piece for almost six years without getting laid to rest?" Romeo asked. "Why do you think that's so?"

" 'Cause I mind my own business," Dollar replied.

"Shit," Romeo laughed. "There's plenty of niggaz up in here minding they own business. That don't mean shit to these killaz up in here."

"I've got a question for you. How is it I've managed to survive in this piece for almost six years without anybody constantly fucking with me besides you?" Dollar smartly replied.

"My point exactly," Romeo said as he walked away.

Romeo actually had Dollar spooked. This was the first time since his incident with Wojo he was feeling the wrath of the prison walls. If someone was out for you in the joint, it was far different than when someone was out for you in the streets. It wasn't about no laying low. There was no where to hide.

Dollar knew that since Romeo was a lifer he didn't have shit to lose. This is what worried Dollar the most. For the first time Dollar knew what it felt like to have genuine fear in his heart and that was some scary shit. It was like being in a pitch-black room with a lion. You could hear his roar as he could hear your every maneuver. It was like walking a mile long tight rope for the first time in your life without a net to catch your fall.

Dollar would soon realize that prison life exists six feet under hell.

***

A couple months later, right before lights out, Dollar was reading one of Donald Goines' old joints when Romeo appeared outside of his cell. Dollar closed the book and sat silently on his cot as he waited to see what fly ass shit came out of Romeo's mouth this time.

Romeo stood quietly as he stared down at the ground. He eventually looked up at Dollar and sighed.

"Truce," Romeo said.

"What?" Dollar asked, just to make sure he was actually hearing what he was hearing.

"You heard me, little nigga," Romeo replied. "I'm done fuckin' wit your punk ass. It ain't even fun no more. Truce."

* * *

The beads of water from the shower spicket beat against Dollar's well-cut physique. Too bad them hoes from the block couldn't reap the benefit from his custom designed body. What was good about Dollar going to prison so young was that he had only been laid a few times. He had let bitches make him sandwiches and suck his dick on an occasion or two, but he wasn't laying pipe to the chicken heads that roamed his block.

Dollar hadn't gotten a taste of the various flavors that pussy came in so the lack of pussy didn't affect him all that much. The few times Dollar had gotten him some it was always from the same girl.

This chick named Pam, who had lived next door to his Aunti Charlene, let him run up in her for the very first time on his sixteenth birthday. Pam was a couple years older than Dollar and had been putting out since she was twelve-years-old. Her own stepbrother had popped her cherry. As a matter of fact, he was the one who hooked the shit up between her and Dollar. It was his birthday present to Dollar.

Dollar was nervous as hell when it all went down, but he managed to get through it long enough to bust his first nut. Pam and Dollar did it right up against the side of Aunti Charlene's house. After that, when it came to Pam, Dollar was like a dog in heat. Whenever his mother would take him and his brother to visit his Aunti Charlene, he would hang out on the porch waiting to catch Pam coming or going. He could smell her coming before he saw her. A squirt of Channel No. 5 that Pam would sneak and use from her mother's dresser always gave her away.

If the timing was right, Dollar knew if Pam's mama wasn't home that Pam would lead him straight to her mother's bed. The bunk bed she shared with her sister, wasn't suffice. The sound of Pam's mother's king size wooden headboard banging up against the wall intensified Dollar shoving his penis into Pam.

They never worried about getting caught because pussy was brand new to Dollar. He never lasted more than two minutes tops (three minutes if he couldn't find the hole right off the bat).

Because Pam lived in Chicago and Dollar lived in Gary, getting between her legs on a regular was difficult. Dollar soon familiarized himself with the technique of jacking off. It became an every day thing almost. This new found skill would pay off during Dollar's years in prison.

Dollar closed his eyes and allowed the shower water to rape him of his sudsy lather. This was the first time he had rested both eyes in what seemed like an eternity. Now that Romeo had declared a truce, Dollar was more at ease.

Dollar aided the water with his hands as he stroked his now 230 pound cut physique. After making sure his skin was squeaky-clean Dollar reached for the shower knobs in order to turn the water off. Just then a striking pain streaked through Dollar's back. It was as if someone had taken a cement block and slammed it into his back with all of their might. The pain was unbearable. Dollar lost all strength as he fell face down onto the tiled shower floor. In and out of consciousness he could see inmates standing over him. Among the inmates, and before losing complete consciousness, he caught view of that all too familiar silhouette.

"*Damn*," Dollar thought to himself as the entire scene faded to black. *"Romeo caught me slippin'*.

Dollar didn't know what Romeo had hit him across the back with, but he knew for certain Romeo had done it. Both angry and in pain Dollar was torn between wanting to die to escape the pain and wanting revenge.

***

In the infirmary Dollar woke up to a blonde hair white girl standing over him. It was Crissy. She was one step up from being like the prison hospital candy stripper.

"Hey now," Crissy said with a smile as Dollar's eyes slowly opened.

Crissy's face was the most pleasant sight Dollar had seen in years. Dollar didn't know if it was because he had been locked up so long, but he never saw a more beautiful white girl in his life. A white chick had never even turned his head before. The only white girls he had ever looked at were the ones on the porno tapes and Playboy magazines he used to jack off to. Crissy was nothing like them. She wasn't trashy looking. She could have been an angel as far as Dollar was concerned.

"Am I dead?" Dollar asked Crissy.

"What?" Crissy smiled.

"Am I dead?" Dollar repeated.

"No, silly," Crissy replied. "Someone busted up your back pretty bad though. I don't know who did it or what they did it with, but they sure got you good. But fortunately, you're not dead."

"Then you shouldn't scare people like that," Dollar said attempting to sit up but prohibited by the pain. "I opened my eyes and saw you, an angel, and thought I was in heaven."

"Good one," Crissy laughed. "But do you really think a man in prison for a triple murder is going to wake up in heaven?"

"You got me on that one," Dollar snickered. "Ouch."

"Oh, you're in pain," Crissy said as she grabbed a hyper thermal needle that was laying on the tray next to Dollar's bed. "I was just getting ready to give you something for that. You're bruised up pretty bad. You must be in severe pain. That's why we've been keeping you out of it. Let me help you try to turn over so I can take care of your discomfort."

Dollar looked at Crissy as if she was crazy as she flicked and plucked at the giant size needle in her hand.

"Oh, you were right," Dollar said. "I am in hell."

"Come on now," Crissy said. "Be a big boy. Roll it over."

"Oh hell no! You gon' stick that in my ass? You are out of your mind. OUCH!" Dollar screamed as the slightest movement sent volts of pain through his body.

"Okay, have it your way," Crissy said laying the needle down and walking away. "I can think of far worse things to get stuck in your ass while in prison."

"Okay, Okay," Dollar said, hailing her back. "Do what you got to do. Just make the pain go away."

Crissy walked back over to Dollar in an *I told you so* demeanor. She picked up the needle and eyeballed Dollar to turn over so that she could stick him in his banana pudding dipped ass. Embarrassed that Crissy was about to see his bare bottom, Dollar hesitated.

"I've been sponging you for a week," Crissy said. "I've seen everything you've got already."

Dollar rolled over very slowly, with Crissy's help, and braced himself as Crissy inserted the needle into his right butt cheek. It was almost instant gratification. Crissy helped Dollar turn back over and get comfortable as his eyes began to prepare themselves for more rest.

"Now that wasn't so bad, was it?" Crissy asked as she ran her hand across Dollar's forehead.

Dollar smiled as false illusions of Crissy in a little white nurse get up danced throughout Dollar's mind. Dollar had a vision in his mind that he was still unable to move, laying in the infirmary bed as Crissy began to tear her clothing off piece by piece. Before Dollar knew it she was straddled on top of him with nothing but a white lacy garter belt with a matching corset and some white, four-inch, ice pick heel pumps.

Crissy's tongue brushed across her cherry red gloss covered lips as she placed her hands behind her back and began to unzip the corset. All the while she was grinding her warm pussy on Dollar's *dude*. As Crissy threw the corset to the floor she took her fingers and pushed her laced thong to the side as she began to tease Dollar with the masturbation of her pink pussy lips. She twisted her clit with her forefinger and thumb and moaned softly. The candy apple red polish on the tip of her nails plunged in and out of her cunt as she began to breath heavily.

Dollar just laid in the hospital bed unable to move; unable to contribute his own fingers in and out of her as his hands were pinned down with Crissy's knees. Crissy began to moan intensely. Dollar knew this was a sign that she was about to cum. Crissy quickly climbed higher up onto Dollar until her pink sticky pussy lips met Dollar's mouth.

"Taste it," Crissy said. "Get drunk off of my cognac."

Dollar realized that he had never eaten pussy in his life. He knew if he ate that pussy right Crissy would handle his dick proper like. Niggaz in jail told him that they stole plenty of niggaz' hoes cause they man didn't go down on them right. "*That bitch, Pam*", Dollar thought. That trick, who had been fucking and sucking dick since she was 12, never once instructed him as to how to eat a woman out.

Dollar's dream of getting laid was now a nightmare. Pussy was literally in his face to do what he wanted to do with it and he was dumbfounded.

"Eat it," Crissy demanded again becoming impatient. "Eat it, Dareese. Dareese, do you hear me? Dareese!"

"Yeah, yeah, what?" Dollar said exiting his dream and re-entering reality.

"Would you like to try to eat, Dareese?" Crissy asked.

"Word," Dollar smiled. No one had called him by his given name in years. Hearing Crissy call him Dareese sounded strange.

"You haven't been able to eat," Crissy said.

"Yeah, I know," Dollar said.

"We've been feeding you intravenously. Would you like to try to eat something."

Slightly disappointed that Crissy was referring to real food and not her private part that she was referring to in the vision he was having of her, Dollar nodded his head in the positive.

"Yeah, that's cool," Dollar replied.

"Don't sound so depressed," Crissy said. "How about we skip this jailhouse food and I give you the sandwich from my lunch? It's salami on rye, decked with lettuce, tomato and onion."

"Yeah, that would be nice," Dollar moaned with a smile on his face.

"Okay, you try to stay awake and I'll be right back," Crissy said heading out the door. "Oh, and Dareese, I was just kidding about that heaven thing. God forgives us all."

Chapter 4

RULES OF THE GAME

It was a couple of weeks before Dollar returned back to gen pop (General Population). He hated that every time an inmate walked by him they hissed and laughed at the back brace he sported.

"Damn, Dollar," this faggot ass dude named Shawny said as he brushed by Dollar with his little tee-shirt tied into a knot at his belly button. "If I had known you put your back into it like that I would have tattooed your name on my ass years ago."

The inmates within ear distance laughed as if they were watching Def Comedy Jam. Dollar just brushed that shit off and went on about his business.

He passed a table where a game of Chess between Romeo and some other inmate was taking place. As Romeo began to make his move he spotted Dollar walking by. A grim grin took over the bottom portion of his face as he declared checkmate against his opponent without taking his eyes off of Dollar.

Dollar stared him down all the same. Fuck it! Dollar looked at it this way; both them niggaz was going to die in jail anyway. They might as well go out gangsta. Although Dollar was in no position to battle, he wasn't going to bow down to no man. The look he gave Romeo confirmed such.

***

Ironically, Dollar's life always seemed to come full circle. Like dejavu, one night, right before lights out Romeo appeared outside of Dollar's cell. Dollar was ready for the old man this time though. Earlier that day, during Dollar's shaving session, he had removed the blade and placed it under his tongue. When he returned to his cell he had inserted it into the bristles of his toothbrush and secured it with tape. Fuck buying a dozen cans of soda pop and loading his pillowcase with them to blast Romeo with. Dollar was going for the jugular. The old man had brought out something in Dollar that he had managed to bury deep inside his soul, the killa in him.

"I bet you think that was me who busted up your back in the shower," Romeo said tooting on a cancer stick.

"Look, old man," Dollar said raisin' up off of his bed. "Fuck you and the mind games you playin'. If you got beef, then come on wit it. Let's do the damn thang."

Romeo couldn't help but burst out laughing. "You little niggaz kill me. What is it y'all call yourselves, hard? Ain't nothin' hard about you hoes except for your dicks when you wake up in the morning. Put the Old G's back on the street and we'll show y'all dumb bitches how the game is played."

"Well from the looks of all the Old G's occupying these prison cells, y'all lost the muthafuckin' game."

"Yeah, but that's when the teachin' comes in," Romeo said exhaling two synchronized streams of smoke from his nostrils. "When you lose, you have time to sit back and think of where you fucked up along the way. Mentally you can correct that shit. Of course you can't go back in time and change things, but you can school the next muthafucka tryin' to come up in the game. Take you for instance. You sat with your back against the world. What kind of shit is that? The world is your enemy and you turn your back to it. You assumed because you *Dolla Dolla Bill*, that shit is tight for you. Son, even Jesus was crucified. You grubbed on your slop thinking there wasn't one nigga up in here wishing you dead. You never forked through your food for foreign objects, you just sat down and ate like it was the last muthafuckin' supper. Do you really think that *if I don't fuck with nobody they ain't gonna fuck with me* bullshit works? Jealous ass niggaz want you dead cause they think your dick is bigger than theirs, but a nigga scream truce and throw up two fingers and you think everything is all good. Just because a muthafucka say they cool with you doesn't mean they cool with you. Just because a muthafucka wanna roll with you don't mean they down for you. Half these niggaz trying to be up in your corner don't wanna be down for you. They only want to be you...recognize."

"So what the fuck, old man?" Dollar said, becoming agitated as if he was attempting to put a Rubics Cube in order. "Why you telling me all this shit? I've survived in this piece this long. I'm doing something right."

Romeo laughed again. His laugh was beginning to infuriate Dollar.

"Back in the day, that Wojo shit," Romeo recollected. "Do you really think them niggaz didn't draw blood out of your asshole because you shouted out a threat or two? When it was all said and done and your asshole was still as tight as a virgin's pussy, didn't you think that God must have been watching over you?"

Dollar thought back at the close calls he had and could have had. He thought back at how he knew God must have been on his side. He looked up at Romeo speechless, not willing to give him the gratification of being right.

"Well, little nigga," Romeo said as he put the lit cigarette out with his index finger and thumb. "I'm God."

* * *

One would have never known Dollar and Romeo had ever had beef. Now days they were joined at the hip. Although Romeo had a twisted way of doing it, he taught Dollar how to survive. He taught Dollar how to constantly watch his back and never, under any circumstance, trust anyone.

Romeo spent hours crowning Dollar with all of the street knowledge he had in him. This was shocking to other inmates. No one knew too much about Romeo, not even his given name. He was never one to brag and boast about his dirt. He never put his business in the yard. But for some reason he had found something in Dollar that made him vocal.

Dollar spent endless hours listening to Romeo's "old school" tales. Romeo did everything from snatching gold chains off of college girl's necks, to mackin' hoes, to robbing banks. Romeo broke down all the things he would have done differently to keep from catching a case, like keepin' his eye on the prize instead of gettin' greedy. He even schooled Dollar on other inmate's fuck-ups, how they had picked the wrong crowd to roll with, how they should have detected that in the end, back stabbin' muthafucka's wouldn't be down for them.

"Loyalty and betrayal are muthafuckas," Romeo said to Dollar as they sat in the yard rappin'. "There are times in life when your head gets all fucked up trying to figure out who you need to be loyal to and who the fuck you just might have to cross. It's even harder trying to figure out who is actually loyal to you and who just might cross you. Eventually you'll have to play both roles. You gotta be that backstabbin' nigga to one muthafucka in order to stay loyal to the next. But you gotta be careful because if you get it twisted, one or the other (loyalty or betrayal) might destroy you...sometimes both."

Dollar would spend his nights dissecting Romeo's words. Romeo had so much he wanted to hammer into Dollar's brain. The main lesson Romeo tried to teach Dollar was to be lowk ey. The less people who knew him, the less people to be jealous of him, the less people to try to put salt in his game.

"Take the game of basketball for instance," Romeo said to Dollar. "Half them niggaz ain't about the team, they about show boating, making a tight play that's going to bring about recognition in the game. They want ESPN play of the week and shit. Them same muthafucka's be the first one's in the spotlight when shit ain't right, rape charges, failing drug test, shootin' they babie's mama's and shit. Now take that cat who just gets out there and does what he's supposed to do, sticks his man, passes the ball, shoots only when he knows he has a sure shot. We hardly know that cat's name. His house is just as big as the next baller's. His wrist is just as iced, but yet we wouldn't even recognize his ass walking down the street. That's the muthafucka you want to be."

Now that Dollar had been let in on the medley of hustles that existed, he wanted to stick his spoon into every pot of hustle there was on the streets and scoop up a taste. But unfortunately, that was no longer an option for Dollar.

Still, that didn't keep Romeo from spoon feeding Dollar knowledge, making him fiend for the streets...making him wish he'd give his left nut to be back on the streets again.

"So how did you finally get caught?" Dollar asked Romeo while they sat at the Chessboard."

"Fuckin' round with other muthafuckas," Romeo said. "They was some iffy cats. I should have known to just do the damn thing without them. Whenever a cat gets iffy on you, like they wanna bitch out, cut 'em the fuck off. They useless."

"So why didn't you take your own advice and cut 'em off?" Dollar asked.

"Because I didn't know then what I know now, lil' nigga," Romeo answered sternly. "I had robbed plenty of spots by myself. I don't know what in the hell made me think I needed to pull them niggaz in on that hit."

Dollar continued to listen to Romeo as he went on about how his nervous ass partners blotched the what could have been "big hit".

Dollar could tell by the way Romeo spoke that he too wished that he could be back on the streets to do shit all over again. Dollar could tell by the intensity in Romeo's tone every time they talked. Dollar and Romeo found that they were so much alike. Hell they even started to look alike.

"Damn," Dollar said one day while attempting to be taught the game of Chess by Romeo. "With all the shit I know now, if I was on the them damn streets today, I'd be a Don."

"Fuck that!" Romeo said becoming angry. "You'd be your own man, not a made man. You little niggaz watch too many Al Pacino movies. You think them Mafia muthafuckas running around talkin' 'bout they wanna be a nigga? Hell no, but you niggaz always want to be them. All y'all worry about is being fly and making sure everybody knows who y'all is. Well, that's where y'all fuck up. The bling bling brings too much attention from the wrong people. Why a hustler would want everybody to know who they are and what they do is beyond me. It's a stupid egotistical mistake. You don't wanna do too much in the game. The less you stand out, the longer your chances are of remaining a player. Get in the game, do what you came to do and get the fuck out!"

"You right," Dollar agreed. "I'd be my own man. Fuck trying to show off to these wankstas. It's all about me."

Dollar dazed off envisioning what he used to know as freedom. Romeo could see the look of desperation in Dollar's eyes. It was as if Romeo was living the street life once again through the dream in Dollar's eyes. Romeo knew that the time had finally come.

"What if I was to tell you there was a way for me to put you back on the streets," Romeo said, pausing from the Chess game.

"I'd say, damn, you really are God," Dollar laughed.

"Seriously," Romeo said with deepest sincerity.

"I'd say do that shit," Dollar turned serious.

Romeo bowed his head and ran his hand down his face. He took a deep sigh and looked up at Dollar. "I got something that the state wants. If I give it to you to give to them, you're a free man."

"But that don't make sense," Dollar said. "If you have something that could make me a free man, then why wouldn't you just use it to free yourself."

Romeo smiled a huge grin. He patted Dollar on the shoulder, who was confused at this point.

"You finally analyzing shit," Romeo said. "See what a game of Chess will teach you?"

"Come on, I'm serious," Dollar continued.

"Because what I have that the state wants is me," Romeo replied.

"The state already got your black ass, old man," Dollar said.

"They got the Romeo that shot and killed a guard and two tellers during a bank robbery," Romeo said. "They ain't got Romeo A.K.A. the Midwest Serial Killer."

Dollar's mouth dropped. He had heard of those killings from years and years ago. Dead bodies of young white females were being found throughout the Midwest. There were a couple of Latino and black chicks too, but the FBI didn't want to taint the Caucasian killings with the minority ones. Each victim's case had similarities. Profilers couldn't piece together a suspect because nothing corresponded with their typical serial killings.

"That's you man?" Dollar shouted.

"Shhh," Romeo ordered.

"Damn, old man," Dollar said. "All this time we been kickin' it you never found the need to tell me that you were a notorious cold blooded murderer?"

"Shit, I figured you were one also so what would it matter?" Romeo said sarcastically.

"I done told you, man. I didn't kill nobody!" Dollar stood up and shouted in his defense. "Besides, poppin' a couple of niggaz ain't shit compared to torturing and murdering bitches."

"Alright. I hear you. Calm down," Romeo said. "It wasn't even like that. Them hoes asked for that shit. Look, little nigga, this is a get out of jail for free card. Do you want it or not?"

Dollar slowly seating himself back down was sign enough that he wanted the card.

"I just can't see you doing no sick ass shit like that, old man," Dollar said.

"It ain't even like that, young blood," Romeo argued. "I didn't just go out stalking and killing girls. It was part of the game. But never you mind the reasoning behind the slayings, you wanna reap from them right?"

"I'm in for a body. How am I gonna get out on a body?" Dollar replied.

"Your bodies, some thugs, criminal niggaz that deserved to be dead anyway as far as the man is concerned. You did them a favor. My bodies, white girls. Over the years these unsolved murders prevented the re-election of two mayors, a governor and the resignation of a Police Chief. There's a million-dollar reward for the arrest and conviction of the Midwest Serial Killer. To make the deal mo' better, you decline the reward money. You do the math," Romeo said.

Dollar listened intensely as he nodded his head. As always, Romeo was making sense.

So do you want the card or not?" Romeo asked Dollar.

"Hell, yeah," Dollar replied.

"Good, then listen up."

For the next several weeks Romeo gave Dollar explicit details of the crimes such as weapons of choice, material used to bound and gag the women, what the women were wearing, etc. He even informed Dollar of a couple of bodies that had not yet been discovered.

Last but not least Dollar and Romeo would have to stage a falling out. The prison would need to see that Dollar and Romeo were no longer on the same team in order for Dollar dropping the dime to be taken seriously.

Dollar and Romeo acted out a fight in the prison yard. Blood was drawn and Dollar even ended up with a month in the hole. This action would validate Dollar's decision to snitch on Romeo and would be sure to guarantee him life on the outside.

* * *

"I got something the state wants," Dollar said to the District Attorney as his lawyer and the prison warden each sat beside him.

Dollar, after a thousand attempts, managed to retain the Similac skills of a public pretender (defender). Dollar needed him to initiate and mediate the game of tit for tat between him and the State of Ohio.

The PD recorded Dollar's statement in relation to the Midwest Serial Killer and researched the facts of the crimes. Sure enough, Dollar's story about the crimes panned out. There were facts of the case that Dollar would have only known if the killer told him or if he were the killer himself.

The PD contacted the District Attorney's office, and after some major convincing, got him to agree upon a meeting with Dollar in the prison warden's office.

"I'm listening," The DA said to Dollar as he tilted his chair back onto its two hind legs. "Get to talking. Time is money. It's not everyday I allot my time to some two bit killer convict."

"My client has the key to unlock a case that has had law enforcement's heads spinning for some time," Dollar's attorney pronounced. "Do you remember those five unsolved homicides here in Ohio and the seven others throughout the Midwest...you know, those nice little Caucasian princesses?"

"The Midwest Serial Killer? Okay, you've got my attention," the DA said, positioning all four legs of the chair onto the floor.

"Do you want them closed after all of these years?" Dollar's attorney asked.

"Don't play games with me," the DA said. "You know God damn well the public and the media was all over our asses on that one. Whenever one of those girl's parents decides to talk to Date Line or Court TV or Oprah or some shit, the shit hits the fan all over again."

"Then I'm sure you'll be willing to sweep the lives of three dead African American thugs up under the rug in exchange for the lives of five beautiful, hell twelve, give or take a few, would be doctors and lawyers, white females," Dollar's lawyer said.

"It's hard telling, sometimes, the difference between when someone's jerking my dick and when someone actually has me by the balls," the DA said. "I want the killer on a platter. No hints, tips or premonitions. I'll settle for nothing less than being the one to shoot the needle into the son of a bitches veins."

"It's hard telling, sometimes, if I'm being made love to or if I'm being fucked," Dollar said. "If I give you the name of your man, I'm screwed. I'm deemed a snitch and risk getting my tongue cut the fuck out. I'm not waiting around for no conviction, trial or any bullshit like that. I turn snitch for the state then the state frees me. I'll give you a minute or two to check shit out, but that's it."

"Look, nigger," the DA said. "Oh pardon me, how do you people like to say it these days, nigga? Anyway, if you can give me the Midwest Serial Killer, then you're a free man, no halfway house, no probation officer, no nothing. In the words of your former great African American leader you'll be free at last, free at last, God almighty, you'll be free at last."

Dollar knew the DA was being a bigot ass prick, but what could he do? He wasn't free yet, not free enough to tie the DA's testicles in a knot for using Dr. King's quote as if it were some lame ass cliché.

"You're already in on three bodies," The DA started to ponder. This could be tough. I mean hell, how can I convince the state to let a killer out for turning in another killer? It just don't add up," the DA said.

"Well, I didn't see the family of those three dead men on television threatening the skills and abilities of the judicial system," Dollar's attorney said. "And just think, the person who finally breaks this case is going to be a Saint in the community, and I'm sure that $1,000,000 reward money, that my client is willing to waive, will find a nice home."

A crooked smile swept over the DA's face. The things he could do with a million dollars. He could figure out some way to bank the million-dollar reward money himself. He would probably have to pull a few strings and pay off a couple of folks with a portion of the reward money, but he just might be able to find a way to make the deal work. He was a politician, of course he could find a way.

"I think we can work this out somehow. I mean perhaps there were some technicalities that were overlooked in your client's case," the DA said with a devilish grin. "But if your client is bullshitting me, then you'll have him to thank for your new position," the DA said to Dollar's lawyer.

"What new position?" Dollar's lawyer asked.

"The one you'll have mopping up floors in the prison toilets you dumb fuck."

Chapter 5

The Deliberate Stranger

Dollar couldn't believe this day was coming to pass. Today was the day he was going to be a free man again. The State of Ohio was throwing him back onto the streets, the streets Dollar would have to get reacquainted with. He knew so much shit had changed over eight years that he would have to perform foreplay on the streets before running up in them again.

Dollar had big plans. He had learned so much from Romeo that the sky was the limit. As he packed up the little bit of shit he owned, all he could think about was all of the tax free mullah in the streets that had his name written all over it. No way was he going to fuck up this time around. This was his second chance to redeem himself to the game.

"I'm a big ass nigga," Dollar said to himself as he buttoned up his blue dress shirt that was compliments of the prison. He flexed his muscles and thought about all the pussy his new build would gain him. There was no doubt in his mind that once he showed up on the block, honeys would be all on his jock.

He entered prison looking like LL Cool J from "Krush Groove", but came out looking like the new buffed up LL. He had picked up an extra 40 pounds of muscle. Yep, yep, pussy and money was all that was on Dollar's mind, but not necessarily in that order.

Dollar brushed his hair then ran his tongue across his perfectly straight white teeth.

"Who would have thought it?" Ed said as he came to escort Dollar out of the prison. "Dollar Bill back on the streets. Where you gon' go man?"

"I'm copping a cot at the YMCA back in Indiana," Dollar answered. When I leave this bitch I get a bus pass and one hundred dollars."

"Then what?" Ed asked.

"Shit, man," Dollar said. "I don't know. I don't give a fuck. All I know is that I'm kissing this place good-bye."

"I'm sure you'll be just fine," Ed said, reaching into his pocket. "But, hey, I got some peoples you might want to contact. They can hook you up with some ole simple ass shit. You know, just something to get you by like cleaning, painting, construction, working at a gas station or what not."

"Good looking out," Dollar said taking the piece of paper Ed had retrieved from his pocket.

"Well, I guess it's that time, partna," Ed said.

"Let's do this," Dollar said grabbing his bag and following Ed's lead.

A crescendo of whistling followed Dollar throughout the prison as Ed escorted him to freedom. He gave dat and pound to some of the inmates. Most of them could care less about Dollar being freed, they were just caught up in the idea of freedom alone. Underneath the whistling there was some hissing, like the sound of a snake. That's one thing Dollar had to mentally prepare himself for, being thought of as a snitch. But he had planned on spending the rest of his life having people think he was a murderer and he really wasn't, what the fuck if they thought he was a snitch?

Dollar had obeyed the street code. He hadn't snitched on his partners. This was different. He couldn't help it if *a get out of jail free* card had been placed in the palm of his hands.

"Yo, Ed," Dollar said. "Where's Romeo?"

"Come on, Dollar man," Ed said. "Don't even think about it. You on your way out of here. Don't start no shit now."

"No, it's cool," Dollar assured him. "Just take me to him."

Ed took Dollar to solitary where Romeo was moved to while he awaited trial.

"Five minutes, man," Ed said noided. "Five minutes and don't start no shit, Dollar, or I swear to God."

Ed left Dollar outside of Romeo's solitary cell as he stood at the corner conversing with another CO.

"Oh Romeo, oh Romeo, wherefore art thou Romeo?" Dollar whispered outside of the steal door.

"You out, man?" Romeo asked through the slot.

"I'm out," Dollar replied as silence fell upon them. "Any last words of advice."

"You know everything I know now," Romeo said. "Be good, Dollar, and be good at it."

"I hate to leave you in solitary like this, man," Dollar said.

"I'm going to have to buy all new shit," Romeo said. "You know them niggaz done had a field day raid'n my shit."

Why, old man?" Dollar couldn't help but ask.

Romeo ignored Dollar's inquiry as he pressed his head against the door holding back his tears.

"Do me a favor," Romeo said to Dollar.

"Anything, man," Dollar replied.

"Make sure the first thing you do is go see your family," Romeo replied.

"No doubt," Dollar said. "That goes unsaid."

"You take care of yourself," Romeo said.

"Peace out, old man," Dollar replied as he prepared to walk away. "Yo Romeo," Dollar said, "What's your real name, at least?"

"Don't matter now," Romeo said.

"Come on, man," Dollar begged.

"Blake," Romeo replied. "Ramelle Blake."

A sudden chill took over Dollar's body. His blood boiled throughout his body and he could hear his heart beating as loud as thunder. Dollar hadn't heard that name since he was three years old. The last time he heard it was when his mother was begging and pleading for his father not to leave her.

"Ramelle Daren Blake," his mother cried. "Don't you dare walk out of that door. Do you think I don't know what people are saying about you out there in them streets? You think I don't know how you come about the money you bring into this house? It ain't from working down at Junie's club like you say it is."

"That money feeds this family don't it?" Dollar's father replied. "So what's it matter where it came from?"

"So are you saying it's true? Is it true what people are saying? Do you have women out there on the streets for you, Ramelle?"

"Don't you question me, woman. Who in the fuck do you think you are?"

Dollar had never heard his father swear at his mother before. He had rarely heard them argue in his few years. The disrespect Dollar's father was showing his mother was the first sign that the streets were taking over him, that the game would eventually play him.

Dollar's mother felt as though her husband had just spit in her face. He had never talked to her that way and now he was scolding her like one of his hoes.

"You know what?" Dollar's mother replied. "You go. You get out of here. I don't want my boys growing up around you. They might mistake you for a man."

"Fuck you, bitch," Dollar's father said to his mother as he exited the apartment leaving him, his mother, and his screaming ten-month-old baby brother for dead.

He never even came back for a change of clothes. Dollar's mother never threw out one thing of his, hoping that one day he might return.

Dollar's body stood frozen. The man he had spent almost his entire life hating, the man that gave him life, was now, once again, giving him life. Dollar wanted to rip Romeo's fucking heart out, though. He wanted to spit on him. He wanted to stomp him for each year his mother spent working in fast food restaurants. He wanted to stomp him for each year him and his brother went without a daddy. In Dollar's head he was envisioning him shankin' Romeo until every ounce of life oozed out of his body. But in reality, he was stiff.

"I know you can't speak," Romeo said. "And even if you could, no telling how cruel your words might be even in spite of the situation at hand. And I wouldn't blame you one bit. Believe me, any hate you've had for me over the years I've hated myself ten times as much."

Dollar was still cold speechless. He couldn't even blink for fear a tear of anger might drop.

"You asked me why, why I'm doing this for you," Romeo spoke. "When you were born I remember watching you sleep in the hospital. I never took my eyes off of you. When you opened your eyes for the first time I wanted to be there. My mother, your Grandma Stevie, told me that you can see your soul through the eyes of your child. When I looked into your eyes I saw everything that I knew I had to be. I didn't see the person that I was, but the person that I needed to be. Sooner than later, the streets started calling me. I wanted so much for you and your mamma. I wanted to give y'all the world, but then your little brother was born and the world was on my shoulders. I couldn't luck up on a decent job and couldn't hold onto a half-decent one. Instead of pushing myself and being strong I answered the call. I answered the calling of the streets. Hell, I don't need to tell you. There was tax free ends to be made out there, but your mama wasn't with that. No way was she going to be a hustler's wife. That's why I told you what I told back when I first started kickin' knowledge to you, if you find a good woman and you love her, then you have to choose. You have to choose either the streets or her. If you really love her then you fo sho don't want to bring her into the life. *You* have to choose. Don't ever make her choose. You won't win."

Dollar listened intensely as Romeo continued.

"Anyway, the first time I looked into your eyes I promised your mamma I would always be there for you. I told your mamma I'd trade in my life for you. I made a lot of promises to her. So far this one, trading in my life for you, has been the only promise I've been able to keep. Go out there, son. Take everything I've given you and rule them streets. The world is your playground, remember that."

Dollar swallowed and stuck his chest out. He regained his composure and looked straight ahead at Ed to signal him that he was ready to walk. He felt as though he had to say something to Romeo. This was his only opportunity to have words with the man he now knew to be his father.

As Dollar proceeded to exit the jail, he said to Romeo, "Don't you ever call me son."

* * *

Back in the day when Dollar first went to jail Jodeci was the male group dominating the charts, now in 2003, these young cats named B2K was rippin' up the airwaves. Dollar bounced his head as one of their songs played on the radio through the Walkman he had copped off of an inmate a few years ago.

The Greyhound bus ride from Ohio to Indiana was like a luxurious limousine ride. Dollar could have rode on that bus forever. Anything but the jail cell was like paradise.

Dollar knew that the bus ticket and one hundred dollars wasn't going to get him far, but it would get him as far away from that jail as possible. He was free and clear of his debt to society. He didn't owe the State of Ohio, or any other state for that matter, shit. He knew he was going to have to stay at the YMCA until he could blueprint some shit out, but he was cool with that. He needed time to think. He needed to clear his mind of what he had experienced for the last eight years and put into action all that he had learned.

Dollar knew that there were three kinds of smarts in the world, street smart, book smart and prison smart. Dollar now possessed a little of each. Once he put things in perspective and learned what was presently going on in the streets, he would be invincible.

When Dollar's bus finally arrived in Indiana he exited the bus and took in a whiff of the smell of the streets. Damn he had missed that scent, the scent of cruddy sewers and cigarette smoke with just a hint of beer that some cat had poured onto the ground for his homies that no longer walked the earth. City life, there's nothing like it in the world.

After taxiing over to the "Y" Dollar was down to $88.21. The taxi fare was only $7.80, but he had purchased an extra value meal from McDonalds at one of the rest stops the bus made. Dollar knew he was going to have to start setting up a hustle, but it was going to be impossible to do it without a crew. With only $88.21 to his name, time was of the essence.

Like Dollar had learned in prison, everyone around him was his enemy. No way could he trust these new age gangstas. These cool ass muthafuckas ain't about nothin' but the bling bling and fucking each other's hoes. He knew that much from the young bucks that were starting to fill the prison. It was time to drop in on Tommy and Ral. Hustling ran in their veins. No matter what they were up to these days, Dollar knew in his heart they would be down for a hustle. Besides, they owed him. The way Dollar saw it, them niggaz owed him the trouble of getting his life on track, for it was his life that spared their own.

First thing was first; he had to look up his family. The guilt of betraying them by being loyal to Tommy put Dollar in between a rock and a hard place. The choice he made meant having to abandon his mother and brother.

How in the hell was he going to explain things to his Mother and little brother? He hoped they would forgive him and understand his reasoning for not wanting to stay in contact with them while in prison.

When he showed up on their doorstep would they believe their eyes? Would they believe him when he told them that he was no longer dead as far as they were concerned, but that he had been resurrected back onto the streets by God?

Chapter 6

Is There A Doctor in the House

"This funky ass place is worse than the joint," Dollar said as he brushed away an oversized cockroach that had made its way up his arm. As it flew in the air he followed it with his eyes. Upon it landing he stomped it dead with his foot.

Dollar scraped the cockroach off of the bottom of his flip-flop. Looking at the flip-flop reminded Dollar of the joint.

"I gotsta get me some real house shoes," Dollar said out loud. Soon enough Dollar would catch back up with the latest fashions. It was now 2003 and shit had changed plenty since 1994. Dollar would be back on top of his game in no time with the right planning. Dollar spent most of his days sketching out different types of stick-ups he could work. Dollar was fiendin' for dem streets. Part of him understood how his father was drawn away by the call of the streets. But the other part of him kept saying "Fuck that! He had a wife and two kids. Something should have eventually brought his ass back home." Now look at him, Ramelle Blake, A.K.A. Romeo, B.K.A. Midwest Serial Killer, had been sucked up by the streets. He had set out to own the streets and the streets ended up owning him.

Yeah, Dollar was glad his father was able to rebirth him, but years of hate for this stranger over powered a few months of liking him. He was glad that man would be sentenced to a slow death. After all, that is the sentence he gave his family when he walked out of that door 23 years ago. Dollar swore he would never abandon his family and to ensure such, he decided that he would never have one, a family. Good conversation and pussy is all any role a woman would play in his life, but a wifey...hell no! He would father no children to abandon and would husband no woman.

So many cats in the prison had gone down because of their so called wifey. Hoes start rattin' them fools out when they knew and had access to what Store N Lock facility the Expedition and $600,000 in cash was located. Dollar wouldn't make that mistake. He wouldn't be one of those cats who spent years risking their lives in the game to feed kids that aren't even his 'cause a bitch done fucked one of his partners and got pregnant and don't know who the damn daddy is. Talk shows and the news brought to light and aided in Dollar's list of do's and don'ts.

Speaking of family, Dollar had already been in Gary a week without looking up his Mother and little brother. It was time to start the preparations for getting his life back. He needed to come at them with more than "I'm out of jail and I'm just hanging out at the "Y" not doing shit with my life." Dollar had to stop staring at the ceiling and make a move.

***

Dollar went into the communal bathhouse at the "Y" and got himself cleaned up. He had spent $33.54 on some clothing items he had picked up from a local thrift store. He pieced together an "I'm looking for a job" ensemble that consisted of some tan khakis and a white three button Henley. He roped a husky brown belt around his waist that just happened to be the same shade of brown as his boots. Dollar armed himself with the $54.67 he had left, the list of job contacts Ed had given him and copped a ride on the city bus to the first address on the contact list.

Dollar hit the buzzer for the driver to stop the bus and

let him off at the next stop. Dollar walked a couple of blocks down Oak Street before he came to the address he was in search of.

"I'm looking for Redd," Dollar said to the group of men hanging outside, in the cold, of the worn down looking building that had a hand painted sign that read "Work for a day".

The men pointed Dollar towards a double glass door. As he walked through the doors he could see, through the reflection, a few of the men screwing up their mugs at him. No one said it aloud, but those of whom he managed to make contact with during his inquiry gave him that "yeah, that nigga just got out the joint" look. People see a buff nigga and automatically assume he been locked up. Although Dollar looked as though he had been in the World Gym training for the Swartzenager Classic, the men were correct in their unspoken assumptions.

"Are you Redd?" Dollar asked the biker type lookin' red neck sitting behind one of the two cluttered desk that were in the office.

"I am," the man answered. "You come for work?"

"Yes sir," Dollar said.

The man laughed and replied, "No need for that sir shit. This ain't IBM or nothing like that. Next thing I know you'll be handing me a resume."

Redd immediately handed Dollar a stack of papers to fill out. He informed Dollar that it was just some general liability waivers and what not. Redd gave Dollar a clipboard and a pen and invited him to have a seat.

"Can you read," Redd asked Dollar.

"Excuse me," Dollar said.

"Can you read?"

"What the fuck kind of question is that," Dollar said taking offense. "A black man walk up in here for a job and you think he can't read?"

"Whoa!" Red exclaimed. "Slow down, brotha. Homeless men and white men with a first grade education come up in here for jobs and can't read, or write for that matter. They get embarrassed and they run out of here and miss out on making money that could have afforded them their next meal. I hired Kera to help out those types. She reads and completes the paperwork for them. That's all I'm saying."

Dollar, feeling a little salty, apologized to Redd and shook his hand. In addition, he commended him for his extra step on helping out cats on the streets and fresh out of the joint. Dollar proceeded to complete the paperwork one sheet after the next. As he completed the final page, which was more so biographical information, a soft aroma filled the air. Redd's Benson and Hedges Menthol light smoke odor had been superseded by J-Lo's Glo, which was similar in scent to the Night Queen oil Dollar's mother would always wear.

Dollar looked up at the sweet young thang that was walking over to the second cluttered desk that sat behind Redd's. Ma had it going on. She was a soft yellow toned, petite flower. She wore her hair in a natural curly bobb that could have very well been wet and wavy weave. She had a medium sized frame with a chunky bootie. You could see her panties because her jeans were gapping around her waist. Obviously she had to purchase a larger size pants to get over her big ass.

"Filet fish with extra tarter, large fry and large sprite," the girl said handing Redd his lunch.

"That's my little girl," Redd said.

"Oh, Daddy," the girl said.

"*Hell, No,*" Dollar thought. He couldn't believe Redd was sticking his finger into the chocolate pot. If this was Redd's baby girl, she had to be by a black woman. The first fine sistah he sees and she's the boss' daughter. There went Dollar's vision of tagging dat ass.

"All finished, sir," Dollar said, handing Redd the

paperwork. "I mean Redd."

"Oh, just give them to Kera," Redd said pointing to her. "Kera this is...I didn't catch your name. I guess I got off track thinking you were going to try to beat my ass after that statement about not being able to read."

"Oh, come on now," Dollar joked. "Let's squash that already."

"I'm just joshing'," Redd said.

"Anyway, it's Dareese, Dareese Blake. But you can call me Dollar. That's my nickname. Everyone called me that as a kid."

"Kera, Dollar. Dollar, Kera," Redd said.

"Nice to meet you," Kera said seductively as she slowly slid the papers from Dollar's hand.

"Same here," Dollar smiled.

Dollar knew that pussy was his if he wanted it. Compared to them raggedy dudes that were standing out front, Dollar was probably the finest muthafucka Kera had seen up in there. Dollar knew he was making an impression as Kera took the papers from Dollar not taking her eyes off of him once. No way was he going to run up in the boss's daughter. That would keep Dollar out of work for real. Love 'em and leave 'em was the game plan. He could see her now crying to Daddy. Dollar had to shake this one off. He couldn't go gettin' caught up with no chick. He had to focus on gettin' that paper.

"So what can you do?" Redd interrupted Dollar's thoughts. Dollar looked puzzled. "What type of work can you do? What was your last job?"

"Oh, uhh...I can uhh....It was uhh..."

"Fresh out the clink, huh?" Redd embarrassed the fuck out of Dollar by asking him that shit in front of Kera.

Dollar didn't respond verbally. He answered Redd with his eyes.

"Thought so," Redd said.

The fact that Dollar was a former jailbird seemed to attract Kera to him even more. Her eyes lit up for this beefed up bad boy. Dollar knew right then and there that she was young, eighteen tops. She had that look in her eyes that little girls get when they get a whiff of a dangerous man, a man who ain't afraid of the streets, a man that would break another man's muthahfuckin' neck for her ass.

"It's cool," Redd assured Dollar. "Not everybody who comes through those doors are on the up an up. People need a break. Hell, I did a dime for the Feds."

Redd looked as though he had done a decade that consisted of ten unrelenting years. This explained his hard look.

"Look, Ed sent me. I don't even know how this type of gig works. I just know I need some cash."

"Ed," Redd laughed. "That's a blast from the past. What's he been up to?"

"Same ole, same ole," Dollar answered. He's still a CO over at Chillicothe in Ohio."

Redd almost choked on his French fries as he started laughing. "He's a CO? He never told me that. Ed used to terrorize the neighborhood. I always pictured him on the other side of the law."

"You know I told you Uncle Ed was working as a CO," Kera added. "That one time I went to visit Mommy in Ohio I told you about Uncle Ed being a CO. He's only been a CO forever and a day."

"Did you?" Redd said. "I don't remember."

"That's why you need to lay off of that stuff, Dad." Redd gave Kera an evil look. He couldn't believe she was putting his business out there like that.

Sensing her father's anger, Kera got prissy, "It's not like he's deep cover. He just got out of jail for Christ sakes."

"You Ed's niece, huh?" Dollar asked.

"He's my ex's brother, Kera's mom's brother," Redd

answered for Kera. "Ed's cool. His sister's a bitch, but I don't hold that against him."

"That's my moms you talking about," Kera snapped.

"Bitch is a compliment," Redd tried to make Kera believe. "You're only seventeen. You'll know what I'm talking about in a few years."

"*Damn*", Dollar thought. "*She's only 17. I ain't going out like R. Kelly, people running around thinking I'm robbin' cradles and shit. Only seventeen years old...damn! Not only is this fine piece of ass the boss's daughter, but she ain't even grew hair on her coochie yet.*"

Dolar's hard dick he had been concealing went limp. He wouldn't be putting it to use anytime soon on Kera. He didn't care if her eighteenth birthday was next week, under age is under age.

"Not for long," Kera replied. "I'll be eighteen in a couple of weeks.

It was almost as if Kera noticed Dollar's loss in interest in her and was aiming her comment more so towards him than her father.

"*Oh yeah,*" Dollar said in his head. "*I guess I can hold off for a couple of weeks. By then that hot little pussy will really be ripe for the pickin'.*"

"Anyway, how this here thing works is that you can come hang out here everyday and wait for some work to come through. It can be anything from cleaning offices to building a deck," Redd said to Dollar. "With your size, I'm sure you'll be the first pick on the kickball team. You staying over at the "Y", a halfway house?"

"The "Y", Dollar answered.

"Well, when you get yourself a phone I can call you up for work. Like I said, with your size, folks will be requesting you by name."

"So, should I come back tomorrow?" Dollar asked.

"Yeah, if you don't want any work today," Redd replied sarcastically.

"So that's what the men outside are doing, waiting on work?" Dollar asked.

"Yeah, the folks who need workers, sometimes just for a day or sometimes for a full project, come through and scoop up workers," Redd said looking at his watch. "Yeah, it's still early enough. Somebody might come through looking for some workers."

Dollar knew he needed some change for his pocket so he decided to go hang out with the other dudes. Dollar felt like a hooker waiting on a trick. After a couple of hours some man pulled up in a pick-up and went inside the building.

"That's Marlon," one of the guys said. "Whenever he's down a man or two who comes by here to find replacements."

"What's the job," Dollar asked.

"Construction," the guy answered. "He frames houses and shit. Do you know anything about that?"

"If it means putting a dollar in my pocket I do," Dollar said.

"That's what I'm saying," the dude laughed. "I'm Jay."

"Dollar," Dollar said shaking Jay's hand.

"You straight out the joint?" Jay asked.

"Damn. Is that shit written across my forehead or something?" Dollar joked.

"You know how it is out here on the streets," Jay said. "You either homeless, a crackhead, or freshly released from that gated community. You don't look like a crackhead and you don't smell homeless."

"Right, right," Dollar nodded.

Just then Marlon and Redd came out of the office.

"Any of you men know anything about tarring and cementing?" Marlon asked.

Of course all the men proclaimed of having such

knowledge. Marlon knew some were lying.

"You, you and you," Marlon said pointing at Jay, Dollar and some crackhead looking dude. "Redd, I need 'em on the set the rest of the week. Write it up for me, okay?"

"You got it!" Redd replied as the four men piled into the pick up and drove off.

Dollar had never worked so hard in his entire life. For four days straight he laid hot ass tar, axed cement, lifted cement blocks and spread new cement. He was not trying to spend the rest of his life working this hard. He had to set some shit up and fast.

The good thing about it was when the job was completed Marlon drove the men back to Redd's and settled the pay. Redd received 30% of what the job paid and the men received the other 70% tax-free. It was the men's responsibility to file taxes at the end of the year as independent contractors. Redd merely served as an agent, a consultant...the middleman. The workers at "Work for a day" were considered self-employed independent contractors. What was even better was that sometimes the men were paid in straight out cash, but Redd had paperwork and receipts on each man and each job that they did through his company just in case there were any questions from the IRS.

Dollar's bank account was now looking at around $470.00. It made him feel good although it wasn't shit. It was enough for him to feel as though he could stand before his mother and little brother. He could tell them he was working and it would be the truth this time.

With a bed at the "Y", a couple of outfits and a job, it was time for Dollar to face his family. Dollar didn't know where to start. He was hoping his mother was still living in the same apartment, and if not, that a neighbor would be able to point him in the right direction.

Dollar took the bus to his old neighborhood. When he

got off the bus, Dollar walked the strip as if he had never abandoned it for eight years. The block hadn't changed. As he approached his old apartment building he stopped at the steps. He recalled the last time he had stepped foot on them. It was when he had been escorted by the Columbus detectives to a downtown interrogation room. Dollar shook off the negative memory and proceeded to walk inside the building.

"Dollar Bill," a voice called before he could make it completely through the main entrance door. "Dollar, dollar bill, y'all. I know that ain't you."

Dollar turned around to find a frail old man approaching him. He was wearing some dirty jeans with holes worn in both knees. The man had on a navy blue fishing jacket with the hood pulled over his head. Dollar didn't recognize the man from back in the day and the expression on his face stated such.

"You don't recognize me, man?" the strange looking guy said. "It's me, Stephan."

As the man walked closer up on him, Dollar recognized him. It wasn't an old man at all. It was his old classmate, Stephan Crouse. He had been one of the smartest kids in school. He had been voted the most outstanding leader of the senior class. It was visible that the streets had eaten him alive.

"Stephan Crouse," Dollar smiled. Ordinarily Dollar probably would have showed him street love with a masculine hug and some dap, but the odor that reaped from Stephan's body prevented him from doing so.

"I thought I was seeing a ghost," Stephan said. I thought you was supposed to grow old and die in the joint."

"Yeah, well," Dollar said.

"What you doing back in the old neighborhood anyway? You ain't no escapee are you?" Stephan laughed as he stroked his index finger underneath his nose and sniffed. "I just saw your little brother about a month ago over at the clinic."

"The clinic?" Dollar said.

"Yeah. He's doing some internship or something over at the free clinic. He been there for a while now," Stephan said realizing that Dollar obviously hadn't contacted his brother.

"Well, I guess I need to go check out little bro," Dollar smiled. "Does my mom's still live up in here?"

"Nah. She ain't lived here in some time. I don't even know where she staying at, man. I meant to ask your brother bout ole Mrs. Blake."

"Well, it was good hollering at you, my man," Dollar said as he headed for the clinic which was only a couple miles away.

Dollar saw a few familiar faces as he strolled the block. He saw girls who had once been the finest now looking like crackhead hoodrats. He spotted some of the old hangouts like Mudbone's candy store. Every city had a candy store ran by some fat dude named Mudbone. The candy was always a front for the dope he sold. Mudbone's lazy ass always hated counting out penny candy for the kids.

Dollar couldn't believe his eyes when he saw that Fat's BBQ was still in business. That was the joint when he was a kid. At least once a month some customer at one of the neighborhood restaurants his mother worked for would give her a nice tip. On her way home from the bus stop she would stop by Fat's and surprise the kids with it. Dollar couldn't resist stopping in for a quarter chicken meal with baked beans, greens and a corn muffin. It brought back some good memories, memories that would soon have a dark overcast.

* * *

"Is there a doctor in the house?" Dollar asked the brown skin Blair Underwood lookin' guy behind the sign in desk at the clinic. People used to always ask Dollar and Klein if they had the same daddy because Dollar had all of his mother's features and Klein had all of their father's features.

"You need to sign in." the man replied as he flipped through a file. "Have you ever been seen here be..."

As the man looked up at Dollar he lost his words. He never expected in a million years to look up and find his big brother standing before him.

"What's up, Doc?" Dollar said.

His little brother still couldn't respond. He wondered if he was dreaming, if he was just imagining his big brother standing before him. When Dollar spoke again as he reached across the counter and put his hand on his shoulder, his brother knew he wasn't dreaming.

"Can I call you Doc? Long time no see, Doc. I know you're speechless right now. Wasn't expecting to see me today, huh, or any other day for that matter?"

"What are you doing out?" his brother replied in a stale tone. "You got life. You didn't...."

"No, man, I didn't break out if that's what you were about to say," Dollar said. "It's a long story, but I'm out legit. I got a job and everything."

The two just stood there, one not knowing exactly what to say to the other.

"What time do you get off?" Dollar asked. "You ate yet? Look, I got you something."

Dollar handed his brother the foam sealed meal he had gotten him from Fat's BBQ.

"Fat's," his brother said nostalgically as a huge grin took over his face. He then looked up at Dollar and the grin vanished.

"Can we go somewhere and talk?" Dollar asked

"Uhh, yeah," his brother replied. "Give me a minute."

As his brother walked away to inform the staff that he would be stepping away for a moment, Dollar observed the patients in the waiting room. There was a pregnant 14-year-old girl in every other chair. There were a couple of whites but blacks and Latinos represented.

"This way," Dollar's brother said nodding his head towards the exit doors.

"You look good," Dollar said scrambling for conversation. He didn't know what to say. His brother wasn't the least bit excited to see him. If anything, he resented the hell out of Dollar for reappearing back into his life. How dare he declare himself dead and then resurface as if ain't shit happened.

Dollar could see that it was going to take way more than a smile and a BBQ meal to break the ice between him and his brother. Dollar knew it was going to take time so he had to just take things slow for now. Something inside of Dollar wanted to just stop and hug his little brother and tell him how much he had missed him, how sorry he was for the way he handled being incarcerated. But Dollar could sense the hostility in his brother's demeanor and knew such actions would be rejected by him.

"Yeah," his brother said as they took a few more steps accompanied by silence. "So you out for good, huh? How'd that happen?"

The two continued walking as Dollar vaguely briefed him on his happenings of getting out of jail. He intentionally left out the part about Romeo being their father, the man who had abandoned them as children.

"I'm just glad to be out," Dollar said. "This is a true blessing."

"Yep, a true blessing," his brother said sarcastically.

With every stale remark his brother made, Dollar was closer and closer to just saying fuck it, walking away and not trying to make amends with his brother. It was obvious his brother was holding onto that grudge for dear life. But first Dollar needed some information from him.

"I stopped by the old apartment to visit ma," Dollar said. "Stephan Crouse was walking by and told me that she didn't stay there anymore. He's the one who told me where to find you."

Doc paused as if he had run into a brick wall. He recouped himself and then proceeded to walk.

"Stephan Crouse," Doc said. "He was up in the clinic not too long ago."

"Yeah, that's what he told me. Anyway, where's ma?" Dollar asked. "Can you take me to see her?"

His brother stopped walking and looked at Dollar with cold eyes. Dollar sensed this and put both hands on his brother's shoulders.

"Look, man," Dollar said. "I know how much my being in prison hurt her. I knew it hurt her even more when I forced her to swear me off as dead. I know you don't understand, but I couldn't allow her to see her eldest son in a place she wore herself ragged trying to keep me out of. But now I plan to make it all up to her, and you. I'm going to do whatever it takes to make you two understand where I was coming from. I'm sorry, Doc."

"It was one thing for you to ask us to forget you ever existed, but for you to do the same to us...sending our letters back and shit," his brother said attempting to catch the curse word he had just spoken.

"I know, Doc, but I thought I was dead. I felt like death," Dollar pleaded. "Prison takes a muthafucka's breath, mind and heart. Without that shit, you are dead. I had no idea I would ever walk these city streets again, ever!"

Doc began walking again and Dollar followed his lead.

"Where you staying at?" Doc asked.

"Over at the "Y"," Dollar answered.

"I tell you what, I'll pick you up in the morning at around 10 o'clock. I'll take you to see Ma," his brother said. "I gotta get back to work right now though."

"It's good to see you, Doc," Dollar said. "It's good to see that you did just what you said you'd do. My little brother a doctor," Dollar said grinning a proud grin.

"Almost a doctor," his brother replied. "I went to school summers and everything to get this far. I'm working at the clinic as kind of like an internship under the supervision of an MD. We almost lost the clinic, but I did a little grant writing and we got some assistance."

"Damn, Doc," Dollar said. "You the man."

"Just giving back to my community in a sense," Doc said. "Well, I guess I'll see you tomorrow. And oh yeah, why don't you stop and get Ma some flowers? She'll like that."

* * *

"Damn, Doc" Dollar said after driving about twenty-five minutes in his brother's Jeep Cherokee. "How far did Ma move away?"

"It's not much farther now," Doc replied as he busted a left off of the freeway exit.

"I can't believe I'm cruisin' the city streets," Dollar gasped as he took in the lovely view. Doc simply looked straight ahead and drove steadily. "You're pretty quiet."

"Still in shock, I guess," Doc replied.

"Yeah, I know. It's hard for me to believe it myself," Dollar said. "For the first few days I kept looking over my shoulder waiting for the man to snatch me up by my collar and drag me back to the joint."

"How long you been out?" Doc asked.

"Not too long," Dollar said. "I didn't come at you and Ma right away because I had to get myself together you know...before I let you and Ma know I was out. I didn't want to be like all these other cats getting out of jail moving into somebody's basement rent free," Dollar said. "Plus, I couldn't just show up on y'all's doorstep. I knew I had to explain a lot to you guys. I just hope Ma understands."

"Umm hmm," Doc said.

"What, man," Dollar asked. "What's on your mind? I can tell something is eating at you. You wanna curse me out, punch me? I don't blame you, man. From your point of view I know I was wrong, but you've never had your life ripped from up underneath you."

"Oh, yeah," Doc said snidely.

"Yeah," Dollar replied as Doc turned into Evergreen Cemetery. "What's going on man?"

Doc ignored Dollar as he maneuvered through the trails of the cemetery roads.

"What's going on?" Dollar repeated.

"You said you wanted to see Ma didn't you?" Doc answered as he parked the car. "Come on then. Let's go!"

Doc got out of the car and walked over to a gray marbled headstone that stood upright. It had a vase attached to it and it read "Ms Sadie Blake... 1958-2000". Dollar got out of the jeep and stood at the hood for a moment. He slowly walked over to the graveside and fell to his knees upon reading the headstone. He choked and lost his breath. Once he was able to clear his breathing passage he roared out in pain. Doc watched his older brother break down and cry just as he had done three years ago.

"Go ahead, Dareese," Doc said. "Give Ma her flowers."

"Why?" Dollar cried. "Why didn't any one tell me?"

"You were dead, remember?" Doc said. "We were dead. As far as you were concerned, that is, we were already dead. It didn't matter to call you. You didn't want anybody coming to visit you, seeing you in your prison fits. I figured you sure wouldn't want to show up at your mother's funeral in chains."

"Damn, Doc," Dollar continued to ball. "When? What happened? I mean, oh my God, my mamma!"

"Car accident," Doc said.

Dollar turned his head to wipe his eyes that had been flooded with tears. His eyes caught the tombstone right next to his mother's that read "Charlene Davis". Davis was his mother's maiden name. He knew the grave belonged to his Aunti Charlene.

"Ma and Aunti Charlene both," Doc continued. "On their way to see you, or try to see you rather. Didn't you wonder why the visits stopped?"

"Oh, Doc. Oh, man," Dollar cried. "Ma, she's gone."

"She said only death could keep her from trying to see her boy," Doc said. "She wanted you to know, she wanted to tell you face to face that she was still proud of you and that she still loved you; that you were her son. She said God told her you were no killer and she'd never believe that you were. She loved you."

"I can't believe no one told me," Dollar snorted.

"I didn't contact the prison," Doc said. "I didn't write you or try to visit either. I was just abiding by your request. You'll be pleased to know that I didn't even include your name in the obituary."

Dollar looked up at his baby brother with discontent. It was as if it was pleasing Doc to see him kneeled in grief at their mother's grave. Before Doc knew it, Dollar had charged him. The two siblings punched and rolled on the ground, on their mother's grave.

Dollar managed to pin Doc down and got a clear shot to punch him dead in the face. Doc saw Dollar's fist clinch and prepare to tag him so he closed his eyes and waited to receive the blow. Dollar held his fist in midair as if he was fighting with an evil entity to keep from bringing it down on his brother's face. Dollar knew in his heart he would have killed his brother. He would have beaten him senseless. Dollar stood up over top of Doc, looked to the sky, beat his hands on his chest and roared.

The sound of Dollar's pain echoed throughout the cemetery as Doc stood watching him. Eventually the two drove off together without saying a single word to one another the entire drive.

***

Hearing bad news while locked up; there's nothing like it in the world. The prison walls close in on you. You can see them coming to smash your mind, body and soul and there ain't shit you can do about it.

Hearing Aaliyah's plane went down, taking the life of the young R&B Princess, while in the joint was emotional. Hearing all those lives were lost and destroyed on September 11th while in the joint was beyond putting in words. But Dollar finding out his mother had passed away was the ultimate.

Unless you're Eminem perhaps, finding out your mother has passed is hell whether you're locked up or not. It takes people a long time to realize that even God's love is greater than their own mother's. That's the pedestal mother's are placed on, like Angels in heaven.

Maybe it was better for Dollar to find out this way. Plenty of times while in the joint Dollar had witnessed inmates receive word that the Chaplain needed to see them. Most of the time, unless an inmate had requested to see the Chaplain, that only meant one thing, that someone had passed.

During the long walk to the Chaplain's office the inmate had too much time to wonder about who had died and out of all their loved ones, who they hoped it wasn't, but if they had to choose, who they hoped it was. Dollar wouldn't have been any better prepared for the walk to the Chaplain's office than for the very moment at hand.

Although Dollar rarely spoke with God, on this occasion he had many words. He had words of anger. Imagine someone cursing God. Again, most likely, Satan and his advocates laughed, "Ah ha ha. We did it again. He's blaming the man upstairs, as they say, for our deeds. We have him right where we want him. I love these niggaz! They make my work so much easier and that much more pleasurable."

Dollar had the worse attitude a young black man on the streets could have. He had that "fuck the world" attitude. He was now dangerous to the world and to himself.

After Doc's, what it seems as though he took pleasure in, telling Dollar of the death of their mother and watching him crumble to the ground, he then supplied Dollar with what Dollar saw as the appetizer to his meal ticket. It was his portion of the life insurance policy of which he and his brother were named as beneficiaries.

Aunti Charlene had taken out a policy for both herself and her sister and had the premiums deducted straight from her own checking account. Aunti Charlene's policy was just enough to cover her funeral expenses. Aunti Charlene always used to say, "I ain't no rich woman while I'm alive, so I sure don't want to make anyone rich off of my death." Plus, it wasn't like she had any kids to leave money to.

Knowing Doc was aiming to become a doctor, Aunti Charlene felt that a $100,000 policy for their mother was called for. It was like pulling hen's teeth for Aunti Charlene to get her sister to sign off on the paperwork to put the policy in effect. She didn't want to think about death. It was the one-year anniversary of the date the policy was signed when the car accident occurred.

Dollar's mother had, in print, named Doc as the sole beneficiary. She spoke words to Doc instructing him that 50% was to go to Dollar in spite of what the policy stated. With Dollar being incarcerated for life, she didn't know what would become of his percentage if she was to list him on the policy. So instead, she left the distribution into the hands of her baby boy. He was to keep Dollars books full, of which he failed to do so. Doc refused to allow Dollar to profit in prison off of the death of their mother. He had no idea what he would do, if anything, with the money, but he knew he wasn't going to document those funds on prison record. So he put away Dollar's portion not knowing that Dollar would someday actually be able to benefit from it.

$46,000 was left for Dollar after funeral expenses. Dollar saw the money not as a new start, but as a foundation to get started...to get started on his bigger picture. The $46,000 was more like the outline that needed filled in.

Dollar needed to get him a quaint little pad. He needed stability and what he referred to as "Uncle Sam hush money" (legitimately earned money to validate his purchases). He needed some new threads. He had to be able to play the role once he hit the streets again. But most importantly, he needed his old running partners. He needed Tommy and Ral.

Chapter 7

Reunited

When Dollar knocked on the locked screen door of the tiny cape cod home, a woman answered. The door was slightly cracked, but Dollar could see that she was fine. She was a beautiful sight and not just because Dollar had been locked up for eight years. She had long wavy locks that she, in sequence, pushed behind each of her ears with her slender fingers. Her natural fingernails, which were formerly rugged and chewed on, were now smothered by the a fresh set of acrylic nails. Her large four-inch in diameter gold hoop earrings dangled from her soft lobes, slightly brushing her cheeks here and there.

"Yes, I was looking for and old friend of mine, Tommy?" Dollar said in awe as he tried to view every inch of the woman through the black metal bars that secured the screen door. Dollar looked down at the piece of paper he had printed off at the library and compared the address on it to that above the mailbox on the house.

"Ha ha, very funny. I see the jailhouse didn't affect your sense of humor," The woman responded as she came closer allowing the daylight to shine upon her soft brown skin.

"Tommy," Dollar shouted recognizing Tommy only by her voice, not her stunning features. "Thomasena McRoy!"

"In the flesh," Tommy said.

"Hell no," Dollar bent over laughing.

Tommy, though both excited and shocked to see her old stomping partner on her doorstep, was becoming angered by Dollar's howling laugh.

"You're a woman now," Dollar said as he fades out his laughter.

"No shit," Tommy said, now full blown pissed and unable to enjoy the coming home of Dollar. "I've always been a woman."

"Oh, my bad," Dollar said coughing his laughter to a complete stop. "But, damn, girl. You was my boy. Now look at you. You clean up real good."

"How'd you really get out?" Tommy asked suspiciously. Before Dollar could prove her suspicions wrong she continued. "I heard a rumor or two, but I know you, D. There's got to be more to the story. What brings you to my doorstep?"

Coming to her own conclusions, all types of wicked thoughts started going through Tommy's head. Maybe Dollar really was a snitch and maybe him turning her over was part of the deal.

"Hold on right there," Tommy said as she suddenly walked away from the door with Dollar still standing on the porch. She returned, unlocked and opened the screen door. She stuck her hand out of it and handed Dollar a brown paper bag, allowing the screen door to close again. Dollar looked inside to find seven rolls of money held in place by rubber bands.

"Take this," Tommy said. "There's about seven grand in there. It ought to get you by for a while. Keep in touch and I can hook you up. There's more where that came from. It just might take me a minute to get that much though."

Dollar began to laugh again.

"What? What's so damn funny?" Tommy said with a twisted mug. "Is it not enough? Look, I said I can get more. Just give me some time."

"I can't believe this, T," Dollar said looking down at the bag of money. "You ain't changed a bit. You still think everyone is out to get you, huh? You would have looked good puttin' this shit on my books over the last eight years."

"You wouldn't accept my letters so I figured you wouldn't except my money either," Tommy said as if her feelings had been hurt by Dollar rejecting her letters. "Look, Dollar, I appreciate everything you done for me back then, you know. And I know I owe you. But I got a life now. A lot of shit has changed."

"Maybe you have changed," Dollar said disappointed. "Do you think I would actually bring you that kind of drama?"

"Well, I have changed. I'm not her anymore. I'm not the Tommy you knew back in the day," Tommy spoke. "Things have changed. I've changed."

"So I see," Dollar said. "Street life got you noided, huh? But don't even worry. It ain't even like that. I'm out legit. I'm free, baby. I didn't have to climb over the gate. They opened it up for me. Now how about you opening up yours for me so I can give you the real on my release."

Dollar nodded his head towards the screen door handle. Tommy slowly opened it for Dollar to come in. Tommy looked to make sure no one was behind him before closing the door tight and locking it back.

"Damn, Tommy," what kind of shit you into?"

"You wouldn't believe the jealous hoes I have to deal with working at The Chocolate Factory," Tommy said. "The niggaz who be up in the bar and they bitches be trippin'. I done had my windows busted out and my car spray painted. I even got jumped coming in the house one night. But I got somethin' for they asses the next time they wanna jump out of a bush at three o'clock in the morning and rob a bitch of her tips."

"Damn," Dollar said. "Tommy gun still keeps the glock cocked, huh? Shit, who would have guessed the life of a bartender would be so dangerous?'"

Dollar pretended to have chills and wiggled his body while hugging himself.

"You's a silly mafucka," Tommy said heading into the kitchen. "I don't bar tend at the The Chocolate Factory. You want a Coke?"

"Yeah," Dollar responded. "I'm a little parched."

"Oh, parched," Tommy said. "Did you learn that word in jail? You got a jailhouse degree that you can't do shit with on the outside and couldn't do shit with on the inside either?"

"Naw," Dollar answered laughing. "I didn't get down with getting fifteen degrees. I mean, what the fuck a felon gon' do with a Master's?" Both Dollar and Tommy laughed. "So what do you do at The Chocolate Factory? You a bouncer? Them chicks be hooking you up like that with tips, just for walking them to their car and shit?"

"Do I look like a bouncer to you, Dollar?" Tommy said putting her hands on her hips. "Besides, what do you know about a bouncer's role in a strip club. It's more than just walking chicks to their car. They're like our own personal body guards."

"Oh, hell no," Dollar said. "You ain't shakin' it up in there are you?" The look on Tommy's face said it all. "You, Tommy Gun, is a dancer now? I knew I must have been dreaming. I ain't really out of jail am I? Satan playing some fucked up practical joke on me ain't he? I mean the next thing you gon' tell me is that you got kids."

Before Dollar could even finish his sentence a little girl, who looked to be around seven or eight years old, came out the bedroom. She was wiping her half sleep eyes with the backs of her hands.

"I can't believe this," Dollar said in amazement. "You really are a woman."

"Aunti Sena," the small child said to Tommy.

"Yes, Heaven," Tommy said as she approached her niece, handing Dollar his Coke along the way.

"I had a dream. We were at a party but nobody was singing happy birthday or nothing. Everybody was sad."

"Well maybe the person whose birthday it was was turning 50," Tommy joked, but her niece failed to see the humor in Tommy's comment.

"My nap is done. Can I watch toons now and have some Blues Clues," Heaven said referring to her Blues Clues fruit snacks.

"Sure, baby," Tommy said. She grabbed a package of fruit snacks from off top of the refrigerator and handed them to Heaven. Heaven went back into the bedroom not once inquiring about the stranger on the couch.

"You baby sitting?" Dollar asked Tommy.

"No, they stay with me," Tommy replied.

"They," Dollar inquired.

"My sister's kids, my two nieces,"

"Oh, what's up with that?"

Tommy paused before replying, "My sister's dead so I took the girls. She was murdered."

"Damn, T," Dollar said. "I'm sorry to hear that shit. How did she die?"

"She was raped and beat to death a few years ago. Her and her boyfriend, the girl's daddy, was staying up over at the Hills. The girls were asleep right in the next room when it all happened," Tommy said as she subconsciously began to crunch the coke can in the palm of her hands. Dollar watched as soda leaked from the can down Tommy's hands.

"So, the girls been with you ever since?" Dollar asked.

"Yeah. The state put me through all kinds of shit about getting custody, but I refused to let them be dumped into the system. That's why I had to start dancing. I had to keep dropping change into the lawyer like he was a fucking parking meter."

"How come the girl's didn't just live with their father?"

"He's the one who raped and killed their mother," Tommy replied. "The girls was so used to them fighting and carrying on all the time that that particular night didn't seem any different than all the other nights they had fought. I tried to get my sister to leave his ass. She couldn't let go. Even after I shot his ass she stayed with him."

"You shot him," Dollar said surprised.

"Man, my sister's face was fucked up. He beat her because when he came home he saw the man who lived next to them leaving out of their apartment. UPS had left a package with the guy next door because my sister wasn't home when they came to deliver it. He accused her of cheating with the man. He beat her and put her out the house butt naked and told the girls he'd kill them if they let her in. Keelah called me...remember Keelah from South High School?"

"Yeah, ole Keelah," Dollar answered.

"She called me and told me that she had looked out her window when she heard screaming and saw my sister beating on the door without any of her clothes on. She said she took my sister a blanket and tried to convince her to come to her house and call the police, but she wouldn't do it. She was afraid he'd do something to her girls in retaliation," Tommy said trying to contain her emotions in order to get the story out clearly to Dollar.

"I headed straight over there," Tommy continued. "That twenty minute drive turned into a two minute drive. When I arrived I told my sister to wait in my car. I went and busted that muthafuckin' living room window out, climbed through that bitch and sent the girls outside to the car too. That punk ass Nigga gon' see my Mag and go lock himself in the bedroom like a hoe. So I'm banging on that bitch yelling for him to come kick my ass, to come fight me. The longer I stood banging on that door the more pissed off I got, but I knew that punk nigga wasn't coming out so I left and went out to the car. It was dark when I got there so I hadn't got a good look at my sister's face. When I turned on the interior light in the car and saw my sister's face," Tommy said as she began to get emotional. "I had to do that nigga, Dollar. I went back up in that house and just start firing at the door. I let all fifteen Mags off through that bedroom door. Do you know only one hit that muthafucka? And in the hand at that, his damn pinkie finger. I blew that muthafucka off though. I got back in the car and drove my sister and the kids to my house. Two days later they were back with him. One month later she was dead."

"Did you do any time for shooting him?" Dollar said.

"That nigga knew better than to report my ass. He told the police some dudes broke in through the living room window and tried to rob his house."

"Damn, T," Dollar sighed. "I'm sorry all that shit had to go down."

"Shit happens," Tommy said. "And you still live."

"Things can't be that bad," Dollar said. "You got G's sitting up in here like everything is gravy. All you doing is dancing ain't it?"

"You know I would never get down like that," Tommy said. "I ain't selling pussy. I sell them niggaz a little weed, but they ain't getting the cat."

"For real," Dollar said. "That's your hustle."

"I don't like that look you giving me," Tommy said. "Talk to me, Dollar Bill. What's on your mind?"

Dollar took a sip from his soda and let out a loud belch. He then looked up at Tommy and proceeded to tell her how he, once again, needed her services.

"You talking about robbin' muthafuckas again," Tommy asked, as Dollar nodded in the affirmative. "Ain't you learned shit? We fucked up the first time and the last time. You don't know these streets now. These cats are ruthless. Niggaz' back up got back up now."

"Introduce me to the streets again," Dollar said to Tommy taking her hand. Dollar proceeded to tell Tommy about the old head (Romeo) he had met in prison and how he schooled Dollar on the game before turning over the wild card to him.

"Reacquaint me to the streets. Allow me to get to know them better," Dollar's said as his words tranquilized Tommy. "You working at The Chocolate Factory, T. I know you know everything that happens in the streets before it happens. The first thing these out of state ballers want to do is go stick they face in pussy. I know they be up in there telling y'all hoes their business."

"Excuse me," Tommy said taking offense.

"Not you," Dollar cleaned it up, "them other hoes."

"Look, Dollar, I'm content with what I got going on. It pays the bills," Tommy said.

"But that's all it does," Dollar enforced. "In all these years all you got saved up is seven grand? So you gon' die here, huh? You just gon' keep paying these same ole bills. So you're like these other wanna be hustlers. You content with some ole two bedroom minimum shit...and there's three of y'all living up in here too? Is this you for life, T? This ain't you, baby. I know you. You like me. We cut from the same cloth. You got caviar dreams. This is fish sticks."

Tommy looked around her spot. Before Dollar had shown up she loved her casa. All of a sudden it was a shack. It was nothing. It was four fucking walls closing in on her. It wasn't what she ultimately wanted and Dollar was there to remind her of just that.

"I got these kids now," Tommy said. "I can't give the county no reason to come scooping them up. I can't, Dollar."

"I ain't talkin' 'bout making no career out of the shit," Dollar said in a convincing tone. "I mean, yeah we gon' have to make a couple lil' hits to get our feet wet again, but I'm lookin' for that big hit that's gonna allow a nigga to retire from the streets."

"I don't know, Dollar," Tommy said.

"I need you, Tommy. I need you to make this happen," Dollar said rubbing her face. "You know when it comes down to it I got your back. I ain't gonna never let nothing happen to you. Haven't I proven that? I can't just go out on the streets and find a crew to run with. I got out of the joint by dropping the dime, Tommy....Snitch, muthafuckas don't care about the DNA of it. Who's gonna trust me enough to have my back? Who?"

Tommy could feel all of Dollar's weight on her shoulders. She knew she owed him. Yeah, she knew the streets like that back of her hand. The streets were her lover. They had gotten her where she was thus far. The streets had not yet let Tommy down and with Dollar by her side she couldn't go wrong. Tommy looked around her house and stared at the picture of her nieces, whom she breathed for and whom she wanted everything in the world for.

"So you in?" Dollar asked, giving Tommy a puppy dog face.

"If I do decide to get down, it ain't gon' be no career move or no shit like that. Just a few times, Dollar. Just enough to make some shit happen, you know?" Tommy said trying to convince herself more so than Dollar.

"So is that a yes," Dollar asked.

"I'm in," Tommy mumbled under her breath.

"What was that?" Dollar asked.

"I'm in, damn'it," Tommy said.

"My nigga," Dollar said picking Tommy up and spinning her in the air. Now alls we need is our third leg."

"Who?" Tommy asked.

"Ral, of course," Dollar replied.

"Oh, we can't fuck with Ral. He's through. The monkey got him," Tommy said.

"Heroin?" Dollar asked.

"That and anything else he can get his hands on to feel good," Tommy said. "I'm surprised he's not dead yet."

Tommy could see the hurt on Dollars face as she shared Ral's current state. Dollar felt as though he had left Ral for dead by going to jail. If he had been on the streets, he would have never let Ral get that bad, bad enough where he wasn't to be fucked with, where he was of no use. Listening to Tommy's words, Dollar thought that maybe Ral would have been better off serving time because, according to Tommy, time was serving him.

"You okay, Dollar?" Tommy asked.

"Yeah," Dollar responded. "I'm cool."

The two sat in silence momentarily. It was as if one was waiting on the other to say the word. Dollar could be a dirty muthafucka and just roll with Tommy or he could be a loyal nigga and go take care of his boy.

"Well, what do you wanna do?" Tommy asked Dollar.

Dollar gulped down the remainder of his coke, set it down on the table and said, "Let's go save Ral."

***

Tommy led Dollar to the spot Ral was known to hang out at. It was an olive green double family home on a street that hosted dozens, in various colors, just like it. As they approached the front door they could hear some laughter and commotion going on. Before Tommy knocked on the door, Dollar clutched her fist and told her to hold up. They walked around to the side of the house and peeked through the side window. What they saw made their stomachs turn. They saw Ral kneeled down on his knees in front of a guy sporting an Outkast velour sweat suit.

There were a couple dames in the living room smoking on a pipe and two dudes cutting lines at the kitchen table. The guy standing in front of Ral was waving a tiny glass valve half way filled with liquid and yanking at his dick with the other hand.

"Com'n man," one of the guys who was sitting at the kitchen table said. "You ain't gonna get him to suck your dick. Ral will knock an old lady upside the head to get high, but I ain't never known him to suck no dick."

"Shiiiitt," the guy standing before Ral said. "I got that hoe, Charise, to fuck a Pitbull last week for some blow. We took pictures of that shit and everything. We had that bitch moaning as that Pitbull pumped his little shit in and out of her. If I can get that pretty ass bitch to fuck a dog, I know I can get this piece of trailer park trash to lick the lollipop."

The guy continued to taunt Ral as the onlookers laughed.

"Com'n, you know you want to get high," the guy addressed Ral.

The guy waved the heroin in front of Ral and started smacking' his dick around Ral's face. Ral turned his head away trying to avoid contact, but the guy made sure he kept up with him.

Ral needed that blow. Ral needed to get high. He didn't even have lent in his pockets. He was too geeked to go out and attempt to steal something, besides, he didn't have the patience to try to sell it for cash or negotiate for a hit. Opportunity to get high was right there in his face, literally.

Dollar and Tommy watched in disgust.

"What you wanna do?" Dollar asked Tommy.

"Save Ral," she replied.

Dollar and Tommy crept around to the backdoor and using all of his weight, Dollar caved in the door.

Tommy, dressed for the occasion wearing some green camouflage pants, a green fishing jacket and a baseball cap, was right behind Dollar with gun in hand, cocked at attention.

Their intrusion was totally unexpected. They heard one of the girls yell "undercover," but before anyone could move, Tommy fired a warning shot. The shot shattered the ceiling fan that was already missing a blade.

"Ral, get the fuck up," Tommy scolded.

Hardly recognizing her, or even aware of what was taking place around him, Ral maintained his position.

Dollar went over and snatched Ral to his feet. The expression on Ral's face was as if God himself had reached a hand down from the heavens to save him.

By this time Tommy had ordered the occupants face down onto the floor. It was now evident that the intruders were no police officers. Tommy looked to Dollar as a question of what to do next.

"Look, man," the guy said zipping his pants up. "I was just fucking with dude. This ain't that serious. Besides, look at him. He ain't nothing but a dopefiend."

Ral dropped his head as his eyes began to roll to the back of his head.

"You holdin'?" Dollar asked the guy.

"Com'n, man," the guy responded. "I work for Ducie. He'll kill me, man. Muthafuckas in wheel chairs for doing that song and dance about getting robbed. Com'n, man."

"Stop crying you bitch ass faggot," Dollar said becoming irritated.

"Come on, D," Tommy said. "You said we was just coming to save Ral."

Dollar gave Tommy the "shut the fuck up, bitch" look. Tommy snapped her neck and turned her lips up at Dollar.

"Take your pants off," Dollar said to the guy.

"What?" the guy responded.

"Did I stutter muthafucka? Take 'em off."

The guy slowly removed his pants and handed them to Dollar. Dollar went through each pocket and took ownership of what was around $6,000.

"This all you holdin'?" Dollar asked. "Oh, you's a tennis shoe dope boy. What do you get out of this, about a grand?"

"Com'n man," the guy begged. "You see for yourself it ain't much. Ducie gon kill me, man."

Dollar looked the guy up and down and began laughing.

"What they call you?" Dollar asked.

"Tyrone," the guy responded.

"Figures," Dollar said. "Well I'll tell you what, Tyrone, you ain't getting this money back."

Tyrone began to cry actual tears and repeat "Com'n, man" over and over.

"You spose to be hard-core ain't you? Yo standing here crying like a bitch. I can see why you like getting your dick sucked by men. You's a hoe," Dollar continued, "See, you caused my boy here a lot of pain and suffering. Tommy, if we were in a court of law, how much do you think a judge would give our friend Ral here for pain and suffering?"

"I don't know," Tommy said. "About $6,000."

"That sounds about right," Dollar replied. "So you see here, Tyrone. I'm gonna be the judge in this case and award my friend here this $6,000 for pain and suffering."

Dollar put the money in his pocket and looked at Tommy as if giving her a cue.

"Oh," Tommy said catching on. "There's always court cost. I suppose your friends here won't mind helping you out with that."

Tommy and Dollar proceeded to strip the occupants of their cash and any jewelry. These were some old sorry ass dope boys paying some bitch's rent to let them hustle out of her shit. Their jewelry pieces combined weren't worth more than

$3,000 all together. Dollar and Tommy took it all the same, along with $4,000 more collected from the other occupants.

As Dollar and Tommy carried Ral out of the house they could hear the cries of Tyrone, "Ducie gon' kill me," Tyrone said. "Ducie gon' kill me."

***

"Where we gon take him?" Tommy asked Dollar as they threw Ral in the back seat of Tommy's Plymouth Sundance.

"We gotta take him to your house to clean him up," Dollar replied.

"I can't take him to my house with the girls there," Tommy quickly said. "You think I want this shit around them? You acting like this fool is drunk and once he throws up he'll feel better. Dollar, he's addicted to heroin. You want him to quit, but he don't want to quit."

"You right," Dollar said taking a moment to think. "This is going to take time. I gotta think. Let me think."

Seeing Ral like this tore Dollar to pieces. He didn't understand how Ral could allow himself to get this bad off. He had a million questions and no answers.

"Where you staying?" Tommy asked.

"I'm at the Y for now, but not for long."

"We can take him to Short Stay Motel on Pike Road," Tommy suggested.

Tommy drove ten minutes to Short Stay where she went into the lobby and got a room for Ral. Short Stay is a cash only, no ID-no questions asked joint. Most of the girls from the titty bars take their tricks there. Some of the girls even live there as roommates. On Tommy's way back to the car with the key to the room, she ran into two chicks of which she stopped briefly to conversate with. At first Tommy felt a little uncomfortable as she thought the girls might assume she was there with a john.

Tommy knew these two chicks were full time hoes their own self so it didn't matter what they thought about her.

Tommy hurried back to the car and helped Dollar carry Ral into his temporary dwelling, room 112. Ral smelled like a baby's diaper that had been sitting in a corner for a week. He hadn't bathed in weeks and the wrenching odor that erupted from his pores confirmed this fact. His teeth were rotted and his hair was an oily pit of dirt. Dollar lightweight had an attitude with Tommy. How had she allowed her boy to get to this point? Why hadn't they stuck together and looked out for one another? Maybe they weren't the loyal road dawgz he thought them to be back in the day.

Ral never spoke a word to either Dollar or Tommy. He moaned and scratched at himself like a dog with fleas. Tommy suggested Dollar put Ral in the shower while she ran to Walmart to grab him some clothes. Dollar gave Tommy $500 of the money he had taken from Tyrone and Tommy headed to the store.

Tommy came back with several Fruit of the Loom sweat suits, some generic brand sneakers, a couple packages of briefs and socks as well as some personal hygiene items. She also stopped and picked up a pizza. She knew nobody was going to deliver to the area the motel was in.

"Damn," Tommy said as she watched Ral's twitching body soaked in sweat lay across the double bed. "He's real fucked up. I told you."

"How long he been getting down like this?" Dollar asked.

"You know Ral always had a thing for street candy."

"Yeah, well if I had been here, there's no fucking way I'd let my boy get like this."

"So what the fuck you trying to say?" Tommy said. "You trying to say this shit is my fault?"

"Look at him, T," Dollar said. "This is your boy. He

supposed to be your boy for life."

"He's a muthafuckin' grown ass man," Tommy said. "I'm raising two kids, sliding down fishy ass smellin' poles, bruising my thighs just to feed them. You don't know what it's like out here. Just trying to take care of my own self is hard. My nieces are my responsibility, not Ral and not you, so fuck you, Dollar. I don't need this shit. I'm saving my money to get out of this hellhole lifestyle for good. I don't care how long it takes me. Fuck this shit. I don't even know how I almost let you talk me into this ghetto ass shit."

With tears in her eyes and a dose of the truth hurts, Tommy scrambled for her keys and headed for the door.

"So it's like that?" Dollar said. "You just gon leave us hangin'?"

Tommy looked into Dollar's eyes and discovered his attempt to remind her of her debt to him. He wanted her to remember that she had shot three men dead and he accepted the punishment for her. Tommy knew she owed Dollar her life. On the same token, she had to be loyal to her nieces. She promised them she would provide them a good life. She promised that someday they would pick up and move to Cali or something, a good part. They would have a nice house, nice clothes, and breed dogs or something. They would be so well off that she wouldn't have to work so hard. She would be there for them when they woke up in the middle of the night instead of being in some bar giving a dude a lap dance.

Fuck it! If it wasn't for Dollar she might not have the girls. They might be dead by now, buried next to their mother. She wouldn't have been there to save them, but in jail instead. She would be there for Dollar, once again, she would commit herself. Just as soon as they made a big hit though, she was gone and would never look back. On that final thought, Tommy dropped her keys and retrieved some cold wet wash cloths from the bathroom to cover Ral with.

Tommy and Dollar nursed Ral. They kept cold rags on him and made him take a few bites of pizza. He kept vomiting and moaning though.

"He can't do this," Tommy said. "He needs help, Dollar."

"I seen cats in the joint go through this same thing," Dollar said. "If he can just get through this first 24 hours he'll be fine."

Ral's eyes began to roll in the back of his head. This episode scared Tommy. Dollar remained calm insisting that Ral could get through his withdraw.

"Dollar, can't you see he needs a doctor. He's sweating bullets, but yet he is as cold as a corpse," Tommy said. "He needs a doctor."

Dollar looked at Tommy who had a frantic look on her face. Maybe she was right, Dollar thought. Dollar's main reason for not wanting to take Ral to the hospital was because he had no idea what kind of shit Ral had been in and how many brushes with the law he had managed to accumulate. What if he had warrants? The hospital was sure to know he was a drug user. Taking Ral to the hospital might have been like checking him into jail. Dollar could see that Ral was slowly but surely deteriorating. Tommy was right, he needed a doctor. This could ruin everything Dollar had planned for the three. He wanted Ral, but more so, he needed Ral alive and healthy.

Ral began to wheeze and vomit. He was near convulsions. Tommy grabbed the toothbrush she had purchased for Ral at Walmart and used the handle to hold his tongue flat so that he would not choke on it.

"Dollar," Tommy screamed. "Please! He needs a doctor."

Tommy took Ral's head and held it in her arms. Was this her fault? Maybe she could have done something. Dollar wouldn't have allowed Ral to get to this point. Ral used to be

Tommy's number one running partner and now look at him. Tommy began to tremble as she rocked Ral.

"Come on, Ral," Tommy said. "I ain't save your life all those times just so you could turn around and kill yourself. Come on, big baby, you can get through this."

Tommy kissed Ral on his forehead and proceeded to give him pep talks. Dollar had never seen Tommy like this. He had never seen an emotional side to Tommy. The scene before him reassured Dollar that he could, in fact, count on Tommy. He watched her repent to Ral a little while longer before giving the order.

"Come on," Dollar said. "We're taking him to see a doctor."

***

"It's four o'clock in the morning. Who in the hell can that be?" Doc said as the repeated beating on his front door woke him. Butt naked, as he always slept, he slipped on some boxers and a tee shirt and headed down the spiral staircase. He separated the blind with his hand and peeked out of the picture window beside the front door to view the side profile of Dollar.

Doc dropped his hands and stood there as Dollar continued to knock. By this time Ral's body was limp and non-respondent. As Doc headed back up the spiral staircase Dollar's knock became harder and more desperate.

"Yo, Doc," Dollar called. "Come on, man. It's me, your big brother. Please open up."

Dollar had driven out near the suburb of Munster, where Doc lives. He had looked up Doc's address in the phone book. He was surprised to find it there because most black people don't list their information, but with Doc being in the medical profession, he was sure enough in the book. Usually folks in the legal and medical profession list their information in the directory.

Hesitantly, Doc reconsidered. He came back down the steps and opened the door. There stood Dollar with Ral limp in his arms. Tommy had Dollar drop her off at her house with the girls and gave him permission to use her car to go get Ral help. When Doc saw Ral he knew that he needed immediate medical attention.

"What happened to him?" Doc said, helping Dollar carry him in, "Is he hit?"

"No, man," Dollar replied. "He's fiendin'. I don't know what to do."

Doc retrieved his medical bag and began to take Ral's vital statistics. Dollar anxiously paced back and forth.

"Can't we give him something like chocolate or something?" Dollar asked.

"How long has it been since he had a hit?" Doc asked.

"I don't know, Doc," Dollar replied. "He hasn't really been able to communicate with me. This is my first time seeing him since I been out."

"Why didn't you take him to the ER?" Doc asked. Dollar's expression answered Doc's question.

"You ain't getting me caught up in no bullshit are you?" Doc inquired.

"You know I wouldn't do that to you, bro?"

"Help me carry him upstairs to the tub," Doc said. "I'll do all that I can do for him, but you're the one who is going to have to stay up and keep an eye on him."

Dollar and Doc carried Ral to the tub and filled it with luke warm water. Doc insisted that Ral's temperature needed to be regulated. He instructed Dollar to drain the water as it chilled and refill the tub. He showed Dollar how to take and read Ral's blood pressure and how to take and read his temperature. He told Dollar to force Ral to drink fruit juice and to secure his tongue if he went into convulsions and if this did occur, he didn't care what Dollar said, he was having Ral transported to the hospital.

All night Dollar nursed Ral like a wounded stray puppy that had followed him home.

***

"Yo, Dollar," Ral said waking up half out of it, still soaking in the tub. "What am I in for?"

Ral's voice woke Dollar from his catnap.

"Huh?" Dollar replied wiping his eyes.

"What am I in the joint for? It was my moms, huh? I told that old bitch I was gonna bring her television set back to her." Ral began to twitch and gag. Dollar grabbed him and positioned him in a headlock to try to gain some control.

"Don't talk. Just don't talk," Dollar said. "Just relax. You're not in the joint, Ral."

"Is we in heaven or hell?"

"Stop fucking around, man. You're sick," Dollar said. "You ain't dead yet, fool. You still in sorry ass G-Town. I got out the joint, man. I'm back."

"Word!" Ral said. "My, *'N' word.*"

"You's a silly muthafucka, you know that?" Dollar said.

Ral looked down at himself fully clothed in a tub of water. Dollar reached for a can of Hawaiian Punch to give to Ral.

"Is this some type of ghetto baptism?" Ral asked.

Doc, hearing voices, entered the bathroom to check on things. He gave Ral some towels and clothing to throw on and moved him into his guestroom. Doc checked Ral's vitals, which were pretty good for the condition he was in. Doc let Dollar know that Ral would most likely go through withdraw for a few days. He also instructed Ral to pay him a visit at the clinic. Doc provided them with information on some rehab facilities where he could go to for help with kicking his heroin addiction.

"I appreciate all this, man," Dollar said to Doc as Ral's body hung off of Dollar's left shoulder. "I really do."

"That's my job," Doc said short and with an attitude. "Let me help you get him out to the car."

Dollar and Doc got Ral into the passenger seat of the car. Dollar laid the seat back as far as it would go, strapped Ral in and closed the door.

Just as soon as the car door closed Doc went off.

"Nigga, don't you ever come to my domain with your ghetto ass bullshit," Doc said. "What the fuck you hanging around trash like that for anyway? Ain't that the same piece of shit you used to run with before you went in the joint? Look; take that money from Ma's death, get you a nice little place, get you some schooling, a steady job and fuck these streets, man. Didn't you learn nothing while you were locked up?"

"As a matter of fact I did," Dollar said opening the door to leave. "As a matter of fact, I did."

***

As Dollar drove Ral back to Short Stay to get him situated in the room, he told Ral all the details surrounding his release from prison. Dollar left out the part about Romeo being his father, as he did with everyone else he relayed the story to. Ral was barely comprehending Dollar's words, but Dollar rambled on and on."

Dollar stopped off at a convenience store so that he could stock the motel room with enough snacks to tie Ral over for a few days. He bought a foam cooler and filled it with ice and beverages.

Dollar ordered Ral to stay put while he handled a few things, and promised that he would come back for him the next day. Dollar soon learned that a fiend don't stay put when he went to the bathroom and came out to find the hotel door open and Ral gone.

Ral hadn't gotten too far down the road before Dollar caught up with him and took him back to the hotel room. It was evident that Dollar was going to have to do some baby-sitting for the next few days.

***

"Good looking out last night," Dollar said, as he drove Tommy to work in her car. "Ral would probably be laying up dead in that motel room if it wasn't for you insisting we get him to a doctor."

"Either that or he'd be some where sucking dick," Tommy said as she looked in the back seat at Ral who was taking a snooze. "One of the two."

Dollar, not finding humor in Tommy's pun, simply gave her a dry look.

"Anyway," Tommy continued, "Shay ain't gon' give a fuck about me saving somebody's life. All she's going to care about is why my black ass wasn't at work last night."

"Shay your boss?" Dollar asked. "Shay from View Point?"

"She manages the joint," Tommy replied. "Her dude owns it. Well he bought it anyway. It's in her name. You know how these dope boys do it once they get big time. They graduate from buying they bitches Tennis bracelets to buying them titty bars, beauty shops, day care centers and shit."

"Then why haven't you snagged up one of them ballers?" Dollar asked curiously. "I know you done bumped into all kind of ballers in the club."

"I can't have that shit around the girls," Tommy quickly replied. "These muthafuckas are ruthless. They don't give a fuck who they shoot up trying to get to a rival nigga or a cat that owe them some money. I can see the girls and me now sitting on the couch watching "My Wife and Kids" and bullets raining through the window. Hell no. It's a known fact, where ever trouble goes, trouble follows. I can't bring it to where I lay my head."

"Yeah, being a hustler's wifey is just as crucial as being the hustler himself," Dollar said.

"If it was just me, hell I'd probably roll with a baller until I got tired of his ass," Tommy said. "Until I got my bookstore anyway."

"What bookstore?" Dollar asked.

"I've been thinking about shit, about what I really want to do. And I want to own my own bookstore. I want to name it after my sister, something to leave for the girls so that they never have to do some of the shit women have to do to survive now days."

"A bookstore, huh?" Dollar said turning into the parking lot of The Chocolate Factory.

"Yeah, all kinds of books," Tommy's face lit up. "Maybe a little café section too, with a stage for some open mic. Yeah, that's what I'm gonna do some day." Snapping out of her daydream Tommy grabbed her duffel bag from out of the back seat and said to Dollar, "Pick me up at 3:00 a.m. Don't be late, Dollar. I ain't trying to be like some of these bitches in here waiting around for their dudes to come pick them up in their own car."

"T, you know I wouldn't play you like that," Dollar said. "Thanks for letting me borrow your wheels."

"3:00 a.m.," Tommy reiterated. "Oh yeah, and Dollar...welcome home."

Chapter 8

A Shot of Henney

"I love these streets," Dollar said aloud as he walked through the city downtown on his way from the Bureau of Motor Vehicles. He had just seen a clean, fully loaded, two year old black Honda Accord at a Buy Here Pay Here car lot. He had to have that shit. It was calling his name. He had the cash, but he didn't have a driver's license. He hadn't gotten around to getting his driver's license so that was the reason for his visit to the BMV.

Dollar's plan was to own a nice set of wheels. He needed transportation first and foremost so that he could maneuver the city easier. It would also make apartment hunting that much easier. That public transportation and walking, while trying to handle his business, was for the birds.

Dollar would be rollin' in that Honda soon enough. This would be the first item he could check off of his "shit to do and shit to get" list he had written up. "*Now I need to get me a crib*," Dollar thought as he stood at the stoplight waiting for the walk signal.

"Excuse me, sir. Do you have the time?" A woman asked Dollar as she fiddled with the watch on her wrist. "Mine stopped."

Honey was the shit. She stood about five feet and six inches tall. She was playing a money green mini skirt suit with a white blouse under it and a matching tie. Her Gator pumps were the exact shade of her suit. Her coffee brown tights complimented her toned scarless legs. Her shiny lips, which wore only colorless lip-gloss, looked like cherries dripping with melted chocolate waiting to be licked.

As the woman stood there plucking at her watch Dollar took in a whiff of her freshly styled hair. He could smell the aftermath of the perm chemical underneath the tangerine scented spritz. Her long brown locks had the Farrah Fawcette thing going on. Each strand was feathered in place. If a tornado had suddenly rolled through, nine times out of ten, still, not a hair would be blown out of place.

"Uhh the time?" Dollar said stunned. He was like a deer caught in headlights. The settle beauty of the owner of the soft voice blinded him. He looked down at the shiny gold watch he had swiped from Tyrone's wrist. Instead of numbers it had small diamond chips. Dollar began counting the stones as the lady stood impatient.

"Don't tell me... you're one of those guys who spends $25,000 on a watch and can't even tell time," she said. "Never mind."

"Damn," Dollar said, as the woman whisked away like Cinderella at the stroke of midnight. Her sassiness/classiness was intriguing to Dollar.

"That shit turns me on!" Dollar said to himself. "Hold up, Miss lady. Don't be so mean."

"Is that the only thing men can think of to say when y'all get shot down by a woman?" The lady said. "I'm not mean. I just don't want to be bothered. I wanted something and you couldn't give it to me. No harm done. Now you go your way and I'll go mine."

Dollar continued following her with a huge grin on his face. Her fly ass mouth, which she probably used on a regular to fight off men, wasn't working with Dollar. Like most men, he was up for the challenge of getting something he liked.

"Why do I feel like the girl in Michael Jackson's *The Way You Make Me Feel* video?" The lady said stopping in her tracks.

Dollar couldn't help but laugh as she stood there dead serious. Eventually Dollar's laughter became contagious.

"I'm sorry for being so rude," the lady said. "It's just been one of those days."

"That's okay," Dollar said. "I recently had a few of those years."

"Pardon me," the lady said confused by Dollar's comment.

"Never you mind," Dollar said holding out his hand. "Dollar. I'm Dollar."

"Dollar, huh," the lady said, showing disappointment that Dollar had given her a nickname, which she thought was most likely his street name given to him by his peer of thugs. "Pleased to meet you. Anyway, *Dollar*, you take care of yourself."

"Don't you believe in reciprocity?" Dollar asked.

The use of the word reciprocity, that Lauren Hill made common and sexy in her song, The Ex Factor, made the lady smile.

"Hennessey," the lady said as she walked away. "Hennessey Monroe."

Dollar watched her walk away until she was out of sight. She damned sure wasn't out of mind.

* * *

Dollar hadn't been to work in four days due to his keeping tabs on Ral. Ral seemed to be through the worst part of the withdraw period and out of the woods. Dollar had to fight him and constrain him a couple of times, but he was willing to do whatever he needed to do to get Ral through this ordeal.

Dollar needed to get back to work. Until he got a chance to start putting the wheels in motion he had to stay on his regular routine. He knew that $46,000 was a lot of money to some people, but on the other hand, million dollar lottery winners have filed bankruptcy only a couple of years after their winning. Besides that, he had already spent a chunk of it on the Honda Accord. Dollar wanted to be sitting on so much loot that he would be able to go to Vegas and lose $46,000 playing blackjack and not even have it put a dent in his finances. All that time he did in the joint was not going to be in vain. It was now time to put everything he learned about surviving and ruling the streets into effect.

Dollar eventually had to have Tommy sit with Ral while he went to Redd's and handled a few other business matters.

***

"Get to packing up yo shit," Dollar said to Ral as he entered his motel room. "You relocating to Delaney."

Dollar threw a bag of clothes at Ral that had a Fubu hook-up inside of it, right down to a pair of Fubu shoes.

"Fubu," Ral said looking inside the bag. "Am I allowed to wear this?"

"Am I allowed to wear Tommy Hilfiger?" Dollar replied. "Come on and get dressed so we can head on over to Delaney."

"Who stay there?" Ral asked.

"You do, nigga, now throw on them rags I just threw at you, get your little bit of shit and let's ride. I gotta go to work."

"Whose name is it in?" Ral asked, as he started to gather his things.

"What, you trying to stay here or something? Let's go!" Dollar demanded.

Dollar took Ral to his new pad. It wasn't much, but he now had a place to call his own. Dollar figured if he possessed a little bit of shit he would start getting hungry for the bigger shit and want to do some thangs. Ral wasn't going to be any good to him as a junkie though. Dollar had to show him that he could enjoy life much more being clean and sober.

Dollar had arranged for some cheap ass Value City Furniture shit to be delivered to Ral's apartment. There wasn't no use buying some expensive stuff to put in an apartment in the projects. Folk will buy a leather sectional in a heartbeat to put up in they low income housing unit. They be having $1,000 cherry wood sleigh beds and shit. They don't realize that no matter what they lace they crib with, it's still in the hood.

Dollar had given Tommy some money to grocery shop for Ral's crib so that he would have the bare necessities, enough to get by. Dollar even bought Ral a $2,200 cross between a get-a-bout and a hooptie to get back and forth from seeing his rehab counselor.

Dollar didn't even have a place for himself and yet he was making sure Ral was straight. The rest of the world may have looked at it as Dollar taking a chance on a junkie, but to Dollar he was taking care of a friend. That's just how Dollar was. He knew that his crew's shit had to be on point before he could feel confident about *his* game. Now Dollar understood why, for all those years, his granny always ate after everybody else had even eaten seconds. She wouldn't have been able to enjoy one morsel wondering if somebody else was still hungry and she had eaten the last bite.

"How'd you do all this shit for me?" Ral asked as he cased his new pad.

"I used your money," Dollar said.

"What money? "

"Let's just say it's restitution."

"Yo, Dollar," Ral said. "Thanks, man. I mean. It's gonna be hard, but I'm going to try to do right. I owe you, man. I don't know what happened to me. I used to feel like I could control the shit. But after you got locked up, the shit start controlling me."

"Must be that Kennedy curse," Dollar winked.

Ral walked over to a corner in the living room where a large box with a television in it was sitting. He and Dollar lifted the television out and set it up.

"This television ain't gon' work without cable," Ral said.

"Damn, I knew I was forgetting something," Dollar responded. "I forgot to call Com Cast."

Ral played with the television until he got a basic channel in which the morning news was on.

"Damn, that's Tyrone," Ral said pointing at the television.

He and Dollar watched closely as the newscaster reported on Tyrone's homicide. He had been found dead. He was murdered execution style. It was reportedly drug related.

***

Kera didn't even look up from the book that her nose was buried in as Dollar entered the office. Dollar cleared his throat to gain her attention.

"Oh, hi," Kera said looking up at Dollar. "I didn't hear you come in."

"Maybe y'all ought to get a bell put on that door," Dollar replied. "You all into that book. It must be good."

"It's very good," Kera said, rolling her tongue across her teeth.

"What's it called?"

"A Hustler's Wife," Kera answered.

"A Hustler's Wife, huh?" Dollar said. "I think I've heard

of that one. What's it about?"

"It's about a young girl who knows what she wants," Kera answered in a rousing tone.

"Oh yeah? Tell me more."

"She meets this guy who's older than her and she falls in love with him. He's not all about the right thing, but he loves her strong."

Kera licked her lips and proceeded to give Dollar the synopsis.

"People think that because she's young that she doesn't know what she wants or what's good for her."

"Not everything we want is good for us," Dollar interrupted, referring to himself.

"She followed her heart and her head and let them lead her in the right direction."

"And what do you follow," Dollar asked, "your head or your heart?"

"It depends," Kera said raising up from the desk to show off her skintight jeans with that sexy ass gap between her inner thighs.

"It depends on what?" Dollar asked.

"On what the final destination is...on where I'm trying to go and who's taking me there."

"Bitches sure have changed", Dollar thought. It seemed as though the chicks now days had much more game than the ones he grew up with. Hoes in the new millennium were bold.

"So tell me," Kera said, "what do you follow? Wait a minute. Let me guess."

Kera walked around her desk to Dollar and looked him up and down.

"Your head," she said with her eyes glued on Dollar's bulge. "Yeah, you look like the type of man who follows his head."

Dollar laughed as he took a couple of steps backwards

away from Kera. "Slow down, little mamma."

"I bet this tenderoni tastes as good as she looks", Dollar thought as he grabbed his nuts. What the fuck was he thinking, knowing Kera wasn't nothin' but a baby? He was a grown big ass nigga. He didn't have time for the games and obsession that came along with fucking a young broad. He would put a hurtin' on that tight ass little pussy of hers. Besides, he had to stay focused and get his shit together. Tommy was already on the up and up and he had gotten Ral settled in. Handling his own business was going to be a piece of cake, especially with those few G's he was sitting on.

He had already looked into a nice spot to live. He didn't want just anything, like what he had set Ral up in. He wanted a nice crib with nice things. He had put in an application at a couple of spots and was waiting to hear back from them. Until he got that call on his prepaid minutes cell phone he had recently bought, he was going to stay put at the Y. He probably could have crashed at Tommy's and he definitely could have chilled at Ral's, but he didn't want to be able to be associated with Tommy or Ral's spot.

Dollar hated the hours he had to waste with a nine to five. He could be spending that time casing the streets...seeing what was what and who was who. He had enough confidence in Tommy though to get the job done and she was in just the right spot to do it. Next to a beauty or barbershop, a skin house was the perfect pair of ears and lips. One heard all and told all up in those types of spots. As tempted as Dollar was to just say "fuck Redd," he knew he had to be on point with his game. One small hole could cause a leak great enough to sink the entire ship. Kera could be that hole.

"Dollar," Redd said entering the office from the restroom. "I thought that was you out here. What's happening?"

"Oh, I can't call it," Dollar said giving Redd a five and a

snap. "What's things looking like today?"

"For the rest of those saps, who knows, but you know you the number one gem around here. Everybody after Dollar Bill," Redd laughed. "I should just get you a desk set up in here."

"Yeah," Kera cosigned. "Everybody's after Dollar Bill."

"Well, I'm gonna head out and shoot the breeze with some of these cats and wait on some work," Dollar said as he turned to the exit. "And, Kera, you're gonna have to let me know how that book turns out."

"I'll give you a blow by blow," Kera said rounding her lips at Dollar then looking to make sure her father was none the wiser of her innuendo.

"Aiight then, little mama." Dollar smiled at Kera and exited the office. When he got outside, Mr. Owens had pulled up in his Lincoln Navigator that all the cats admired. They admired his whip and his habit of paying cash to Redd for the men's services, who in turn, Redd then paid the men in cash. Seeing cash switch hands for their services made some of the men feel like hoes being pimped, but what the fuck? Half of them bastards didn't have a bank to cash no check at and the other's desperately needed that $20 check cashing fee the check cashing place was raping them of.

Mr. Owens only needed three men that day and had picked them already when Dollar came out of the building. One of the three men knew they were about to get the boot and be replaced with Dollar just as soon as Mr. Owens noticed him. Dollar was a strong hard worker. He managed to do the work of two men.

When Mr. Owens spotted Dollar he gave the third guy, who was fixin' to hop into the Navigator, a "beat it" stare. The guy mean mugged Dollar as he walked back over with the other unchosens.

"Nigga what?" Dollar said. "You got something to say

then say that shit."

The man twisted his lips up at Dollar and sucked his teeth as he proceeded to walk on.

"Man, I ain't even on that bullshit you screamin'," the guy said.

"You don't want none of this," Dollar said, getting in the last word before closing the door.

Where was all this cockiness coming from? Dollar had only envisioned his master plan, he hadn't put shit into play and already he was starting to act like the muthafuckin' man. As far as Dollar was concerned, he had a win-win plan. He was going to make sure his shit was airtight this time around. As they rode off, Dollar thought about the long hours and hard work he was about to put in and this only motivated him more.

"I gotta stop off at my house first, fellas," Mr. Owens said. "I left my keys to the property we gotta work on."

Dollar nodded in the affirmative as if he was giving Mr. Owens' permission to make a detour. He then continued on deep in thought.

Dollar thought about how once he, Tommy and Ral successfully completed their first hit for that paper, Dollar's pockets would be cool enough to show up at Redd's every other day or so. Once they really put in work he was only gonna fuck with Redd on the weekends. But for now, he had to pay homage to one of his strongest traits of which spending time in the joint forced upon him, patience.

Dollar had nothing but time. Haste makes waste. This was his second opportunity, his golden opportunity to redeem himself to the streets by proving that he wasn't some young thug who couldn't even pull off a simple ass robbery. No, this time he would do everything by the book. When all was said and done the streets would belong to him.

"*Fuck it!*" Dollar thought to himself as he rolled down the window. "*The Streets are already mine.*"

***

Dollar always wanted to know what the inside of The Chocolate Factory looked like. As a kid, he had heard stories about what went on up in that spot. He witnessed a lot of men's clothing flying out of apartment windows because of those stories. Their wives must have heard them too.

The Chocolate Factory was a pretty cool looking joint. From the outside it looked like just another hole in the wall, like one of those raggedy ass titty bars on Bourbon Street in New Orleans, but on the inside it looked like some Vegas type shit was jumping off. Disco globes hung about the ceiling that whirled around and around, giving a hypnotic affect. There was a live DJ instead of some jukebox. He spun the beats the bitches shook they ass to from a muthafuckin' sky box. Some smoke still filled the air where you could tell the last dancer must have crooned her body through. Dollar was sure things had changed since back in the day, but if this was the type of shit the old playas fell victim too, he could almost see why them niggaz left home and never came back.

"These bitches is tizight," Dollar said to himself, grinning from ear to ear. He copped a seat at the stage and looked around for a barmaid. Fine ass women were in every corner of the room talking shit to niggaz. Dollar felt like he was a wishing well filled with dimes. That's exactly what the bitches up in that piece were, dimes...perfect asses, perfect breast, stomachs and teeth. They didn't have any stretch marks, their weave looked believable and their cosmetics were flawless. Whoever hired these hoes must have worked at Baskin & Robins at one point because every flavor represented.

While Dollar was turned to his left signaling the

barmaid, on his right a dancer sat down next to him. With skin the tone of a Vanilla Wafer, her Alicia Keys braids flowed down her back like a waterfall. Her Janet Jackson baby hair gave her a look of innocence while her Aliyah smile had already earned her three fifty dollar drinks that night. This black mixed with Indian lookin' young miss was on point.

Dollar looked her up and down. She looked like she had just stepped out of a Frederick's of Hollywood catalog. Peeking through her long hot pink, sheer cover up was a hot pink little two-piece liquid leather number. Her five-inch ice pick heels were the narrator to the story her body would soon tell.

Dollar tried to find a flaw on her, but it was a downhill battle. She was perfect, right down to her edible toes that hung slightly over her shoe...in a sexy way...for them foot fetish muthafuckas. She was whole thangin' it, no doubt.

"Sup, Poppa?" she smiled.

"You, ma," Dollar said, as the barmaid approached him. *"This bitch think she got perfect timing"*, Dollar thought to himself referring to the barmaid.

"What can I get you?" the barmaid asked Dollar.

"I'll take a shot of Hennessy, straight, no ice," Dollar requested.

"And for the lady," the barmaid said looking dead at Dollar. Out of the corner of his eye he could see the dancer giving the barmaid a "good lookin' out" wink.

"Ah huh huh huh," Dollar laughed. "Get ma a $20 spot of whatever she's drinking."

"Thank you. I'll have my regular," the dancer said as the barmaid nodded and walked away.

"No problem," Dollar said gazing into the dancer's eyes. "Don't I know you from somewhere?"

The dancer laughed at Dollar's use of the most abused and corny ass line in the book.

"I ain't never seen you before so I know you ain't never

seen me. Although I could be that girl you been dreaming about all of your life."

"That's cute," Dollar said.

"So are you," the dancer smiled.

"What's your name?" Dollar asked. "Wait a minute, let me guess. Is it Lexus? Is it Mercedes or is it Delicious?

"Storm," the dancer said.

"So, why they call you that, Storm?"

"I come across soft, like a light rain or a summer's mist," the dancer said as she put her hand on Dollar's knee. "But I cum like a storm, a drowning rain or a roaring wave on a Cancun beach."

Just as Storm's hand began to make its way up Dollar's leg the barmaid's arm cut between them as she proceeded to place their drinks in front of them. Dollar paid for the cost of the drinks plus a $3 tip for the barmaid. Dollar took a sip of his drink as the DJ introduced the next dancer.

"Like her name, she's intoxicating," the DJ said. "Fellas, fuck dem dolla bills, y'all better pull out them tens and twenties because our next dancer, repin' the chicks in da club, is the one and only Wine."

As the stage went black a figure could be seen taking its place on the stage. She strutted like she was modeling for the new Victoria Secret line. As the theme song to her act began to play, the fellas in the club got hype and drew all their attention onto the main act.

"*Hoe's in da club show love, shakin' that ass sho nuff nigga what. Hoe's in da club show love, shakin that ass sho nuff nigga what,*" the male patrons sang along.

As the lights pulled up slowly the crowd was in awe. Before them stood a bad ass bitch in spiked red thigh high boots. Her red hot pants covered only the top portion of her ass allowing for her chestnut ass cheeks to hang out. The matching bandeau squeeze her pretty brown browns tightly. As she stretched her arms high to grab the pole on each side of her, the fellas were hoping them coconuts would pop out. But she had so much grace it was as if she was rising from the ground like magic. Once she reached the ceiling with poles in hand the lights came completely up. She swung her legs up so that her ankles grasped one pole and saw to it that both her hands secured the other. Slowly she slid down piercing Dollar with her eyes the entire way down.

"Son of a bitch," Dollar said once he realized the dancer was Tommy. He couldn't believe his eyes. For one minute he imagined the trick on the pole sliding right down onto his dick, come to find it was Tommy, someone who was like one of the boys as far as he was concerned. On that note Dollar gulped down his drink and raised his glass to the barmaid for another.

Dollar couldn't wait for Tommy to dance her two songs and get off the stage. Shit only got worse though. On the second song the hot pants came off and all of Tommy's ass was revealed, compliments of the matching G-String.

As "It Seems Like Your Ready" by R. Kelly played, Tommy maneuvered her body in unimaginable positions. Niggaz was filling those boots and G-String with bills. They swarmed the stage like vultures. The hoes was even showing Tommy love with all the "work it, girl" and "do that shit" shout outs. Tommy was putting her heart into that little show. She was working it like she had never worked it before.

Dollar tried to occupy his time by slamming down shots of Hennessy. Thanks to Tommy's rump shakin' ass, he had spent $60 on Storm's drinks.

"You know her or something?" Storm asked Dollar. "Is she who you want? You wanna buy her drinks? You wanna fuck her?"

"Slow down, baby," Dollar said.

"You my girl or something? Bitch, I bought you a drink, not a fucking wedding ring," Dollar said with attitude.

"I'm sorry, Poppa," Storm said. "It's just that I get so jealous. I mean, you so fine and all."

"You got game, ma," Dollar laughed. "It's cool. You do your thang. I respect that."

"So we cool?" Storm said, running her hand down the back of Dollar's neck.

"We cool," Dollar replied.

"Let me dance for you," Storm said, getting out of her seat and pressing her pussy up against Dollar's knee.

As Dollar licked his lips he couldn't help but being slightly turned on.

"The game is crazy," Dollar said. "You wanna dance for me, love?"

"Oooh I do," Storm said as she closed her eyes and allowed Dollar to finger her pussy through her costume bottoms.

"Cool," Dollar said.

Dollar finished off his drink and followed Storm into the Champagne Room. He threw the one hundred-dollar bill at the bouncer who was guarding the entryway and proceeded to get his sweet bud satisfied.

"Oooh oooh oooh ahh ahh ahh yeah yeah yeah what what what" were the words that crooned out of the ceiling speakers of the passionate room that was lit with one lamp that had a purple light bulb in it. The room was about the size of Dollar's old jail cell, but it was plush. It looked like something from out of the 70's. The lamp set on a glass end table with a black metal frame next to a big velvet like couch with purple satin pillows to match the lighting. The walls were painted a shiny black and the floor was covered with black furry rugs. Across from the couch was a mirrored bar with a black pleather ice bucket sitting on it. Inside the ice bucket was a bottle of Asti.

Storm headed straight over to the bar and grabbed two of the champagne glasses that were lined up on the bar. She filled them to the top and then walked over to the couch where

Dollar had sat down and made himself comfortable.

"Cheers," Storm said, as she handed Dollar a glass of champagne. "Drink up baby, but allow *me* to intoxicate you."

"Go on and talk that shit," Dollar winked as he spread his legs, sat an elbow on each one, and with the hand free of champagne, cupped his chin.

Storm began to roll her hips and allow her tongue to stroll across her top lip. All Dollar could imagine was her tongue strolling across his tip.

"*I'm just an R&B thug babe, tryin' to get some ass babe, do you wanna thug babe*?" Dollar lip-synched to the song. It must be a crime not to have R. Kelly's shit in a strip club. This ain't the place for Luther. R's shit made a nigga wanna stop whatever he was doing and fuck. Damn that making love and making babies shit Luther specializes in. Gangsta niggaz wanna fuck. And for another Benji that's exactly what Storm offered.

Dollar never thought in a million years he would trick, pay for some muthafuckin' pussy while there were hoes giving the shit away. But he had been locked up for eight years and the pussy was in his face. No nigga in their right mind, in his situation, could have turned that shit away, no nigga in their right mind.

Dollar went in his pocket and pulled out a wad of money. He peeled a one hundred-dollar bill from the wad and placed it in Storm's hand. Then he pulled out his dick. It was hard from just thinking about getting ready to run up in some pussy. He had even pre-ejaculated in his drawz.

After properly placing a Magnum style condom on Dollar's penis, Dollar watched as Storm's pussy sucked in all ten inches of his dick. Dollar felt like he was watchin' a mafuckin' magic show the way Storm made that shit disappear.

Storm put on a brief rodeo show for Dollar. She wrapped both legs around Dollars neck and bounced it out.

Dollar watched as his dick went in and out of her, pussy juice flowin'. Then Storm flipped it on him backwards so that her ass smacked down on Dollar's six pack. That's when Dollar exploded. She rolled them hips like an ocean and Dollar couldn't hold back the tidal wave.

Storm could feel Dollar's muscle flexin' inside of her so she proceeded to make the appropriate moans and groans to enhance his climax. Her pussy was workin' Dollar's dick like it was an old Atari 2600 joystick and she was playing Centipede. Once she knew Dollar had shot out all the juices he could, she then rested back on his chest and wrapped his arms around her body.

It didn't last as long as Dollar would have liked it to, but it had been a while since he busted one up inside some pussy. There was no way to prolong it. It was quick, easy and greasy, but it was pleasing.

"Did you like that, baby?" Storm asked as she sucked on Dollar's middle finger. "Did you, Poppa? Did it feel good to you?"

"You know that shit was on point," Dollar moaned while kissing Storm's neck.

"Stop it. That tickles," Storm giggled putting her head down and getting from off top of Dollar.

"Oh, now you wanna get shy."

"So when you gonna come back and see me?" Storm asked as she began gathering her costume, which was Dollar's hint to move the fuck on.

"I ain't really into trickin', ma. This was just a one-time thang, but I'll hook you up with a drink or two the next time I roll through. Is that alright? Is that alright with you?" Dollar said zipping up his pants.

"Yeah, that's what they all say," Storm said. "But you'll be back. Trust me...you'll be back."

Storm vanished into the changing room and Dollar let

himself out of the Champagne Room. The first thing he saw was Tommy hugged up with some gold tooth grill dude. Dude was all up in Tommy's face, playing in her hair and shit.

Dollar took a seat back at the stage and made eye contact with Tommy. He widened his eyes and nodded his head as a sign to let her know that he was waiting to talk with her.

Five minutes went by and Dollar was becoming inpatient. Eventually Tommy stood up and headed Dollar's way, but the dude that had been hawkin' her was right behind her. Tommy looked at Dollar and held up her index finger telling him to wait a minute. It didn't take Dollar long to figure out that she was headed to the Champagne Room.

Just then everything started going in slow motion. Dollar pictured ole dude doing to Tommy what he had just done to Storm. That shit wasn't about to go down with him up in the spot. Dollar got up from his chair and approached Tommy and as she was just about to head inside the Champagne Room.

"Yo, T," Dollar said. "I need to holla at you for a minute.

"It's Wine," Tommy corrected Dollar.

"Yeah, whatever. I need to holla at you real quick," Dollar replied.

"Is this yo man or somethin'?" the dude said to Tommy with a crooked face.

"Naw," Tommy replied. "We just friends."

"Then your friend needs to step. You workin'," the dude said pushing Tommy on into the room.

"Mafucka, you don't know nothing about this here," Dollar said pointing to Tommy and then to himself.

Smelling that some shit was about to go down any minute, Tommy put her hand on Bear's, the bouncer, chest to calm him as he began to flex.

"Look, let me talk to my homie for a minute. You go in there and wait for me," Tommy said to the dude. "When I get back, I'll play an extra song for you, baby."

Dollar wanted to puke, but he laughed instead. This scene was unreal.

"It's cool, Bear," Tommy said.

The dude followed Tommy's instructions and once he was out of sight Tommy turned towards Dollar with devil eyes and said, "Follow me!"

Tommy escorted Dollar out to the parking lot of the club. She was steaming mad. She couldn't wait to get his ass outside so she could let him have it.

"Do I come up on your job and interrupt what the fuck you doing?" Tommy scolded as her breath created a fog from the cold.

"Look, my bad," Dollar said. "You right. I don't even know what got into me. I just couldn't sit out there and wait for you while you went in that room to do God knows what."

Tommy was silent. She looked at Dollar in disgust.

"Is that what you think of me? You think I was about to fuck ole dude just because I was going into the Champagne Room with him? Why, because you fucked Storm?"

The look on Dollar's face gave Tommy the answer she was looking for.

"You triflin' ass," Tommy said. She shook her head and looked down at the ground. "Well, I'm not like Storm. I get paid to dance and that's what I do. That's all I do and I'm offended you would think otherwise. Yeah, I sell a little bud on the side to some of these cats, but that's it."

"T, I'm sorry," Dollar said with his head down like a puppy dog.

"Sorry for what, fucking Storm or thinking I'm a slut?"

"Whoa," Dollar said. "I don't have to apologize to you for who I fuck, do I?"

"I didn't mean it like that so don't flatter yourself. Besides, Storms a dyke anyway."

"You said that like a true hater. Is Tommy jealous?" Dollar said cooing at Tommy like she was a little girl.

"Hell no I ain't jealous. What do I have to be jealous of? Storm is really a dyke."

"She might be bi, but she sho ain't no dyke," Dollar said grabbing himself as to insinuate that he had beat that shit up.

"Remember when we checked Ral into Short Stay and I was talking to those two chicks? Well, Storm was one of them. The other one was her wife, girlfriend or whatever. Her name is Thunder. They been together for four years. Storm does dick on the side for money only. Thunder is straight pussy. And them bitches is raw."

"I knew I recognized her face from somewhere. They live at that hotel?" Dollar asked.

"No. They work up out of there. They got a nice ass crib out there in Merrillville. Storm got two daughters who go to private school. The girls call both Storm and Thunder Mommy."

"But I thought you said ol' girl was a strict vegetarian, no meat," Dollar said.

"She is. Thunder don't get down with men. Them kids are Storms. When the two of them put in work, they Ecs'in a nigga," Tommy replied.

"What?"

"They getting' a cat high off that liquid ecstasy and robbin' his dumb ass. Storm does what she needs to do and Thunder strips him for his goodies. Don't let them find out the muthafucka married. They will black mail his ass 'til Kingdom Come."

"Hell, no. Them bitches got hustle like that?" Dollar was impressed.

"As quiet as it's kept, they done put a couple of fools to sleep on that Ecs. They don't even look like the type, especially when you see them out with their daughters. They be lookin' like the perfect little mother's. Up in here, we call them Murder

Mommies."

Tommy could see the wheels in Dollar's head churning.

"What you thinking?" Tommy asked.

"Oh, nothing. I'm just storing this info for future reference. You never know when a couple of hit hoes might come in handy," Dollar winked. "Damn!" Dollar said turning his attention to a girl getting out the passenger side of a yellow Hummer in a full-length mahogany mink coat. "Who's that lookin' like Lil' Kim?"

"That's Becka. Her brother, Wayne, the guy dropping her off, he sells them coats. She's his walking advertisement," Tommy answered.

"Oh yeah... legit?" Dollar asked.

"Actually, he does sell them legit. Their dad has a store in Chicago. He gets them for next to nothing. You know how they do it in Chi-Town with the furs. I hear they're nice. Tiwana, the barmaid, her boyfriend is getting a load of them. He's going to try to push them up North for double what he pays for them."

"When's he supposed to be coppin' them?" Dollar asked.

"I don't know."

"You need to find that shit out so we can just happen to be around when the transaction takes place."

Chapter 9

Back In Business

It was midweek, about 7:45 p.m. Dollar wasn't comfortable with an early evening stick up his first go round since 95', but hell, he was confident with his game. He would have preferred a midnight or early a.m. stick-up, but who in the fuck runs around selling furs at midnight, legit ones anyway?

Dollar's big buff ass was crammed in Ral's little hooptie. He felt like a clown at the circus in one of them lil' buggy cars. He had just dropped Ral off around the corner. All the pieces to the game were in place with the exception of the queen, which was Tommy. Dollar was awaiting her call on his cell.

"Damn," Dollar said fiddling with the radio dial. "This bitch ain't even got a tape deck in it. What was I thinking hooking my boy up with some shit like this?"

As Dollar tapped his fingernails on the dashboard he noticed how dull and rigid they were.

"My nails are fucked up," he said out loud as he began to gnaw on them. "I'm trippin'," he laughed. "Since when do I give a fuck about my fingernails? I'm acting like a hoe. Just relax, Dollar. Just relax."

Dollar continued to tap his nails on the dashboard. For some reason, even though he was playin' a ridiculously overpriced Phat Pharm denim hook-up, some clean ass And 1s, and a nice fresh cut which left him with a shiny bald head, his nails were fucking up his total look.

"Niggaz, get they nails done too," Dollar said trying to convince himself. "Fuck it! I'm gettin' these shitz did."

Just then Dollar's cell phone rang and he answered it.

"He just dropped Becka off, so it's on," Tommy said.

"Good lookin' out. Peace," Dollar said closing the flap on his cell phone.

A few minutes went by before Dollar saw the bright yellow Hummer H2 pull up across the street from him and park. Dollar sat at attention.

"Dis mafucka rollin' an H2 in the heart of the hood," Dollar said laughing as he used his cell phone to call Ral's pager and key in the code. "This cat deserves to get got."

On cue Ral cleared the corner. He was wearing an olive green Down Coat with feathers poking out, some dirty ass jeans and a funky baseball cap. He was looking like the recovering addict he was. He killed time by digging in garbage cans, collecting cans and whatnot. In the meantime Wayne had gotten out of his Hummer and knocked on the door of Tiwana and her boyfriend's apartment. Once assured that Tiwana's boyfriend was home, Wayne returned to his truck and with three coats in arm and a total of four trips, he hauled the minks into the apartment.

Back in the day Dollar would have probably pretended to be a customer looking to buy some furs. Once Wayne showed up, Dollar would have robbed him for whatever he had on him, but according to Romeo, that was one of Dollar's mistakes. There wasn't a need to befriend a mafucka and play pretend. Just sneak up from behind and handle they ass. All that other bullshit takes up too much time and leaves room for error. Romeo brought up the point that if Cartel and his boys hadn't of been shot dead, they would have known exactly who to retaliate against. Now, with the situation at hand, if anything, Wayne would feel as though he had been set up by Tiwana's boyfriend and that's who he would look to seek revenge on.

On Wayne's final trip, Tiwana's boyfriend closed the door behind him. That was Dollar and Ral's sign that money was about to exchange hands. After ten minutes the apartment door opened and Wayne exited.

As soon as he opened the door to the Hummer, Ral caught him off guard.

"You got some change?" Ral asked. "Driving a fine automobile such as this, I know you got some change."

"Man, kick mud," Wayne said. "I ain't got shit for you."

"Then maybe you got something for me," Dollar said coming up behind Wayne and placing Tommy's gun to his back.

"Oh, shit," Wayne said being caught off guard.

"Yeah, oh shit is right, nigga," Dollar said cocking the gun.

"Here's my keys," Wayne said. "Take it. Fuck it. Just don't kill me."

"Look, we don't want to kill you and we don't want your truck," Dollar said. "Just empty your pockets."

"Empty my pockets?" Wayne repeated.

"Yeah, pull 'em out, nigga. Turn 'em inside out."

Wayne nervously put his hands down in his pockets and said, "Don't shoot. I'm just doing' what you said. I'm going in my pockets."

Wayne pulled his pant pockets inside out and gave Dollar the contents, which was only a few hundred dollars.

"Empty those pockets too," Dollar said pointing to Wayne's jacket pockets.

"These pockets too?" Wayne repeated.

"What the fuck are you, an echo?" Ral added. "Yes, them pockets too."

Wayne emptied his inside jacket pockets where there was a total of $32,000. Meanwhile, Ral had raided the truck and retrieved a woman's long black mink coat.

Dollar forced Wayne to get into the back of his Hummer and ball up in a fetal position on the floor.

"Count to 100 Mississippi's before getting up," Ral

ordered Wayne. "If you get up, our other partner who's watchin' all this go down is going to blow your muthafuckin' head off. You got that?"

"Yeah, yeah," Wayne said nervously. "One Mississippi, two Mississippi, three Mississippi..."

As Wayne continued counting, Dollar and Ral headed for Ral's car. Ral had trouble lugging the huge mink that was secured inside a clear clothing bag. Since Ral was frail, weighing in at about a buck twenty-five, the weight of the coat slowed Ral down. He even tripped and fell running with it and had a hard time getting the car door closed because he kept shutting the coat in the door. This scene from the three stooges was starting to piss Dollar off.

"Why the fuck you always gotta do some extra shit?" Dollar asked. "We got the money. You need to learn how to keep your eye on the prize. That's what fucked us up eight years ago. We doing' things different now, Ral."

Dollar steered the car with one hand while fondling the coat on Ral's lap with the other. That's a bitch's coat anyway. What the fuck you gon' do with a woman's coat?"

"Do you know how much pussy this can get me, amigo?" Ral replied.

"Man, Ral, don't fuck with me."

"Seriously, how much loot we get away with from ol' dude?"

"I don't know. It looks like it's about $30-$35,000," Dollar said handing the wad to Ral to count.

"So that means dude bought a dozen of these bitches for around $3,000 each. Shit, I know I can get between $4-$5,000 for one."

"I swear to God, Ral, if I find out you swapped that coat for a hit...."

"Come on, man," Ral said. "Give me a little bit more credit than that. I ain't did no drugs man. No hard shit anyway.

Yeah, I might have blazed on a couple of those fat ones, but that's it. You can ask your lil' bro. He checks my piss every time I go to the clinic. He done already warned me about the bud leading me back to more glamorous pharmaceuticals. But I'm straight. Ask him, man."

"I'll take your word for it," Dollar said.

"What's the deal with you and your bro anyway, man?"

"I ain't trying to talk about my brother," Dollar said becoming a little uneasy. "I'm trying to talk about money."

Dollar knew damn well that he wanted to talk about his brother. He wanted to ask Ral if he had asked about him. He hated the fact that he would probably never have the kind of relationship he longed for with his brother. But Dollar couldn't let that shit weigh on his mind. It was impossible for him to turn back the hands of time. So for now he decided to keep his mind on money.

***

"So, what's our next move?" Ral said as he studied the food menu at Jimmy's Coney Island.

"These cats from T town (Toledo, Ohio) rolled through the bar last night. They were ballers on their way to cop some of them thangs," Tommy said taking a sip of her ice water.

"What the hell some dudes from Toledo stopping off in Gary for?"

"Making a lil' pit stop," Tommy answered.

"So did all that pussy up in the spot get them cats to telling they business?" Ral asked.

"Well, I know that some dude named Ant over in T-town is expecting about 30 G's via Fed Ex," Tommy said in a bragging manner as if it was her pussy that was responsible for the lead. "

"Okay, keep the info coming," Dollar said as he listened intensely. The talk of money made Dollar's dick hard. Contrary to popular opinion, fuck dogs...money is man's best friend.

"I know dude stays by a park on Hollywood and is expecting the loot next Friday," Tommy said. "Ol' dude was making it a point to let me know that throwing 30 at his boy wasn't nuthin' but a thang."

"Show off niggaz," Dollar said. "These young bloods don't know shit about the game."

"Oh well", Ral said. "That's where we benefit."

"Y'all know what y'all want yet," the waitress asked with pen and pad in hand.

The three proceeded to order their soul food entrees and discussed their next move as they waited on their meals to be prepared. Like a game of Chess, Dollar was meticulous about the moves that were to be made. He didn't want to do too much too fast. Actually he didn't want to do too much at all. He wanted to hit the jackpot, some big type stick-up that would put them on easy street for a long spell. He would then turn around and invest his money in some investments that would pay off well enough to take care of him for life. But no amount sounded remotely enough to take care of Dollar for life. Nah, he wanted too damn much. He wanted to live like one of the Good Fellas, although Romeo had warned him that that type of attitude leads to downfall. But, of course, Dollar's attitude was *fuck it.* He wasn't like these Similac drinking' wankstas. He would take heed to the words of the elders. He would be the exception to the game. He would win.

Just as the waitress brought the food out to their table, through the restaurant window Dollar noticed a familiar face walking by. He never forgets a face, especially one belonging to such a beautiful body. Obviously she recognized him too because as she entered, she told the girl who she was with to grab a table while she hollered at Dollar for a minute. Dollar acted like he didn't see her coming his way as he took a bite of his collard greens.

"Excuse me, sir, do you have the time?" the soft spoken voice said over Dollar's shoulder.

Dollar looked up and replied, "It's time for you to get a new watch," and continued eating his food.

"I see you holdin' a grudge," she said smiling.

"Naw, Miss lady," Dollar said cracking a smile, the "I'm that nigga" smile. "I'm just messing with you."

"Hennessey, right?"

"Umm, you're good. Yes, Hennessey Monroe," she said turning her attention to Tommy and Ral who were sitting across from Dollar. Tommy was eyeballing Hennessey from head to toe, checking out her Donna Karen casual pantsuit, Donna Karen purse and Donna Karen casual like flip-flops.

"Ahem," Tommy cleared her throat.

"Oh," Dollar said, "forgive me for being rude. Hennessey this is Ral and Tommy."

Hennessey stuck her hand out to shake their hands. The diamonds from the five-karat tennis bracelet that appeared to be making love to her wrist damn near blinded them. Tommy really wasn't feeling Hennessey's presence so she left her hand hangin' and gave her a "what up" nod instead. Ral's hand was greasy from the fried chicken, but that didn't keep him from giving Hennessey a courteous handshake.

"Oh, my," Hennessey said as she looked disgustingly down at her greasy hand. Tommy couldn't help but giggle. Dollar was embarrassed.

"Uhh, yeah. These are my boys," Dollar said as Tommy kicked him underneath the table. "Well, this is Tommy, he's a girl...I mean she's a girl. We're all just friends."

"Oh, very nice," Hennessey said. "Well, I'm here with my cousin, Trini. She lives around these parts."

"And what part do you live around, Miss lady?" Dollar inquired.

"I'm over in the windy city," Hennessey replied. "Well, I just wanted to say hey. I better go join Trini now."

"Well, it was nice meeting you, bye-bye," Tommy said rushing Hennessey off.

"Uhh, let me walk you over to your table," Dollar said excusing himself and at the same time giving Tommy and evil look.

"Oh, well thank you," Hennessey said as she turned to Tommy and Ral. "It was nice meeting you both. Take care."

"Tah, tah," Tommy said sarcastically under her breath as Dollar and Hennessey walked away. "I don't like that bitch."

"You don't even know that bitch," Ral said sucking the grease off of his fingers.

"I know her alright. I know her kind and I don't like her kind."

"What's her kind?" Ral asked.

"Bitch. She's a bitch who thinks she better than everybody else. But underneath it all she's got something to hide. I can tell she's fake. I just hope Dollar can tell too."

***

Stickin' up the Fed Ex carrier was the easiest $30,000 the trio ever made. Dollar, Ral and Tommy drove over to Toledo on Thursday night in two separate cars and camped out on Hollywood. The park split the street so each car manned one end of the block. There was no way they were going to miss the Fed Ex truck turning into the neighborhood.

The Fed Ex driver didn't put up a fight. Hell, as far as he knew it was a set of stainless steal pots in the package and his life was worth more than that. He turned over the package with ease and even offered them all of the other packages he had in his truck waiting to be delivered.

Dollar felt bad holdin' up the driver. He looked like a little young brotha tryin' to make a living, trying to earn money for college or some shit. He reminded Dollar of himself. Dollar tucked five Benjis in the Fed Ex guy's uniform pocket before they dipped and apologized for the inconvenience.

It had been over six months since Dollar had been released from prison. He had been content bankin' his ends while living at the Y. But that shit was old. Dollar used his entire cut from the Fed Ex hit for the security deposit and first three months rent for some little ass apartment near the shore in Chicago. Dollar couldn't believe how high rent was in Chicago. He paid three times as much for the monthly rent for his place than he had put down on Ral's and Ral's place was bigger. You couldn't compare the atmosphere though. Dollar's bachelor pad was like his little kingdom. He fell in love with it the first time the manager showed him around. He was nervous as hell that his application wouldn't get approved. Although he hid his history from management, he didn't know just how extensive their background check on him might be.

Dollar convinced Redd to nigga rig some paperwork for him stating that he had been doing work for his agency for the past three years. Dollar agreed to work for Redd on a 50/50 cut for an entire month in exchange for the favor.

Dollar's credit was clear because he didn't have any. He concealed his felony bid from the apartment manager and spoke of how he had gone to school and graduated from the Ohio State University. It was a partial lie. He put in a few years in the state of Ohio, but it damn sure wasn't at the university.

Dollar bragged to the apartment manager of how he had briefly played football for the university, but had injured himself during a practice. The injury would end his football career. The apartment manager praised Dollar for continuing his education in spite of his football let down. As far as Dollar was concerned, doing time in the pen was like schooling. It was the school of hard knocks. He learned how to survive. No university could teach him that there shit.

Dollar enjoyed creating a new life for himself. He felt like Omar Tyree, the Urban Griot, making up stories, telling people what they wanted to hear. Dollar had plenty of tales and very little of the truth. He started to believe the shit he was making up himself. Dollar's demeanor and attitude began to change to accommodate his fables. He was on top of the world. He was about to have his shit on lock. Do it easy-easy does it, is what Dollar had to remember. He couldn't rush. He had to take his time and do the damn thang right, no gorilla style type shit.

***

"Damn, my nails are shiny ain't they?" Dollar asked Mya, the nail technician at the salon.

"Sir, they'll stay shiny for about two weeks," Mya replied as she continued to massage the smooth side of the buffer over Dollar's thumbnail. "Do you want a clear coat of polish on them? That will keep them shiny and strong for a long time.

"Naw, I'm straight on that, ma" Dollar replied.

"You ready for your pedicure, sir?" a small Asian lady said to Dollar.

"Yes," Dollar said, but at the same time Mya replied for him as well.

"No," Mya said. "I haven't given you your hand massage yet."

"Oh, that's okay. You did good," Dollar pulled out a ten-dollar bill and placed it in the palm of Mya's hand. She clinched the tip and thanked Dollar with a stimulating smile.

"It would have been my pleasure. Enjoy the rest of your treatment." Mya then brushed a piece of her long blonde hair from her face and turned to the little Asian woman to say, "He's ready."

"You follow me now, sir," the Asian woman ordered Dollar.

She led Dollar over to a small refrigerator and offered him a drink and some fruit before taking him over to the massage spa chair. She then ran water into the attached foot tub and poured some lilac smelling powder into the water, which formed a layer of suds. She showed Dollar how to operate the massage control buttons on the chair and then pampered him with a forty-five minute pedicure.

After paying for his services, and tipping the women $10 each, Dollar went on to get his head conditioned and massaged. This is how Dollar spent every other Saturday. Afterwards he would normally cop a DVD, some grub and then head back to his spot. But Dollar thought it was safe, and about damn time, to start finding him some hoes to keep company with.

This Saturday night would be different. Dollar was going to find a club that was jumpin', but not thugged out. He didn't want to fuck with the baller's scene. He just wanted to go somewhere where he could groove to a little bit of R& B hip-hop with a touch of jazz, clock some hoes and not have some ole' jealous niggaz mean muggin' him.

Dollar decided to go to one of Chi-Town's low key spots called "The Art Bar" and cool out. He heard it was a nice chill spot, not uppity, but not ghetto either. It was a mixed crowd.

When Dollar arrived at the club in his black long sleeve CK dress shirt and black CK dark dress pants, he turned every woman's head up in the spot. And once he was out of their sight, the scent of his CK1 cologne left them with something to remember him by.

Dollar found an empty stool at the end of the bar and

hugged it all night. Honeys deliberately brushed up against him while in an attempt to get the barmaids attention to order a drink. This made Dollar smile, but none of the women coppin' free feels had "it". Some of the girls were tight, but Dollar would have rather paid for some ass than to have to listen to some gabby ass chick talk about nothing, have to buy her a couple of drinks and take her to the Waffle House before knowing if he even had the slightest chance of fucking her. So he decided to call it a night. He swallowed down his last taste of Hennessy and went for his wallet to leave the barmaid a tip. As he pulled his wallet out, a small body bumped into him.

"You got that out to buy me a drink?" the owner of the small body said. "I'll take Sex on the Beach."

"Sex on the Beach, huh?" Dollar said.

"Yeah, and after that you can buy me a drink," Kera winked as she slightly stumbled. Dollar grabbed her arm that was hanging out of her short sleeve, dark colored, Coogie dress in order to help her balance.

"You're not even old enough to drink," Dollar said grabbing hold of Kera's arm to aid in balancing her wobbly ass. It was obvious she had had a little too much to drink already, but yet here she was in Dollar's face beggin' for a drink.

"I'm old enough to do lots of stuff," Kera giggled.

"How did you even get up in here? You're not even old enough to be in here," Dollar said to her.

"Shhhhhh," Kera said spraying Dollar with spit.

"Who you wit?" Dollar said, standing up from the stool in authority.

Kera looked around and replied, "See that little number over there on the dance floor in that sky blue tube dress?"

Kera pointed and Dollar's eyes found the girl she was talking about.

"Is that who you're with? Wait right here," Dollar said as he stomped towards the dance floor.

"No, wait," Kera said trying to grab hold of Dollar before he took off. She wasn't quick enough though. Dollar had already walked over to the dance floor and began talking to the girl in the sky blue dress. The conversation was intense as Dollar pointed to Kera and then scolded the girl for allowing Kera to get to the drunken' state she was in. The girl began to snap her neck and scold back at Dollar. This went on for a couple of minutes before Dollar returned to the bar where Kera was standing. Dollar was plum red and Kera was laughing hysterically.

"That wasn't cute," Dollar said.

"I tried to stop you," Kera replied. "Nobody told you to race over there and play daddy."

Just then a tall dark skin girl in a red one-piece pants suit came over and tapped Kera on the shoulder and said, "You ready to go?"

"Leece, this is Dollar," Kera introduced the two. "Dollar, this is Leece, the girl I'm really here with."

"Nice to meet you," Leece said before turning to whisper in Kera's ear. "Girl, you were right. He is a fine ass LL Cool J looking muthafucka."

"It's nice to meet you too, Leece," Dollar said. "You don't look old enough to be in here either."

"Thank you for the compliment," Leece said. "But I just turned 21 today."

"Go Shawty, it's your birthday," Kera sang. "We gon' party like it's your birthday."

Kera and Leece continued on with their version of "In Da Club" that would have made 50 Cent proud. They had everyone within ear distance shouting "Go head, Go head."

"That's enough, ladies," Dollar said as Kera and Leece high-fived one another. "I hope there is a third party with you two because neither one of you look like you're in any condition to be leaving up out of here alone."

"We cool," Leece said. "My man and his boys are up in here. We ridin' out with them back over to Indy."

"How many of his boys?" Dollar asked, worried about Kera being taken advantage of in the condition she was in.

"Oh, we straight. I ain't gonna let nothing happen to my girl," Leece said.

"Oh, I can see how well you take care of your girl," Dollar said sarcastically. "I'll take care of Little Mama here. Kera, I'll see to it that you get home. Do you need to get your coat from coat check or anything?"

"No, I'm straight. Are you sure you don't mind seeing to it that I get home?" Kera said giving Leece a thumbs up on the low-low. "I don't want to put you out or anything."

"I'm sure," Dollar said. "Leece, where's your man? I want to make sure you straight too."

Dollar saw to it that Leece caught up with her man, then he led Kera outside of the club and immediately hailed a taxi. The taxi driver pulled over and asked Dollar, "Where to?"

"Where do you stay?" Dollar asked Kera as he scooted into the taxi and held his hand out to help her in.

"A fucking taxi," Kera said. "You offered to see to it that I get home and you didn't even drive your own shit. I stay all the fuckin' way over in Gary. You gonna pay my fare?"

"Look, fast ass," Dollar said. "We in Chicago, not Alaska. Gary is 30 minutes away. Even if you lived right here in Chicago, *like me*, you'd still take a taxi. Half the muthafuckas here own a car and still take public transportation. Parking is always a bitch. Now you can get your ass in this taxi or catch up with Leece and chance getting gang raped by her man's boys."

Kera huffed and puffed but eventually hopped into the taxi. It seemed as though every time she rode over to Chi-town to club it there was some extra drama.

"Now, where to?" Dollar asked her.

"I'm going where you going," Kera said, closing the door as the taxi driver pulled off.

"The hell you are," Dollar replied.

"Why, yo bitch laying up waiting on you?"

"Ain't nobody waiting on me, but your ass is going home."

"I can't go home. My father would kill me if I came home drunk. Just let me sober up at your spot...pleazzzzze," Kera pleaded with her big innocent eyes.

She looked too damn good in that Coogie dress she had on and she was giving Dollar mad sex appeal. He knew that if he took her home he'd want to do her. If only she was a little older. Young girls don't know the true definition of a one-night stand. She'd be sweatin' him and he knew it. So taking her back to his place was out of the question.

"Pleazzzze," Kera said, poking out her lips and rubbing on Dollar's knee.

"Stop whining," Dollar said pushing her hand off of his knee.

"Look, seriously. I can't go home like this. Redd will trip. I just turned eighteen and I want him to trust me."

"The meter's running and I'm just driving around. Are we sight seeing, folks, or are you going to tell me where you want to go?" the taxi driver said.

Dollar directed the driver to his apartment off of South Shore Drive.

***

"*Damn she got a tight ass pussy,*" Dollar thought to himself as he placed the tip of his penis inside Kera.

Dollar tried not to think about how his actions were

violating everything he said fuckin' with Kera would lead to. It was getting easier not to think about it as he was succumbed by the warmth of Kera's pussy. Even through the condom, the shit felt proper.

Once Dollar and Kera had arrived at his apartment, tucking Kera in on the couch wasn't good enough for her. Dollar should have chained her ass down. It was a matter of minutes before she appeared butt ass naked in his bedroom doorway and shortly thereafter, in his bed.

There wasn't any foreplay or nothing involved. Kera just jumped in the bed and started ramming her tongue down Dollar's throat while fondling his dick. What did Dollar have to lose at this point, he thought. This was easy pussy, the next best thing to easy money.

"*Ease up, Dollar Bill. Just the tip. Just the tip. Damn this shit is wet. I love the sound of a sloppy pussy. Sounds like waves smacking up against the shore of an ocean. Alright, she's moaning and squirming so that must mean this dick is feeling good to her. She can stand another inch or two. Let me kiss her on her forehead. Hoes like that shit. Makes 'em feel safe and secure. Now her eyelids, then her nose and next her lips. I knew she was gon' stick her tongue in my mouth. She sticking it deep down my throat which means I can stick this dick deep in her pussy now.*"

Dollar positioned himself to be able to drive his dick inside of Kera while watching her facial expressions. She wanted the dick so bad, well he was going to give it to her. Seeing the expression of pain on her face let Dollar know that Little Mama had bitten off more than she could chew.

"OOOUUUU," Kera screamed out as Dollar attempted to insert more of his penis into her. "Be gentle, it's my first time."

"What?" Dollar said in shock.

"Despite what you may think of my fast ass, I'm a virgin," Kera said.

"Then what are we doing?" Dollar asked as he started to remove himself from of top of Kera. "Why didn't you tell me? Little Mama, we can't do this. You're first time can't be some drunken' night you won't even remember. Your first time should be special."

"Was yours?" Kera asked.

'Naw," Dollar sighed.

"You are special, Dollar," Kera said rubbing his face. "That makes this special."

Kera pulled Dollars face to hers and began kissing him.

"We can't do this, Little Mama," Dollar said as he breathed heavily. "We gotta stop."

"No," Kera said. "I want to do this. I really want to do this with you. It's too late already. You've already been inside of me a little bit. I can take it. I can take it all. Please don't stop. Please don't stop," Kera repeated over and over as she began to roll her hips. She wasn't throwing that thang like no virgin. She buried her hands into Dollar's ass cheeks and pulled him into her gently. Dollar would dip in and out of her softly until she would pull him inside of her even more. Then finally half of his penis burst through her walls. Yep, she was a virgin.

The entire situation was blowing Dollar's mind. He imagined that Kera probably felt the same way he did when he got his first experience of the birds and the bees with Pam. He just wanted to get it over with so that he could peel the "V" (Virgin) off of his chest. That's probably what Kera wanted to do with her hot ass, rid herself of virgin status so that she could go on a fucking spree. All of a sudden Dollar felt used, but fuck it. He was damn near all the way up in her now. As he pumped in and out of Kera he didn't mind being used. Her pussy sucked in his dick like a leach until he exploded inside of her. Hell, he wished every 18-year-old female virgin would use him.

The feeling of Dollar busting through Kera's walls and her screaming and tearing down his back with her nails aided in his ultimate climax. After he and Kera had sex, Dollar led her into the shower where he washed her down with his hands and a bar of Irish Spring soap.

At that moment Kera felt like a woman. She felt special, that she was probably one of the very few people Dollar had let into his world. Dollar played in Kera's hair, her beautiful hair that curled up even more from the moisture of the water.

"So what were you in jail for?" Kera asked.

Dollar paused at Kera's candidness. "It don't matter."

"I just want to know," Kera smiled. "I mean I just gave you my virginity. You can't answer me a simple question."

Dollar told Kera, in very little detail, about his spending years in jail. He had already fucked her, why complicate the situation even more by laying all his business out on the table. But she already knew he had done time in jail so he fed her some insignificant details to satisfy her craving.

Dolar's story to Kera was that he got pinned for a murder that he didn't commit and copped a plea on the advice of his lawyer. Being the young, naïve, *I just want a bad boy*, type of girl, Kera was, she ate the story up and digested every word of it.

Dollar felt a degree of guilt as he held the young innocent thing in his arms. She had given him her virginity and he had given her lies and false hope. "*Poor thing*," Dollar thought to himself about Kera as he squeezed her tightly. He felt bad in advance for breaking her heart.

Dollar's conscious didn't keep him from running up in Kera one mo'gen before sending her home in a taxi with a $50 bill for fair. The second go round Dollar had to get Kera wet before he could stick it back up in her. He wasn't about to go down on her so he put his fingers in his mouth then massaged the saliva onto Kera's private spot.

Kera wanted to prove to Dollar to some degree that she wasn't all little girl, so she went down on him. Dollar could tell she didn't really know what the hell she was doing, but she did well enough to make him cum all over her face. Kera did more lickin' and kissin' all over Dollar's dick than she did just straight out sucking it. When he felt a nut cumin' on he held her head stiff on the tip, forcing her to keep her lips in one place and suck until he came.

For the next couple of weeks Dollar avoided Kera at work. The more distance he kept between the two of them, the more quickly Kera would realize that her night with Dollar was just that, *a night*.

Dollar would show up at Redd's and wait outside with the other fellas instead of going inside the office first like he usually did. He wanted to keep from running into Kera. She hadn't done any unannounced drive bys by his apartment like some other chicks might have and she never came outside to see if Dollar was around. Perhaps Kera wouldn't be a problem after all.

Chapter 10

What's Good To You

Turning 18 didn't make Kera feel like a woman as much as being with a man for the first time did. Kera couldn't get Dollar off of her mind, off of her tongue. She would go over to Leece's house just to talk about Dollar for hours.

"He's poison, girl, I'm telling you," Leece said, as she and Kera sat on her bed eating a bowl of cherries.

"Nuh, huh, girl. He's the antidote," Kera said as she sucked a cherry off the stem, spit out the seed and placed it in a napkin. "And the way he calls me Little Mama, girl, it's so cute."

"I just can't believe you finally did *it* You've been like the biggest tease in the world. Clockin' dollars and shit from niggaz on the hope of them gettin' some pussy from your ass."

"Girls need to learn that they can play the hoe, they don't necessarily have to be the hoe."

"I guess you got tired of role playing.....hoe," Leece laughed.

"You stupid," Kera said play punching her on the shoulder. "This is different. Dollar ain't like all them wanna be wankstas I done fucked with in the past. They deserved to get played. Dollar's been there and done that. I can see that he ain't about the drama, the games and shit. And girl, he don't have no kids."

"Fine ass catch like him and he ain't got no babies mama's running around Gary? What's his story, Kera? Come on, girl, you can tell me. He got a wooden leg don't he?"

"Will you stop being stupid?"

"A glass eye?"

"Damn'it, Leece," Kera paused. "Okay, okay, girl. I guess I have left one thing out."

"I knewed it, I knewed it!" Kera said. "Go on, spit it out." Leece watched Kera fondle a cherry with her tongue before sucking it off the stem. As she slushed it around her mouth, trying to weed the seed out, Kera spoke.

"He been locked up the last few years," Kera said very quickly as she spit the seed out into the napkin.

"Oh, an ex-balla, huh?" Leece said. "Once a balla always a balla, you know that shit. You know he probably just using your pop's business to keep the Feds off his ass. I thought you was through fuckin' with them street pharmacist."

Kera listened to Leece without making eye contact and continued sucking down cherries.

"Why do I have the feeling that you still leavin' some shit out?" Leece said without getting a reply from Kera. "What?"

"He wasn't in jail on no drug charges. He was kinda in jail for murder."

"Get the fuck out of here," Leece said. "That fool done killed somebody before?"

"More like killed three people," Kera said nonchalantly as she put another cherry to her lips.

"Bitch, are you crazy?" Leece said snatching the cherry out of Kera's hands.

"He didn't really do it?"

"Oh, 12 jurors and a judge just locked him up for being so damn fine?" Leece said sarcastically.

"That's why I didn't tell you. I knew you were going to over react and try to rain on my parade. It's not even like that. He really didn't do it. He didn't want to risk the death penalty so he copped a plea. You know black men are guilty until proven innocent."

"I can't hardly believe you," Leece said taking offense.

"So you caught that fish hook, line and sinker, huh? His word is bond, huh? I'm your girl, I'm going to always have your back. But I'm not going to sit back and watch you fuck around with no killer. How long he been out? Is the fucker rehabilitated or what? I ain't feelin' this, K."

"Dollar's a good man. If you could just look into his eyes and see what I see. He's good "

"He ain't good for you. You need to spit his ass out the same way you spittin' those seeds out. Walk away from this one, baby girl. Write it down in your diary for memory sake. You ain't ready for him."

"What the fuck is that supposed to mean?" Kera said, not giving Leece a chance to answer. "I'm a grown woman. I can handle anything. You know what? I don't even want to talk about it anymore. Jealousy is one thing I can't deal with."

"Jealousy!" Leece said. "Oh, now I'm jealous because you got drunk and gave up your virginity to someone who you hardly know?"

"Fuck you!" Kera said as she got up from off the bed and began to gather her things to leave. "I knew I should have hung around white girls. They don't hate like black girls do."

"And they won't beat your ass like a black girl, either," Leece said raising up off the bed in flex mode. "Nigga, what?"

"Look, I'm out," Kera said as she walked over to the door with her sweater, purse and car keys in hand.

"Oh, so now you gon' run away. Stick around and let's deal wit this woman to woman. You a woman now ain't you? Isn't that what you wanted, someone to make you feel like a woman? A man, a real man like *Dollar!*"

"I hate you so much right now," Kera said as her eyes began to swell up with tears.

"You can hate me all you want, but I'ma keep lovin' you. You my girl. I'm not about to sit back and watch you get hurt. Every since you've laid eyes on him your entire conversation has been Dollar this and Dollar that. How many times do you think your name comes up in his conversations?"

The tears that had weld up in Kera's eyes were now rolling down her face.

"How often does he call you?" Leece continued. "Has he ever called you?"

Kera stood there looking stupid.

"It's obvious he already got what he wanted. He's done, Kera. You be done."

"I am done......I'm done with you," Kera said slamming the door to Leece's room behind her.

***

“Hey, it's me, Kera,” Kera said through the phone receiver.

“Hey, what's up, Little Mama?” Dollar replied rolling his eyes up in his head. He had seen her phone number pop up in his caller ID and had avoided answering it. This time she had called from an anonymous number and caught him off guard.

“Nothing, just wanted to see what was up...what you were getting into.”

“Oh, uhh, I'm bout to head out to the movies,” Dollar replied.

“Oh,” Kera replied, wanting so badly to ask Dollar who he was going with. But hell, it was 10 o'clock, at night, of course he was going with a female.

“What are you going to see?”

“Uhh, uhh, what's it called?” Dollar said, “Oh, yeah, Deliver Us From Eva.”

“*A chick movie on top of that*,” Kera thought to herself.

“Oh, okay, well, I won't keep you. Call me sometime,

okay?"

"Yeah, yeah, sure," Dollar replied.

"Okay, well then...."

"Aiight, Peace out," Dollar said hanging up the phone.

Kera hung up the phone and sat staring at it in disbelief. She couldn't pick which emotion she wanted to keep company with. Instead of being angry or hurt she convinced herself that Dollar and her didn't have any ties so he could do what he wanted to. But still, everything in her wanted to go over and camp out at Dollar's apartment and stalk him to see if he was with a bitch or not.

While Kera fed herself excuses why she shouldn't be hurt, Dollar had rolled over and gone back to sleep, which is exactly what he was doing when Kera had phoned him. It was exactly what he had planned on doing for the rest of the night.

Chapter 11

He's Got Game

Although Dollar wanted to scream out to the world his existence in the game, he didn't want a reputation. He didn't want niggaz knowing how hard he was, therefore it would be easy to walk up on them fools and catch 'em slippin'. Nobody living the street life really knew him, maybe a few cats from back in the day, but that's it. As far as he was concerned, Dareese Blake was a dead soul rotting away in jail. Dollar Bill was back...reincarnated. He would be a shining light to the game of life. Not the one that can be bought in the stores, but the one that is learned then earned on the streets of Gary, Indiana.

Moving from Gary to Chicago gave Dollar a piece of mind. Gary was too damn small, it cluttered his mind and didn't allow him to think. Dollar liked living in Chicago and wished he had grown up there. It had way more opportunities than little ass Gary, Indiana had. Dollar was actually born in Chicago, but his father convinced his mother to move away with him to Gary. Dollar's father wanted to get his mother as far away from her controlling overbearing parents as possible. Dollar's mother believed in that bullshit emotion called love and followed her heart, which meant following her man. So they up and moved from Chicago to Gary.

Shortly thereafter, Dollar's grandparents, Grandpa and Grandma Davis, his mother's parents, passed away. They died in their sleep of Carbon Monoxide poisoning. Aunti Charlene took over their house and tried relentlessly to get her only sibling to move back home to Chicago. She even said that she could bring her husband with her. Dollar's father convinced his mother that Aunti Charlene only wanted to pick up where her parents had left off, that she wanted to control their life and would probably eventually break the two of them up. So Dollar's mother decided against moving back to Chicago. Instead, she lived in a one bedroom run down apartment in Gary with her husband and baby.

Dollar could only imagine what life would have been like if his mother had moved in with Aunti Charlene. So much would have been different. But no, she had to be a down ass chick and have her man's back. And in the end he left her hanging'. Define irony.

***

It was Sunday morning and Dollar had been out the night before with Mya, the manicurist from the nail salon. He knew it was only a matter of time before he hit that. He could always tell that she wanted him by the way she gave him an extra ten minutes on the hand and wrist massage. Mya had the same unspoken persistence as Kera did, so like Kera, Dollar had to break Mya off a lil' somethin' somethin'.

The evening before, Dollar had only gone into the salon for a manicure, but he left with Mya. Dollar had been Mya's last client for the day and she had insisted on taking him out to have a drink. After several drinks he found himself in her apartment, then he found himself between her thighs.

As Dollar pulled the cover from over his head, through the cracks of the window blind, the sun screamed, "Wake up, Nigga!" Dollar laid in bed wearing nothing but a morning hard on. He stretched and flexed his muscles as one of them popped, causing an ache.

"Damn," Dollar said to himself. "I need to find a gym or

something. Get this body back in shape. It sounds like a box of Rice Krispies, all this damn snap, cracklin' and poppin'."

Dollar looked over at his digital clock that read 11:45 a.m. After a night of wild sex with Mya, Dollar was exhausted, and to add to it he had a hangover. He thought back of all the positions he had Mya's limbs pinned up in during their sexcapade.

Dollar rubbed his penis as he thought about how Mya would allowed him to cum inside of her and would then suck the juices off of him. The taste of her own pussy was like a delicacy to her. She managed to get all ten inches of Dollar down her throat without even gagging. Dollar felt like he had a staring role in one of his "Jake's Freaks, Hoes and Flows" porno tapes.

What really tripped Dollar out was that as small and petite as that lil' white girl was, she took it in the ass like a champ. Dollar had never gone there before and probably never would again, with a sistah anyway. It didn't matter how long he had been locked up in prison, it was common knowledge that a guy had to be extra careful of what sexual acts he asked a sistah to perform. Hell, they take offense to all kinds of shit. They don't even like for a man to ask them to suck his dick. "Don't ask me to do it. Just let me do it on my own," they say. And God forbid a man tries to push their head down to his spot. A sistah will straight clown. So asking a sistah for some anal sex might get a brotha cut. They always talking about they saving that ass for their husband. But Mya was an exhibitionist. Dollar couldn't believe half the shit they had done and on top of that, he couldn't believe he had gone up in her raw.

"*What in the hell was I thinking*?" Dollar thought as he laid in bed and rested his body a little while longer.

Dollar's mind managed to drift into thoughts of his little brother. Ral bringing up Doc's name the other day must have struck a cord with Dollar because ever since then, Dollar caught himself thinking about Doc constantly. He and his brother had been inseparable as kids. They were each other's keeper and now here they were living a half-hour from one another but yet a world apart.

Dollar desired to have a good relationship with Doc. Hell, he wished they could ride together. But he knew that him and Doc were living in two separate universes. Maybe once Dollar went legit he could see to it that things between him and Doc were on the up and up. But until then, it wouldn't hurt to at least try to carry on a decent conversation with him. So Dollar decided that he'd invite Doc to play a game of ball with him. He was the older brother. He could at least make the first attempt to warm down the ice.

Doc had made it a point not to give Dollar any of his contact information. He knew that right now he wasn't ready to have a relationship with his brother. He didn't know if he'd ever be ready.

Since Doc was nearly a practicing physician at the clinic, he was in the book, so Dollar looked up his home phone number as he had done to get his address the night he went to his house with Ral.

"Hello," Doc said almost out of breath. He had just walked in the door from visiting their mother's grave, which is what he did every Sunday.

"Hey, little brother," Dollar replied. There was silence on the phone. "You busy? You sound out of breath."

"I'm just walking in from church. I heard the phone ringing."

"Oh, cool. That's cool. I was wondering if you knew of gym or some place with a court," Dollar asked.

"Where you staying?" Doc asked.

"The shore...North," Dollar replied.

"Yeah, they got a California Fitness not to far from where you at. It's about a mile from the pier.

"How about you meet me over there for a game of ball?"

"Man, I haven't shot baskets in years."

"Oh, you chumpin' out on me? You sceered?" Dollar joked.

"I didn't say I couldn't play. You know ballin' for me is like riding a bike. I ain't forgot how it's done."

"So does that mean I'm gonna see you up at the gym?"

Doc paused while he contemplated and replied, "Give me an hour."

"See you then," Dollar said hanging up the phone. He took a deep breath and hit the shower to rid himself of Mya's scent.

When Dollar got out of the shower he threw on his black and white And 1 Tee shirt with the cut off sleeves, the matching shorts and his And 1 black and white kicks. When Dollar went to leave he noticed a pink envelope laying in front of his door. Someone had obviously placed it through his living room door mail slot. Dollar picked it up and was greeted by the scent of the sweet flowery scent of the envelope. He knew by the scent who the note was from:

"The Gift"

Sleep don't come easy with you on my mind
I think I've found something it takes most people years to find
You tell me things so smooth and so clear
You make me feel like I have nothing to fear
Dreams of giving you my body, all of me, the way I thought making love should be.
My insides are burning as I explode in ecstacy
This feeling I'm feeling is greater than any feeling I've ever felt

Then I feel a sweet release and I start to melt
Stroking your hand through my hair, holding me knowing I need you there
Kissing my neck, nibbling my ear, your arms around me, keeping me near.
I've given you all of me and all I want is for you to, at least, think about me every day
Cherish, adore and please dont throw my gift away

Love Always, Kera

Dollar closed his eyes and put his hand on his forehead. What he had expected from fuckin' wit a young broad was coming to pass. Dollar balled up the note, pitched it into the trash, and then headed out to meet up with his brother.

***

"You don't want none of this. Buuuyaaa...nothin' but net," Doc said as he dunked on Dollar, who was sticking him.

"Oh, you showing off now," Dollar said as he dribbled down the court, followed by the other players.

Before Dollar could get half way down the court Doc stole the ball from him. Doc took the ball to the hole.

"Game point," Doc said, showing his pearly whites.

"You da man," Dollar said, giving Doc a five.

The two shook hands with their teammates and headed into the locker room to shower and get changed.

"You wanna go get some grub?" Dollar asked.

"Nah, I gotta study for my classes I'm taking over at North Western."

"How many years of school do you have to do?" Dollar

asked.

"Well you know I skipped my senior year. Hell, I earned college credits my junior year."

"Get out of here," Dollar said.

"Yeah, I got to graduate with the current seniors while I was a junior. Man, ma was so proud."

"I'm proud of you too, man," Dollar said sincerely. "I just wish I could have been there. My brother, an MD."

"Yeah, I still have a lot of schooling left before I can put an MD behind my name, but I'm getting there. I'll be an MD in no time and it will all be worth it." Doc smiled. "That's why I gotta hit the books."

"Oh, alright then. Well, maybe we can go some other time."

As the two continued to get dressed Doc noticed the disappointing look on Dollar's face. He had enjoyed spending time with his big brother, but a game of basketball was different than having to sit across the table from him. Doc could handle constant activity between the two, but he didn't know if he could hold a conversation with Dollar without it turning sour. As Doc focused on Dollar's expression he found himself staring at Dollar and noticing how much he looked like their mother.

"You've got her nose," Doc said to Dollar.

"Huh?" Dollar replied

"Sadie...you've got her nose."

Dollar didn't reply to Doc's comment. He grabbed his gym bag and pulled out his keys.

"I guess I'll talk to you whenever," Dollar said.

"Yeah, I guess so. Take care, man."

Dollar and Doc gave each other pound and Dollar headed towards the locker room exit.

"I guess it don't make since to try to study on an empty stomach," Doc said.

A huge grin took over Dollar's face as he replied, "Fat's

BBQ."

"And you know this, man," Doc said, as he grabbed his belongings and followed Dollar out.

Dollar and Doc talked and laughed over their quarter chicken BBQ dinners. Holding a pleasant conversation didn't turn out to be such a hard feat after all.

"So, Doc," Dollar asked tearing a piece of chicken off the bone with his teeth. "You got a woman in your life?"

"You mean a girlfriend?" Doc said.

"Yeah, man."

"Nah, don't have the time. Relationships take too much time and effort. I only have enough time and effort for success right now."

"But I thought every man needed a good woman in their life," Dollar smiled in a suggestive manner.

"I do have a woman in my life," Doc replied. "Mama. I visit her every Sunday, just to talk. Her spirit guides me, you know?"

"Yeah, I know what you mean," Dollar said.

"Mama pushed me to this point and supported me to the end. I'm not going to let anything stand in my way."

"Mama was always there backing up every one of our big dreams," Dollar said. "Remember when we set up that lemonade stand? Mama helped us with the sign and everything."

"Man, do I remember. We used to do some crazy stuff trying to get money," Doc replied.

"What about that time we tried to sell decorated Easter eggs for a dollar each?" Dollar laughed.

"Yeah, and you forgot to boil them."

The two laughed hysterically. Dollar almost choked.

"The things a little nigga gotta do to make it out of the hood," Dollar said, after clearing his throat.

"Tell me about it. I remember when Mom wouldn't buy

you that MJ jersey. You were set on getting it yourself so you sold sips of Canadian Mist to the dunks in the hood from an old bottle dad had left behind. You charged them one dollar a sip. You got your name honest, Dollar. You probably would have sold nickels for a dollar if you could have. Selling sips of liquor for a dollar...you was crazy. I thought Ma was going to kill you when Old Lady Parker ratted you out. Man, Ma was heated. I remember her saying how if dad were still around she would have had him beat your tail black and blue. But then she thought about it and said, "Boy, if your daddy was around, all he'd probably want to know was how much money you made so you could split it with him."

Doc began laughing. He found himself laughing alone.

"I don't have a dad and neither do you," Dollar said as he stood up and walked over to the trash can to throw away the remainder of his meal. He had suddenly lost his appetite.

Dollar returned to the table where silence was still present.

"What are you going to do with yourself, Dollar?" Doc asked with sincerity. "You just gonna walk around mad at the world, holdin' grudges?"

"Why not?" Dollar replied. "Ain't that what you doin'?"

Doc sighed and continued, "Why don't you go to school, man?"

"Me, go to school," Dollar laughed. "School ain't for me."

"You've got a brain don't you? You're capable of thinking aren't you? So why isn't school for you?"

"I don't know nothing but street, Doc. I mean, I read a lot, but even that is just some ole' gangsta shit," Dollar said.

"You know just as much as me."

"Yeah, right," Dollar laughed.

"I'm serious, man. Remember when I was younger, before you went to j.... Well, anyway. You used to ask me all of those questions and pay me $25 if I answered them correctly. A couple of times I gave you the wrong answers and you made me find out the true answer. I used to give you the wrong answers on purpose, just to see if you even knew the answers to the questions you were asking me. And you did know."

"Yeah, I did, didn't I?" Dollar said grinning proudly.

"Yeah, you did."

"Well, that was then and this is now," Dollar said, becoming more adamant. "School is not an option for me. That's your thang."

"And what's your thang?" Doc said waiting for Dollar to respond. Dollar simply looked away. "Oh let me guess, the thug life is your thang...big ballin' and shit. Fuck that street life, man. Fuck the streets."

"Fuck the streets," Dollar repeated angrily. "The streets is all I got. I love the streets and the streets love me back. Besides, I don't see you inviting me to come live out there in the burbs with you."

Doc couldn't say anything. Dollar had shut him down.

"Well, I guess I better get going," Doc said. "It's getting late and I uhh..."

"You have to study," Dollar reminded him.

"Yeah, I have to study."

Dollar stood up and took Doc's trash to the garbage. He walked back over to the table where Doc was preparing to leave.

"You always been a friend to the streets, Dollar. I know this. I know you missed your freedom on the streets, but it ain't the answer," Doc said. "The streets don't love nobody. I'm stitching' up bullet wounds, knife wounds and treating AIDS patients daily. Do you think the streets love them? Look at Stephan Crouse. He sleeps with the streets every night. Does it look like the streets love him?"

Dollar looked away from Doc in silence.

"Look, Dollar, man. I'm not trying to end this on a sour note," Doc said as he turned to leave. "So let's just squash it. It was good kickin' it with you."

"Yeah, me too man."

"You got a number or something?" Doc asked.

"Yeah, I have a cell phone."

"No home phone?" Doc inquired.

"Naw, all I need is a cell phone. The Feds can't tap that," Dollar joked.

"You staying over by the shore. That must mean you're job is panning out pretty good for you. Those places over there are high as hell. You gettin' lots of gigs?"

"I can't complain. What about you? How's work at the clinic?"

"Oh, it's good. We just got a new grant from a private donor."

"Well that's good. Hell, free money is always good," Dollar said.

"Not always," Doc replied. "Not always....Well, uhh, I guess I'll holler at you later," Doc said.

"Yeah, man." Doc gave Dollar a hug. A passionate brotherly hug. He looked up at Dollar then walked away.

"Yo, Doc," Dollar called to him. "What athlete was on the cover of Sports Illustrated more than any other athlete?"

Doc stood and thought for a minute. "I don't know. Who?"

"Muhammad Ali," Dollar replied.

"Oh yeah, that's right," Doc said winking, knowing the answer all along. "Muhammad Ali."

Dollar smiled and watched his little brother until he was out of his sight, taking in the words his brother had just spoken to him. Perhaps Doc was right. Maybe the streets don't love nobody. Dollar's ego wouldn't even allow him to entertain this concept. Of course the streets loved him.... didn't they?

Chapter 12

NO SEX IN THE CHAMPAGNE ROOM

"Did I look sexy up there for you," Tommy said to her perspective Champagne Room client.

"Oh, hell yeah, ma," the man who called himself Kube replied. "You looked good as hell dancin' up there on stage."

"I bet you would like to take me in a dark room and let me give you a private dance, huh?"

"Yo, you'll do dat shit?" Kube said with his New York accent telling on his city of residence.

"You see that room back there?" Tommy said pointing. "I can make it happen right there for you, baby."

"You gon' take some shit off?"

"You tippin' proper?"

"Fo shizzel," Kube said fondling the toothpick with his tongue and rolling it with his fingers.

"Aiight then," Tommy replied. "You and Benji follow me."

"Benji?" Kube questioned.

"Ben Franklin," Tommy said screwing up her mug.

"Damn, it's gon' cost me a hundred?"

"Oh, you a baller on a budget?" Tommy asked.

"No, ma. It ain't even like that," Kube replied.

"Oh, you one of them cheap ass wankstas frontin' like a gangsta."

Tommy knew the more she insulted his pockets, the deeper he would go into them to prove her wrong.

"You see this shit right here?" Kube said pulling out a thick wad of cash. "Do this look like fake money?" Kube proceeded to peel off twenties and throw them at Tommy who kindly scooped them up. "Let's go."

Kube took a sip from his drink and signaled to his two homeboys he had rolled in with that he'd be right back.

Tommy showed Kube the way to the Champagne Room where Kube paid Bear $100 to enter. Tommy led him over to the couch and fetched the champagne.

Kube sat on the puffy black couch that many of niggaz and hoes had fucked on over the years. He bobbed his head to the beat as he stroked one of the purple satin pillows that was on the couch.

"That's my shit," Kube said referring to the song that was coming through the speakers. "Can you turn that up?"

"Sure, baby, whatever you want," Tommy said turning the music up. With her back towards Kube she began to pour the champagne.

"Can you turn it up a little more?"

"Just a little more. I want you to be able to hear me when I talk shit in your ear," Tommy joked.

As soon as Tommy turned the music up a notch she felt Kube's hands groping all over her.

"Slow down, baby. Let me finish this here and I'll be over to do my thang. You just go back over to the couch and wait for me."

"I want my shit right here, right now," Kube said.

"You want me to dance for you right here?" Tommy asked. "Don't you think the couch would be more comfortable? You can sit down and..."

"Bitch stop playing games," Kube said cutting Tommy off. "I ain't pay no $100 to get back here for no dance. Hell you could have danced for me out here. A nigga trying to get some ass."

"Well, you got me bent," Tommy said. "Ain't no sex in the Champagne Room with me. You get a dance and that's it, nigga."

"I thought hoes play when ballers pay," Kube said as he placed his hand down Tommy's crotch.

Tommy fixed her mouth to start cursing Kube out but when she went to open her mouth he rammed his tongue down her throat. Tommy knew if she got herself in the right position she could take Kube, but the fucker had caught her off guard. The feeling of Kube's fingers plunging in out of Tommy made her want to throw up.

Tommy was able to draw her hand up and slice her nails down the side of Kube's face. In retaliation, Kube grabbed Tommy by her hair and pulled her down to the ground, still kissing her and using his other hand to finger her. Tommy's resistance, only excited his sick ass more.

As Kube was forcing Tommy down to the ground she managed to grab onto the neck of the champagne bottle. Taking the bottle of bubbly down with her, she cracked Kube right over his head. This dazed him momentarily.

"You fucking cunt," Kube said grabbing his head as blood streamed down his face. "You're dead, whore. You hear me? You fuckin' dead!"

Tommy had already made her way to the door and summoned Bear to handle that nigga. Bear took one look at Tommy's desperate face and knew some shit had gone wrong. He picked Kube up like a rag doll and escorted him out of the Champagne Room. The two dudes Kube was with noticed the commotion and darted from across the room to have their homeboy's back. The two dudes were no match for Big Bear, who put all three of they asses out the club. Their punk asses knew they didn't want none of Big Bear. But at least they had the heart to run up on him.

"You alright, girl," Storm said comforting Tommy, who

was more pissed off than anything.

"Girl, yeah, I'm alright," Tommy replied. "Son of a bitch. Niggaz kill me thinkin' just cause you dance for a living you fuck for a living or that a big tip equals a quickie. Fuck this shit!"

"He didn't fuck you did he?" Storm asked in a demanding tone.

"No, but he was kissing me and he stuck his fingers...,"

"It's okay, Wine. It's okay. Girl, it's gon' be alright," Storm said hugging Tommy.

"I'ma get that New York bastard," Tommy ranted.

"Girl, you know how these niggaz are. They think they can cut through our neck of the woods from the big city and treat us like trash. Fuck'em, girl."

"I want you to handle his ass, Storm," Tommy said.

"Girl, you just scared and angry right now," Storm replied.

"No, I want you and Thunder to handle that fucker. How much is it gon' cost me? I got money."

"Come on, Wine. You trippin'."

Bear knocked on the door and peeked through.

"You alright, Wine?" Bear asked Tommy.

"Yeah, I'm cool," Tommy replied.

"I got that buster's license plate number and shit if you wanna press charges or anything."

"It was probably a rental," Tommy said pessimistically.

"Naw, that shit was customized," Bear responded. "It wasn't no rental."

Bear handed a piece of paper with the license plate number on it to Storm, who was closer to him, to give to Tommy. Storm took it from his hand and Bear closed the door behind him. Storm tried to hand the piece of paper to Tommy, but Tommy pushed her hand away.

"Naw, you keep it. You gon' be needing it to track that nigga down. How much?"

"You know what, bu? This one is on me," Storm said grabbing her purple Crown Royal bag and sticking the piece of paper down inside it along with her tips. "As a matter of fact, by the time I finish cleaning out that nigga's pockets, it's gon' be on him."

"I want the full package, you know, M&M (Murder Mommies)."

"Don't you worry. We gon' melt in that mafucka's mouth for sure."

***

Dollar was standing outside of the work building talking to Jay when Kera walked up.

"*Please don't let her walk over here and speak to me. Please, God,*" Dollar thought as he continued on with his conversation with Jay.

"Hey, Dareese," Kera said as she approached Dollar.

"*I knew it. I knew it,*" Dollar thought to himself as he ignored her. "*I told myself not to fuck with no young girl. Getting' rid of her is going to be like getting rid of ants at a picnic.*"

"Dollar," Kera said putting a little bass in her force.

"Oh, hey, Kera, hey...uhh yeah, hey," Dollar stuttered. By this time all eyes were on the boss' daughter. All eyes were green. Every one of them guys had used Kera as a motivating factor to jacking off. Their dreams were Dollar's reality.

"Yeah, uhh hey," Kera replied as they each stood in silence. "Well, I just wanted to say hey."

"Hey," Dollar said.

"Hey," Kera said looking stupid as she walked away in humiliation. As she entered the building she could hear the men begin to whistle and salute Dollar for his conquer.

"What's the matter, baby?" Redd said to his baby girl, seeing that she was a little disturbed.

"Nothing really," Kera hesitated. "Daddy, can we talk?"

***

"Yo, T, come on. Answer the door. It's me, Dollar," Dollar said knocking on Tommy's door like he was SWAT. After a few more pounds the door cracked open.

"Damn, girl, what took you so long? You ain't answering your phone or nothing," Dollar said, but before he could get another word out of his mouth he saw that the person who answered the door wasn't Tommy. It was her older niece.

"Hi," the girl said. "You Dollar?"

"Yeah, I'm Dollar."

"My aunt always talks about you. I'd know you anywhere. She has pictures of you in newspaper articles. You were going up the courthouse steps in one picture. You were in the courtroom in another. You look bigger in person"

"Yeah, I'm a little bit bigger?" Dollar said. "Where is your aunt?"

"She's not feeling well. She's sleep, but I'm sure she'd want me to wake her up for you."

"Is something wrong with the phone?" Dollar asked. "I tried calling."

"Oh, the ringers are off. The phone kept waking her up. Do you want me to get her?" the girl said.

"No, it's cool," Dollar said. "Just let her know I stopped by to talk about some work I got lined up."

"K," the girl said as she watched Dollar walk away.

Dollar walked back to the car where Ral was waiting on him.

"She ain't home?" Ral asked.

"Yeah, she's home. She ain't feeling well or some shit."

"So you still wanna head over to Jimmy's to grab a bite and talk business?"

"Yeah, we can do that," Dollar replied.

Dollar and Ral went on to Jimmy's, without Tommy, so that they could discuss their next move. The stick-up Dollar had lined up was one that Ral and Tommy could handle solo. Dollar wanted them to rob Mr. Owens. Dollar knew for a fact that Mr. Owens always carried a good amount of cash money on his persons and another good amount in the glove box of his Navigator. He wasn't a check writing or credit card using man. He liked dealing with straight up cash. Mr. Owens always said that when you use cash money you get more for less because money talks. Dollar knew that they'd get no more than $9,000, but he still upheld the theory that free money was always good money.

***

After a couple days of cooling off from her awful experience with Kube in the Champagne Room, Tommy put her high-heeled boots back on and hit the grind. She also handled her business with stickin' up Mr. Owens. She and Ral pulled off the robbery with ease.

They caught Mr. Owens first thing in the morning, 6:00 a.m., as he was getting ready to pull out of his driveway for work. Dollar had been to Mr. Owens' house before and had given Tommy and Ral directions on how to get there. It just so happened that Mr. Owens was making a bank deposit that day and had an extra few grand on him, which made the total stick up worth $13,000.

Dollar took his share and purchased some odds and ends for his place and tightened up his wardrobe. He invested in a 14kt gold Figaro necklace and bracelet set. He wasn't trying to fuck with that platinum shit that just drew attention to a nigga.

It hadn't taken Dollar long at all since his release from jail to get a nice place to rest his head, a nice lil' ride and a nice lil' wardrobe. He had a couple of options on pussy and he looked good as hell. On top of all that, he had a legit job so Uncle Sam couldn't fuck with him.

Dollar kept a nice little bank account, but he kept his real loot in a safe at his apartment. He made it a habit to always deposit one half of the money he made working at Redd's into his bank account. He didn't deposit the money from his mother's life insurance policy. This way he could always say that any purchases he made were made with that money.

At this point, Dollar felt all he needed was one big hit. Redd had been talking to him about some investments he had made that damn near quadrupled his money and Dollar was looking to do the same. With the money he earned from his investments he wouldn't mind opening up a spot similar to Redd's. Maybe he could open up a barbershop-massage parlor or something. Dollar didn't know what he was going to set up for himself, but he knew that he had to do something. Dollar knew that all good things came to and end and he wanted to be the one to put an end to them, not the police and not some jealous thug. He would live the good life, but on his own terms.

***

The line at the bank was long as hell and Dollar was becoming agitated. There were two security guards on duty.

One in particular, who was standing at the bank entrance right underneath the surveillance camera, kept eyeballin' Dollar. The security guard didn't try to hide his suspicions, as he never once turned his eyes away from Dollar, even when Dollar decided to stare back at him. Dollar wanted to go over there and whoop his ass. After all, he was standing underneath the camera so the ass beating wouldn't get caught on tape.

Dollar should have known better anyway than to go to the bank at lunchtime on a Friday afternoon. There were only five more people ahead of him out of the 11 that were initially standing in front of him. Although Dollar had already been waiting a half-hour in that line, he didn't think he could stand to wait much longer. Just as he decided to pull out of line someone tapped him on the shoulders.

"I didn't mean for you to have to stand in line, you can come back to my desk now," Hennessey said winking at Dollar.

"*Damn, here she is again,*" Dollar thought to himself.

"Right this way," Hennessey said signaling with her hand for Dollar to follow.

Dollar smiled and followed Hennessey back to a cozy little office where she offered him a seat.

"I didn't know you worked here," Dollar said. "I've never seen you before."

"That's because you've never looked into investing in your retirement," Hennessey said. "That's what I do here, make sure people are taken care of when they're old and gray."

"I'm anything, but that," Dollar said with conceit, which light weight turned Hennessey off.

"Are you making a deposit today, Mr. Blake?" Hennessey asked Dollar.

"Yeah, but how did you know my last name?" Dollar asked.

"It's not that hard to read upside down you know," Hennessey said referring to the personalized pre-printed pink deposit slip Dollar had in his hand. "I can make that deposit for you."

"How do I know you're not going to run off with all of my money?" Dollar joked.

"You don't know, do you? I guess you'll just have to trust me," Hennessey said holding her hand out to take Dollar's deposit.

Dollar stuck his hand out to give Hennessey his deposit but instead he grabbed her by the arm.

"Fuck the deposit," Dollar said looking into Hennessey's eyes. "Let me take this money and spend it all on you."

Hennessey couldn't help but laugh as she took the deposit out of Dollar's hand with her loose hand.

"That's quite alright, Mr. Blake," she said as she proceeded to log the deposit into her computer.

Dollar watched her pounding away at the keyboard. What he wouldn't do to get with her fine ass. She was playing hard to get, but he could tell that she wanted him. *"But for what?"* Dollar second-guessed himself. *"What could I possibly have to offer her? I'm not exactly company Christmas party material. "Hello, I'm Dollar. I do construction for a living and oh yea, on the side I rob people*," Dollar laughed to himself.

"Something funny?" Hennessey asked.

"It's funny why you won't go out with me," Dollar answered. "Come on, just dinner."

"Nah," Hennessey said. "You look like the type who might feel as though I'd owe you something afterwards."

"Naw, Miss lady. It ain't even like that. It will be kinda like me returning the favor of you rescuing me from that long ass line out there."

Hennessey proceeded to log in Dollar's deposit and hand write him a receipt.

"Here you go, Mr. Blake," she said slightly smiling and blinking almost in slow motion.

"Thank you," Dollar said. "But anyway, that was good looking out not making me stand in that line."

"It wasn't a problem," Hennessey said. "I'm glad I could be of some assistance."

Hennessey started typing away at her computer. Dollar stood before her not knowing what his next move should be. He wasn't used to waiting around for a woman to say something to him. What was it with her? Dollar was going to make it his personal mission to find out.

"Can you find your way back out?" Hennessey asked.

"Oh yeah, yeah," Dollar said. "I see you're busy, so yeah, I'll just go ahead and find my way back out."

"Alright then," Hennessey said as she continued typing. "Oh, and, Mr. Blake."

"Yeah," Dollar said stopping in his tracks.

"Can you close the door behind you?"

"Uhh, sure. And thanks again."

"Anytime," Hennessey said as Dollar walked out of her office and closed the door behind him.

"Damn, I can't believe I froze up," Dollar said as he looked down at his deposit receipt. Underneath his deposit verification was a note that read:

You can return the favor at 8:00p.m. tonight. 1777 Lake Wave Loop.

- Hennessey

- 855-2755

***

It wasn't as chilly as it had been the past few nights as the cold season was coming to an end, so Dollar sported his Fonzy, from Happy Days, leather jacket over his V- neck long sleeve ribbed sweater and Hard Knok Life Wear jeans. He couldn't wait to meet up with Hennessey at her place.

Dollar wasn't sure exactly how to get to Hennessey's address so he left his house a few minutes earlier than he had originally planned. He only had to stop and ask for directions one time when he saw that there was a chance that he might be late. Hennessey didn't seem like the kind of chick that would wait around on a late ass nigga. She was the type that kept a brother in check, on his toes. Perhaps she was what Dollar needed in his life.

Hennessey was smooth like the cognac she was named after, but Dollar knew her chaser was bitch mode. Her words were fly as if they were rehearsed. This is one of the things that attracted Dollar to her.

When Dollar finally turned onto Lake Wave Loop he saw that the scenery wasn't residential at all. There were hotels, cafés and drug stores. Dollar followed the numbers carefully until he found 1777. It appeared to be a lovely high-class hotel.

"That's what I'm talking about," Dollar said out loud as he searched for a parking space. As he drove by the hotel he realized that it had valet parking. He turned his car around, drove up to the hotel door and utilized the valet services.

Dollar walked into the hotel and headed straight towards the registration desk to find out what room number Hennessey was in, probably waiting for him butt ass naked.

"May I help you, sir," the clerk asked Dollar.

"Yes, can you phone Miss Hennessey Monroe's room

and let her know that Mr. Blake has arrived?" Dollar replied.

The clerk punched a few keys on her computer before saying to Dollar, "I'm sorry, but we don't have a Hennessey Monroe in this hotel."

"Well, there must be a mistake. I'm sure she's here."

"There's no mistake," a voice crept up on Dollar from behind.

Dollar turned around to see Hennessey standing in a black, floor length halter gown with a split in the front that almost played peek-a-boo with her kitty-kat.

"You look good," Dollar said to Hennessey.

"Thank you," Hennessey replied. "You're lookin' fine."

Hennessey licked her lips and winked, "I hope I don't have to come out the heels tonight and beat down nobody over you."

"Would you do that for me, baby?"

"Umm hmm," Hennessey smiled.

Hennessey had a smile that humbled even a hard head dude like Dollar instantly. The contour of her lips allowed for just enough of her beautiful white teeth to show. She had a memorable smile, like Laci Peterson, the woman who's smile was plastered on every news channel and news paper when her husband was accused of murdering her and her unborn child.

Dollar stood before Hennessey, being mesmerized by her smile. The two stood there looking each other up and down. Hennessey especially admired Dollar's chest muscles peeking up out of the V on his sweater. She could have stood there and counted every chest hair if time had permitted.

"We should head to the hotel restaurant," Hennessey said. "We have reservations so we don't want to be late."

Dollar followed Hennessey over to the restaurant where the hostess led them to a quaint table for two.

Dollar slightly nudged the hostess, who was about to pull Hennessey's chair out for her, and pulled it out himself. He then removed the little black evening bag she was carrying from her shoulder and placed it on the back of her chair by it's gold chain strap.

"Thank you," Hennessey said, surprised at Dollar's mannerism.

"It's my pleasure, Miss Lady," Dollar replied.

The hostess presented them with menus and said, "take as much time as you need to look over the menus. Your waiter will be right with you."

As the hostess began to walk away, Dollar stopped her.

"May we see the wine menu?" Dollar asked.

"Certainly," the hostess said. "I'll bring one right over."

Dollar allowed Hennessey to scan the wine menu and order once the hostess brought it back over to him.

Dollar and Hennessey shot the breeze over a bottle of Zinfandel and a nice eloquent dinner that consisted of steak and lobster, preceded by an appetizer of crab stuffed mushrooms and followed by a delicious dessert of cheesecake covered in caramel syrup.

When the waiter brought out Dollar's and Hennessey's main course, Hennessey sent her steak back to be prepared a little longer. Instead of diving right into his delicious looking food, Dollar waited the ten extra minutes for Hennessey's plate to be served and then ate with her.

After feeding Hennessey the last bite of the cheesecake the two had shared, Dollar signaled the waiter over to the table. He was ready to get out of there in hopes that Hennessey would invite him back to her place...*just to talk*.

"Is there anything else I can get you two tonight?" the waiter asked.

"No, we're fine," Dollar said sticking his hand out. "Unless the lady would like something to go, for perhaps a midnight snack or something."

"Oh, no thank you. I'm fine," Hennessey said.

"Then I'll just take the bill," Dollar said to the waiter.

Hennessey stuck her hand over top of Dollar's and accepted from the waiter the black leather billfold, which contained their dinner bill inside. She then reached into her little black evening bag for money.

"Hey, I thought I was supposed to be returning the favor," Dollar said.

"You did by having dinner with me. Your company is opulent. I feel like a priceless angelic antique."

"Well, damn, does that mean we fuckin'....I'm playing," Dollar said as Hennessey shook her index finger at him."

"You are so bad," Hennessey said smiling. "But that's how I like 'em."

"Really, Miss Banker with a personal office throwing words around like opulent and angelic and shit."

Hennessey couldn't help but laugh as Dollar imitated her.

"Shut up, Eddie Murphy, and kiss me."

"Huh," Dollar said being caught off guard by Hennessey's forwardness.

"Lay one on me. Pucker up. Stick your tongue down my throat. Am I speaking your language now?"

Dollar looked around the restaurant to see if anyone was watching them.

"You embarrassed?" Hennessey asked.

"Who me?"

"You know what? Forget about the kiss. I'm sorry for putting you on the spot like that......excuse me, waiter," Hennessey said.

"You mad, baby. Well, I'm sorry I'm not one of those guys who kiss on the first date. You think just 'cause you buy me an expensive meal I'm supposed to let you stick your tongue down my throat?" Dollar said, enjoying him and Hennessey's role-play.

"I understand. I ain't trying to rush things. I don't want you to do anything you don't want to do. It's cool," Hennessey said winking at Dollar.

When the waiter came over to the table Hennessey handed him the leather billfold with the bill and two one hundred-dollar bills inside of it. Dollar tried to leave the tip, but Hennessey wouldn't allow him to do so. Hennessey laid a $30 tip on the table and excused herself to go to the ladies room.

Dollar stood up when Hennessey stood up to excuse her. Upon her return she and Dollar exited the restaurant and hotel.

"So where did you park?" Dollar asked Hennessey. "I'll walk you to your car. Or did you valet?"

"It was much too lovely of an evening to drive. Besides I just live a few blocks around the corner," Hennessey said.

"Then let me walk you home," Dollar insisted.

"No, that's okay. But if you're up to it, I wouldn't mind going for a walk. There's a little park behind the building with a penny fountain. I'm in the mood to make a wish."

Dollar obliged Hennessey by walking her to the fountain. He dug all of the change from out of his pockets and he and Hennessey threw coins into the fountain and conversated.

"So *Dollar*," Hennessey said. "How did you get the name Dollar?"

Dollar laughed and replied, "When I was a kid I had big dreams, dreams of becoming a thousandnaire. I did and sold everything I could think of to try to make a dollar. I would try to sell eggs to a chicken if I could. And no matter what it was I was selling, everything had the same price."

"A Dollar," Hennessey jumped in.

"You got it," Dollar said mocking his days as a child. "Dollar bill. It's just one Dollar Dollar bill y'all. Pretty soon folks in the neighborhood start calling me Dollar."

"Oh, I bet you were so cute," Hennessey said pinching Dollar's cheek.

"Well, Miss *Hennessey*," Dollar said turning the table. "How is it you were named after an alcoholic beverage?"

"Actually I'm not named after an alcoholic beverage. My name is spelled "ey" at the end instead of just "y"."

"Okay, aaannnd.... it's still pronounced the same."

"Let me finish why don't you?" Hennessey continued. "My mom was going to be a lawyer if it was the last thing she did in life, only she could never seem to afford law school. So until the day she could afford it she studied law by watching every court show that existed. The last name of one of her favorite characters on one of the court shows was Hennessey, therefore, naming me Hennessey. My mom was a homebody. She had no idea that Hennessey was a cognac."

"Nice story," Dollar said.

"It's the truth," Hennessey said play nudging Dollar on his shoulder.

"I know baby, I know. I'm being serious," Dollar said. "It's like that Justice shit in that movie with Pac and Janet Jackson. What was it called?"

"Poetic Justice," Hennessey laughed. "You know I never thought of it like that."

"Well, did your moms ever make it to law school?" Dollar asked.

"I'm putting her through it now," Hennessey said proudly, almost as if she wanted to cry.

Dollar turned Hennessey's face towards him with his hand and kissed her softly on the cheek. The tear that had made its way from her eye slid onto his lips. The warmth from the tear melted Dollar. He could feel where Hennessey was coming from. His own mother had been his motivation in life. Dollar wanted so badly to share his thoughts with Hennessey, but for the first time in a long time, he was afraid. He felt that there was something special about Hennessey. Dollar couldn't risk losing something before he even had it. He wasn't going to make the same mistake his father made.

Dollar sat holding Hennessey for a few more minutes. Hennessey ended up walking Dollar back around to the hotel where he waited on the valet driver to bring his car around. As the driver drove up in Dollar's car he exchanged the $20 bill in his hand for the keys to his car.

"Well, Ms. Monroe, we must do this again sometime."

"We must," Hennessey said placing a pliant kiss on the side of Dollar's neck. Dollar tried to push up on her, but Hennessey pulled away, leaving him with a hard dick.

As Dollar drove off he was in complete bliss. He looked in his rear view mirror at Hennessey who was standing in model stanza, leg stretched out of the slit, one hand on her hip and blowing him a kiss goodbye with the other. He wanted so badly to catch it in the air and place it on his lips, but he knew that would be some corny ass shit. So instead, he drove on.

Honey had Dollar cheesin' all the way home. Just the thought of Hennessey put a smile on his face. She was beautiful and smart like his mother and no-nonsense like his Aunti Charlene. She was the two of the most influential women in Dollar's life rolled up into one. And on top of that, Dollar saw that same look in her eyes, that determination to do anything she could for her moms by any means necessary. That same look he used to posses.

Dollar made it up in his mind that Hennessey was going to be his main girl. He liked her style. She wasn't necessarily going to be the only one, not just yet. But she damn sure would be number one. Maybe eventually the little spark that existed between the two would grow into a flame. Who knows what the future holds?

Chapter 13

Hit Hoes

"So how was you and your wife's little trip to the NYC?" Becka asked Storm as they got dressed in their dance costumes.

"It was very productive," Storm replied as she looked over at Tommy who was lining her lips with a chocolate Mary Kay lip liner. "I ran into a dude there that said he had been up in here the last time he came through the city."

"Oh yeah," Becka replied. "Small world. Well, I'll holler at y'all hoochies later. It's showtime."

Becka put on her cover up and walked out of the dressing room.

"By the way," Storm said to Tommy. "This is yours."

Storm handed Tommy a wad of cash. Tommy flipped through it puzzled.

"What's this?" Tommy asked.

"That dude I ran into," Storm said, as she headed for the door, well he said the last time he was here he forgot to tip you. He wanted you to have that."

Tommy's eyes watered as she flipped through the $3,000 Storm had just handed her. Storm winked at Tommy and then closed the door behind her.

"Now that's a down ass chick," Tommy said to herself. She tucked the money in her Crown Royal bag that was down inside her gym bag. It was almost show time for her as well.

That night at the club Tommy was supposed to handle a situation with some young buck named Rob from LA. It was something Ral had hooked up. Through some cat Ral used to cop crack from named Kill Dog, and was now making runs for here and there for a little change, Ral learned that Rob and a couple of his boy were going to be hitting Chi-town to check this nigga named Steelo's shit in. Supposedly Steelo had set up a deal that went raw with some boys from LA. The LA boys were paying them Chi-town niggaz a personal visit. Ral was getting paid to be their host while in town. Of course, after the hit he would lead them straight to The Chocolate Factory, where they, themselves, would get hit in the parking lot. As it turned out, Ral and Rob and his boys were a no show.

***

"Ral been spending mad loot lately," Dollar said to Tommy. "Have you noticed? He got all kinds of shit up in his place, and did you see the sounds he got installed in his lil' ride?"

"Umm, not really....Well, I guess," Tommy replied, focusing on the television show she and Dollar were watching. "I mean, I heard he been trickin' like mad lately, but what's new? As long as he ain't fuckin' with that shit, he straight. He could have bartered for half the shit he got. You know how he is. He'll sell a rope to a man threatening to hang himself."

"Word," Dollar replied.

"This is the funniest show in the universe," Tommy said as she continued watching television.

"Yeah, that's a funny ass muthafucka," Dollar said, referring to David Chappel of The David Chappel Show. "Ral probably just been holding on to his loot from the hits, huh, and that little bit of change he gets making runs for Kill Dog? You know how sometimes people get the urge to just start spending? Yeah, he's probably just going through one of them phases."

"Yeah," Tommy replied half-listening to Dollar. "Ah ha

ah ha. I love this show. Dis nigga crazy!"

"You probably even dip into your stash every now and then to treat you and the girls to a little something nice, huh?"

Tommy took a deep breath and looked at Dollar. She picked up the remote and turned the television off.

"Dollar, what's on your mind? Just spit it out. What are you trying to say?"

"Things just ain't been feeling right lately. I mean, there's been too many interferences and circumstances. Like when we was gon' stick up kid from LA, but he turned out to be a no show...like somebody gave him a heads up, dropped the dime or something."

"Ral said them niggaz wanted to handle their business and dip. What's so strange about that? Shit happens," Tommy said in Ral's defense.

"I know, but now all of a sudden Ral got all this spending money. I guess I just been adding two and two together."

"So what you trying to say?" Tommy asked. "You think Ral getting paid behind our backs, that he don't want to split the pot no more so he handling shit on his own? That's ridiculous. You just noided. That means it's time for you to give this shit up, especially if you gon' start worrying about how much money your boy is spending."

"It ain't like I'm clockin' his dollars. I'm just saying..."

"You just saying what? Next thing I know you'll be thinking Ral getting paid to talk, like he's some informant involved in a conspiracy to put you back in the joint," Tommy chuckled.

Dollar remained serious as he glared off into space.

"I was just joking. You can't honestly being thinking that," Tommy said.

"Lately I just can't erase the thought that Ral was a hard fiend. The shit a fiend would do for a hit...you'd never know."

"Yeah, but not turn on their partners. Not Ral. He'd die first. Besides, it wasn't a concern back when you wanted him on the team, so why should it be a concern now? He's the same Ral."

"Yeah, you right. I'm trippin'," Dollar said. "Turn that show back on."

Tommy turned the show back on and in moments was back to laughing hysterically. Dollar tried to enjoy the show and Tommy's company, but something was itchin' at him. That something was Ral. Dollar couldn't help but think that his loyalty to Ral, to clean him up and help him get his shit together, might have gotten in the way of his better judgment.

"So what's been up with Storm and her girl?" Dollar asked out of the blue.

"They cool," Tommy said. "Why do you ask?"

"No reason," Dollar replied with a snide look in his eye. "No reason at all."

***

"Yo, Dollar Bill," Redd called to Dollar who was getting ready to climb inside of Mr. Owens' Navigator. "I didn't know you were out here. You didn't come in today. Can I talk to you for a minute...just real quick?"

"Oh shit," Dollar said under his breath. "I hope I ain't gon' have to throw these thangs at this fool over no chick."

"Yo, Mr. Owens. Can you hold up a sec?" Dollar asked Mr. Owens, who he now felt slightly awkward around knowing that he had set him up for a robbery.

"Sure," Mr. Owens agreed. Dollar then followed Redd into his office.

Redd sat down at his desk, took a long deep breath

then stared at Dollar. He paused momentarily before speaking.

"I won't beat around the bush with this," Redd said. "So, I'll just get right to the point. Kera had been acting really strange lately..."

"Look, Redd..." Dollar interrupted.

"No, let me finish," Redd continued. "I could tell she was hiding something from me."

"Redd...," Dollar tried to intercept.

"Just listen. Kera told me about the night at the club and I'm not going to lie. I was completely shocked."

"I can explain," Dollar said.

"No need to explain. I mean, hell yeah I'm pissed that you didn't tell me. But teenagers need someone they can trust and I'm just glad she chose you."

At this point Dollar was mystified. Since when does a father approve of who takes his daughter's virginity?

"I still can't believe my baby snuck into a 21 and over club and drank alcohol," Redd said. "If you hadn't of been there to see to it that her and Leece got home safe, then I don't know what could have happened to my baby girl. Some pervert probably would have taken advantage of her and I'd have to go back to prison on a 187."

Redd began to laugh as Dollar contributed his fake laughter.

"Well, Mr. Owens is waiting on you so you better get to going. I just wanted to say thanks for looking out for my baby girl. I'm glad I can trust you. Loyalty is priceless."

"No need to thank me, sir...anytime," Dollar said as he headed back outside.

"By the way, did you hear what happened to Mr. Owens? He got robbed. Two thugs did it I think. It's a fucking shame," Redd said.

"Yeah," Dollar added. "A fucking shame."

***

Dollar and Tommy became a little nervous as they sat in Jimmy's waiting on Ral to show up. He was already twenty minutes late.

It wasn't Ral's absence that had them nervous. It was the fact that two cops came in and were dining at the table right behind Dollar and Tommy's.

"You two ready to order or do you still want to wait on the other person?" the waitress asked.

"Uhh, actually he just called me on my cell phone," Dollar said. "He's stranded so we have to go pick him up."

"Yeah," Tommy said as she stood up from her chair. "We got to go pick him up. Thanks anyway though. If it doesn't take too long we might be back."

Dollar and Tommy exited the diner suspiciously. Tommy was walking 100 miles per hour.

"Calm down," Dollar said to Tommy. "Relax."

Tommy slowed her pace and began to take tiny deep breaths.

"Now what?" Tommy asked, as Dollar walked her to her car.

"Let's just drive to your house. We'll talk there."

"Not my house," Tommy said. "What if they follow us?"

"Girl, you talking silly," Dollar said.

"Meet me at the DQ on Broadway."

"Okay," Dollar agreed. "Drive slow. Stay calm and relax damn'it."

Dollar followed Tommy to the DQ where they each ordered a small vanilla ice cream cone and sat in Tommy's car to eat and talk.

"Now you see what the fuck I'm talking about when I

say interference and circumstance?" Dollar said to Tommy.

"What's going on, D?" Tommy said confused. "I mean, Ral should have at least called you on your cell or something."

"I paged him on the way here and he ain't hit me back yet," Dollar said. "I should have listened to you in the beginning. You said we shouldn't fuck with Ral."

"What we gon' do, D. I'm sick of this shit. I can't do this."

"Come on, T. Be cool. Everything is going to be okay."

"I don't want the cops sniffing around my tail, and for what, a few punk ass stick-ups? I got enough saved to maybe start doing my own thing. Fuck this shit!"

"Damn'it, Tommy, stop talking like that," Dollar said. "We can't let one monkey stop our show."

"We not fucking teenagers anymore, Dollar. Can't you see that? I might as well had done that fucking bid nine years ago because I'm locked up anyway. I'm locked up between these fucking city walls. They trapping me, man," Tommy said out of frustration. "I don't think the game was designed for us to win, D."

"Stop pumping' out that negative energy," Dollar snapped. "We can do this shit. Just you and me. We can make shit happen."

"Yeah, but Ral knows everything. He knows what we're about. If he's playing us while he's part of the plan, imagine what he'd do if we cut him off."

Dollar sat listening to Tommy who was on the verge of frantic. His soft serve vanilla ice-cream cone began to melt down his hand.

"Well," Tommy interrupted Dollar's thought. "What are we going to do about Ral?"

"We don't have a choice," Dollar said. "He's poison. We got to spit his ass out."

***

"I told you that you'd be back," Storm said as she straddled Dollar who was sitting on the couch in the Champagne Room. Storm slowly crooned to the music.

"I guess you were right," Dollar replied as he stuck a twenty dollar bill between Storm's breast.

"I'm always right."

Storm put her hands behind her back and began to untie her bikini top. Dollar grabbed her hands and stopped her.

"What's wrong, Poppa, don't you want me?" Storm said, as she pulled Dollar's head to her breast.

"Yeah, I want you," Dollar said as he began to lick them. "I want you to do something for me."

"Anything. Tell me what you want and tell me how do you want it," Storm said as she began caressing Dollar's penis.

"I want M&M. Ecs...overdose," Dollar said while pulling Storm hard against his penis.

Storm immediately pushed away from Dollar and got off of his lap. She went and poured her a glass of champagne and started drinking it.

"Did you hear me? M&M."

"I don't know what you're talking about," Storm said, as she took another sip of her champagne.

"Oh, you don't hear me, now? It ain't like I'm muthafuckin' 5-0. Don't even try to front. I already know underneath all that sex appeal, you ain't nothin' but a hit hoe.

Storm continued to ignore Dollar.

"Well maybe you'll hear this," Dollar said as he pulled out fifty one hundred-dollar bills and waved them in Storm's face.

"Well, as they say, money talks," Storm said removing the money from Dollar's hand nice and slowly.

Never once did Dollar think twice or even reconsider his decision. Ordering a hit on Ral was preventative maintenance. As far as Dollar was concerned, it was only a matter of time before Ral killed himself anyway. Ral had been missing meetings with the drug counselor and was now lacing his blunts with cocaine. Dollar felt that Ral's destructive ways would somehow be the downfall of his mission. Boys or no boys, friend or no friend...Dollar couldn't just sit back and let that shit happen. This was his second chance at the game and he'd be damned if he let a dopefeind fuck it up for him.

Dollar paid Storm a portion of the money for the hit up front and promised her the rest once he received the call from her stating that the deed had been done. And on that note, Storm let Dollar hit it from the back on the strength.

Chapter 14

Pro-Choice

Dollar had finally given in to Kera's persistence. She wasn't going to stop hounding him until she got with him again. Dollar had already hit it once, so why not hit twice. Kera wasn't anything he couldn't handle. So he invited her into his home to fuck. No dinner, no movie, no nothing. Dollar refused to butter up to Kera. If she wanted to be like Stevie Wonder and pretend she couldn't see the real, then that was her own mistake. Like all sleeping beauties, Kera would someday find that prince charming to wake her up with a genuine kiss. Until then, Dollar might as well keep beatin' that thang up.

Dollar couldn't really enjoy being inside of Kera. His thoughts were on Hennessey. He had been kickin' it with her for a minute now and yet he hadn't gotten into her head. Fuck that, he hadn't gotten into her drawz.

Dollar would have definitely wanted to spend most of his time with Hennessey, but she always made it seem like she was so damn busy. The most time she would allot Dollar was lengthy conversations on the phone. It seemed like that was the closest he was going to get to her. Talking dirty after dark just wasn't doing the trick for Dollar. One could say that Hennessey had Dollar questioning his manhood.

Hennessey was a real woman, not like Kera and Mya who were barely a class up from being chickenheads. As Dollar laid on top of Kera, the more he thought about Hennessey and how she continued to reject him, the deeper he shoved himself inside of Kera.

"Oh shit, Dollar," Kera cried out.

"Umm, you like that, bitch?" Dollar said pumping harder and harder. "You like that shit?"

"Dollar, stop it!" Kera cried out. Her cries were silent to Dollar's ears as he aggressively assaulted Kera's insides.

Kera had showed up at Dollar's house that evening on the inevitable drive by...no call before coming...just an "I was in the neighborhood". All that meant was that she wanted to be fucked. This was the third time she had pulled this stunt.

"Oh shit. I'm cumin'," Dollar roared. "I'm cumin'." He wrapped his hands around Kera's throat as he ejaculated.

Tears of pain and anger strolled down Kera's face as she laid beneath Dollar who was breathing heavily. Eventually he got up and showered. Normally he probably would have led Kera into the bathroom with him so that they could shower together. Just like the last time she would have probably let him let one more off up in her, but this time Dollar showered alone, leaving an emotional Kera alone in his bed.

As the water ran down Dollar's butter pecan toned six pack, for the first time, he saw his life for what it was. He had put in work hustling. He had the riches, jewels, and a nice crib out of the hood and yet his mind was still in the ghetto. Did he ever really want to leave the streets alone, no matter how much money he had? It must be true what they say about being able to take the boy out of the ghetto, but not being able to take the ghetto out of the boy.

Dollar realized why a lot of cats didn't leave the hood. It was like an addiction, a fear. Scared to leave shit you learned to love and that loves you back. Dollar loved the streets. He was married to them, forsaking all others.

After Dollar got out of the shower he dried himself off and wrapped the towel around his waste. He went back in the bedroom to find a fully dressed, teary eyed Kera grabbing her purse and sweater.

"Aren't you going to take a shower?" Dollar asked Kera.

"Fuck you, Dollar," Kera said.

"Baby, what's wrong, Little Mama?" Dollar said none the wiser to the situation at hand.

"What's wrong? I don't know what that shit was," Kera said as tears flowed down her face.

"What what shit was?" Dollar asked completely ignorant of what was going on in Kera's mind. "You didn't cum?"

"That sex, fucking, screwing or whatever you want to call it. It sure wasn't making love."

"Making love," Dollar laughed. "We ain't never made love. People who care about each other make love. You and me ain't like that."

"You are one big piece of shit, do you know that? I can't believe I fell for you. Fuck you, Dollar. You don't ever need to say two words to me."

"Am I supposed to be mad? Are my feelings supposed to be hurt? Ma, this was just a fuck thang. I thought you knew," Dollar said, spelling it out in black and white to Kera.

Dollar's words were destroying Kera. He felt it was time to get rid of her anyway so he might as well go for the gusto.

"You let me hit that the first night you were ever with me. That was a hoe move. Did you think I was going to make a hoe my girlfriend?"

Anger took over Kera's emotions. She looked around the room to see what she could pick up to throw at Dollar. Her eyes settled on a crystal base lamp that was on the nightstand Dollar, noticing Kera's intentions, quickly walked up on her.

"Bitch, don't even think about it," Dollar said.

"Now I'm a bitch too," Kera cried. "I can't believe this is happening. What's happening to you?"

"You talking like you know me. You done popped over here a few times to get laid and now you know me? You don't know me, girl. I'm Dollar Bill. I'm that muthafucka. You lucky to be one of my chosen ones."

"Well, I don't feel so lucky. I feel like I've just been raped."

"Oh, so now you 'bout to pull a Mike Tyson situation and scream rape. I guess I better walk you down to your taxi so that I can avoid catching a case," Dollar said.

"Funny you should make the comparison. You're an animal just like him, and it didn't take twelve jurors to convince the world of that."

"Here, call 911," Dollar said throwing the phone at Kera, breaking one of her nails. "If you think I raped you, go ahead and call the police on me. Put me back in jail. But don't play games with me, girl. You really don't know who you fuckin' with. I'm a grown ass man. You do what you need to do. Either call the police or step. You make the choice."

"Nah, I don't need to call the police," Kera said. "Your punishment will come from a much greater wrath. Mark my words."

"Then get the fuck out," Dollar said, throwing himself on the bed as if nothing mattered to him in the world.

Kera began crying harder. She watched Dollar lay on the bed as if he could do no wrong, as if he had done no wrong all of his life. How could he be so cold? Kera asked herself this question over and over as she walked outside to her car.

The people she walked past looked at her with such pitty. A couple even stopped to ask her if she was okay.

Kera knew in her heart, and her head, that this would be the last time she would ever make the walk from Dollar's apartment and that she would never hear him call her Little Mama again. But fuck that shit! She wasn't going to be the young and dumb little number Dollar had taken her for. She wasn't going to keep fallin'. Her actions weren't going to mimic the words to Alicia Keys hit song.

Kera jumped into her white Saturn that was parked a couple of blocks down. She could hardly get the key in the ignition. She started the car then sat there and allowed the words her mother had told her when they had *the talk* to absorb: "The man that breaks your cherry will break your heart, and even ten years down the road when you bump into him on the streets, he'll still make your heart beat fast and your palms sweat."

Instead of going home, Kera went where she could be comforted. She needed someone to talk to who would understand what she was going through.

Kera pulled up to Leece's house and parked on the curb in front. Kera's legs wobbled the entire journey to Leece's doorstep. Kera hesitantly knocked on the door.

Leece rushed down the steps, wearing her girlie pink J-Lo terry cotton short set, and peeked through the peephole. When she opened the door Kera was standing there with her head down. She had tried to stop crying long enough to say hello and to say "I'm sorry" to Leece, but she couldn't.

Leece's eyes watered and her bottom lip trembled at the sight of her heartbroken friend standing before her. Leece put her arms around Kera as Kera broke down in a sob.

Leece stood there holding Kera for what seemed like forever holding back the words, "I told you so."

***

"You haven't been in the salon in a while," Mya said to Dollar as he sat down at her table to get his fingernails worked on.

"I been busy," Dollar said short.

"Too busy to call?" Mya pried.

"Something like that."

"I tried calling you all last week," Mya said, as she placed Dollar's hand in a bowl of water that she knew was too hot.

"Damn!" Dollar said, jerking his hand out.

"Oh is that too hot for you?" Mya asked sarcastically

without getting a rise out of Dollar. She poured some of the water out and added cold water to the bowl. She then placed Dollar's hand back into the bowl.

"Is that better?" Mya asked.

"That's cool."

"But, like I was saying," Mya continued. "I tried calling you all last week."

"Oh, for real?" Dollar said, knowing damn well he had seen her number on his cell phone's caller ID and ignored the calls. "Ouch."

Mya had *accidentally* jabbed Dollar with the nail file. He pulled his hand away from her and checked out his finger to see if any blood had been drawn.

"Is there something on your mind?" Dollar asked Mya. "If it is just cut the crap and spit it out, ma."

"I need to talk to you," Mya said.

"I'm listening," Dollar replied.

"Not here. Can we get together tonight?"

"Here you go," Dollar said throwing his hands up.

"And what is that supposed to mean? Oh let me guess, you just get women left and right wanting to talk to your fine ass huh? Well you best believe what I got to say is far more important. Trust," Mya said, trying to act black.

"Let me just go on and put it out there. The shit was good, ma, but I ain't really trying to get down...."

"Don't fucking flatter yourself," Mya said raising her tone. Customers and workers turned their attention to her.

"I'm sorry," Mya apologized to the onlookers before gearing her words back to Dollar. "Look, what I have to say won't take up much of your precious time."

Dollar could tell Mya was becoming emotional. "*That's what I get for fucking with a white girl*," Dollar thought to himself. "*The two types of women brothas definitely need to stay away from, young girls and white girls.*"

"I'll meet you at your spot at about 9 p.m. tonight. Is that cool?" Dollar said.

"Yeah," Mya replied. "I'm sorry for raising my voice and cursing at you."

"No problem," Dollar replied. He knew Mya's dramatics were just an excuse for her to get Dollar back over to her place and in bed again. He didn't blame her for being addicted. Hell, she had gone black so she couldn't go back. That was a well-known fact.

***

When Dollar showed up at Mya's she had a candle lit dinner prepared for the two. Dollar gobbled down the roasted duck, red potatoes and greenbeans. He wasn't impressed, he was simply hungry.

During dinner, Mya went on and on about her sister and her husband and two children, about how happy they were. Dollar could have cared less. He had no intentions upon ever meeting them.

After dinner the two engaged in intercourse that wasn't even worth describing. It was off the hook the last time, maybe all that liquor had something to do with it. Dollar humped on Mya for about two minutes before he felt himself ready to cum. He snapped the condom off and jerked on Mya's belly. Dollar then got up, went into her bathroom and cleaned himself off. When he returned he had a towel in his hand that he had already used to wipe himself off.

"Here you go, ma," Dollar said throwing the towel at Mya. "Here's a towel to clean yourself up. I'm fixin' to go."

Dollar was hoping that Mya caught on to the significance of him throwing in the towel. He was finished with her. As a matter of fact he was finished with hoes period. He wasn't about to let them fuck up his game by fucking with his head with all of their emotions and shit.

"Dollar, remember, I invited you over here to talk," Mya said, getting up from out of the bed to slip on her robe.

"Well then talk. I have a lot I have to do tomorrow."

"I'm pregnant," Mya blurted out.

Dollar stood speechless momentarily before bursting out laughing.

"You're kidding right?" Dollar continued laughing. "And I guess I'm the daddy."

"Of course you are," Mya said. "I haven't..."

"Been with anybody else," Dollar mimicked.

"How much is the abortion going to run me?" Dollar said, pulling his money out of his back pocket.

"I'm having this baby. I can't have an abortion," Mya cried to Dollar as she sat down on the bed. "It's against my religion."

"Oh, and having sex unmarried isn't?" Dollar said.

"Mya, you don't even know me. I'm just some dude you slept with."

"And that's my fault. I'm the one who will have to explain that to the world. But why should I punish this unborn child?" Mya said, rubbing her belly. "I can't do it. I won't. Abortion is murder."

"I don't even know why you're laying this on me," Dollar said. "We were only together one time."

"News flash...all it takes is one time."

"And I'm supposed to believe the baby is mine?" Dollar asked.

"Don't go there," Mya said. "Please don't go there."

"Look, Mya, honey, sweetheart," Dollar said in a condescending manner. "I've never wanted kids. I don't want any kids now, tomorrow or yesterday. This baby, if it is mine, ain't gonna happen."

"Dollar, I understand where you're coming from, but you don't have a choice at this point. I'm having this baby."

"It's a no win situation with bitches," Dollar snapped. "When y'all get pregnant, the man doesn't have any choice over whether or not he wants to be a father."

"The man has a choice before he lays down and sticks his dick in a woman," Mya retaliated. "You made a choice not to wear a condom. That's where your choice started and ended."

"I am so not hearing this. I am so not fucking hearing this," Dollar said swinging his fist in the air. No way in hell was a kid in the plan.

"I'm sorry this happened. I didn't plan for it to happen," Mya cried.

"Yeah, right," Dollar said, disbelieving every word Mya uttered.

"Fuck it. You don't have to be a part of this child's life. This child never has to know you existed. I'll tell him you were a casualty of war or something." Mya paused. "I knew telling you was a mistake."

"You're not paying attention, Mya," Dollar said. "This baby is not going to happen. No seed of mine is going to produce. You feel me?"

"I'm sorry, but you can't tell me what to do with my body. The baby didn't get to choose whether or not it wanted to be conceived. It's not fair to take the baby's choice of life away."

"That's all good, but I believe in Pro-Choice," Dollar said. "Abortion isn't always bad depending on the circumstance. And in this circumstance, where the father doesn't want the baby or the mother, abortion is the answer."

"I'm not asking you to want *me*, Dollar. I believe in Pro-Choice too and my choice is to have this baby. Abortion might be the answer for other women, but not me. I won't have that on my conscious."

By this time Dollar is heated. His conversation with Mya wasn't going anywhere. This dumb ass white girl is determined to have this baby. He didn't want it to get to this point, but it was time for him to pull out his wild card.

"Well since you believe in Pro-Choice," Dollar said as he flipped through his wallet, "here's $500. Bitch, it's your life or the baby's. You make the choice."

Dollar threw the money at Mya who had the fear of death in her eyes. She stood trembling as she didn't mistake Dollar's words as an idle threat.

Dollar walked up on Mya slowly as he stared her down.

"Here's another $200," Dollar said throwing the money at Mya. "This is for the couple of days of work you might have to miss."

Dollar kissed Mya on the forehead then left her apartment.

"*A baby,*" Dollar thought as he stood outside of Mya's closed door. "*Maybe a lil me wouldn't be so bad. But what the fuck do I have to offer a kid? What could I teach a kid, how to hustle? That's about the only damn thing my old man taught me. Maybe things would be different between me and my kid, though.*"

Dollar contemplated walking back into Mya's apartment. He was so torn at this point. The fate of another human beings life was in his hands. Dollar turned around and put his hand on the doorknob to turn it. Mya, who was standing on the opposite side of the door contemplating going after Dollar, watched the knob turn. Maybe she wouldn't have to go after Dollar after all. Maybe he had changed his mind on his own.

Just before pushing the door open Dollar said to himself, "I can't curse my baby. I can't bring no child into this ghetto ass shit. Naw, it's better off dead."

Mya could hear Dollar's footsteps walk away. She leaned up against the door and slid down to the floor. Her wailing filled the apartment. She knew what she had to do.

***

Dollar was tossing and turning as sweat dripped from his body. He opened his closed eyes, which weren't asleep-just closed, and looked at the clock. It was two o'clock in the morning.

Dollar's concerns about Ral had been eating at him. Shit with Ral just didn't feel right anymore. Dollar remembered Romeo once telling him that if shit don't feel right, then it ain't right.

But this was Ral, not some new jack on the street. This was the same comrade Dollar traded in eight years of his life for. This is the same comrade he had invested so much time in saving. This was his best friend, Ralphie Boy from the playground.

Dollar felt like someone had put a dinner plate covered with delicious foods in front of him right after he had eaten a large pizza. The dilemma between throwing the food out or just eating it so that it didn't go to waste was tormenting Dollar's soul.

"I should have listened to Tommy in the first place," Dollar laid in bed thinking. *"Ral was a fuckin' junkie. He wasn't no good to us. I tried to fix him. I tried. I did my part, didn't I? I gave him a chance. It's only a matter of time before Ral fucks up and takes Tommy and me with him."*

Dollar had to do something. Sleepless nights for Dollar was becoming a problem. He didn't have a choice but to eliminate the problem.

***

Dollar, Ral and Tommy sat in the living room of Ral's crib. Since Dollar's and Tommy's scare with the po-po at Jimmy's Coney Island, they hadn't met back up there since. Dollar suggested they meet at Ral's until they decided upon a new location to discuss dealings. Ral was clueless to the fact that Dollar and Tommy had no intentions on ever meeting with him again.

"Damn," Ral said. "I didn't even think you remembered my birthday."

"That's from Dollar and me," Tommy said, referring to the gift certificate for a suite at the "W" in Chicago that Dollar had just handed Ral.

"I'm glad you like it," Dollar said.

"A suite at one of the dopest overnighters in the city, shiiitt...there's only one other thing that could top that," Ral said raising his eyebrows.

"You think I ain't up on top of that?" Dollar winked at Ral. "I knew you'd get lonely up in a big ole place like that so I arranged for you to have a little company."

"See, that' why you my mafucka," Ral said beating on his chest with one hand while pretending to wipe away tears from his eyes with the other.

"That's all men think about," Tommy said.

"And good thing we do or else you wouldn't have a job," Ral said. "Y'all excuse me. I have to go to the bathroom."

Ral got up from the couch and went into the bathroom. Tommy waited until she heard the bathroom door close before she spoke.

"I knew one of the two would be Ral's downfall," Tommy said to Dollar. "Pussy or drugs."

"Yeah, but who ever thought it would be both?"

***

Tommy had already bumped her head twice on the pole. She even stumbled and almost fell off the stage.

"Wine," the DJ chuckled, "I think you done had a little too much of your name. Tiwana, just give that hoe Shirley Temples the rest of the night." The patrons in Chocolate City laughed along with the DJ as Tommy exited the stage and went and sat next to Dollar in a corner booth.

"You okay?" Dollar asked a nervous Tommy.

"Hell no. Are you?" Tommy replied. "He's our boy, D. Maybe we should have just talked to him."

"Talk is cheap, Tommy. Unless you up in a piece like this, talk is free and gets you nowhere."

"Look, I can't think straight. I can't be up in here, not tonight. I'm gon' go tell Shay I need to go home. Tommy excused herself and headed towards Shay's office.

Dollar sat at the table looking at his watch, knowing that in a few minutes, like two-day-old milk, Ral would be expired.

"Hey, Dollar, right?" some cat said as he strolled up to Dollar. Dollar put his hand on his chin and eyeballed this cat up and down. He didn't recognize this fool whose pants were about five sizes too big.

"Who wants to know?" Dollar said.

"Oh, it ain't like that, partna. I'm Kill Dog, ya dude Ral's boy. I've seen you with him a couple of times."

Kill Dog put out his hand to shake Dollars. Dollar reluctantly did so.

"Ral talks about you twenty-four/seven. It's good to meet you up close and personal. I'd expect to see some gleaming halo over your head, a beaming light behind you like you Jesus or some shit," Kill Dog laughed.

"Oh, yeah," Dollar lightweight laughed.

"Word. Ral's my boy, with his crazy ass. That wigga would take candy from a baby and sell it to its mother if he had to. He's good peoples though. Always got a mafucka's back."

Kill Dogs words were starting to eat away at Dollar. They only reminded Dollar of how loyal Ral was and had always been. But hell, people change. The game changes people.

"Me and my girl had got into it and Ral was there to have my back," Kill Dog continued. "Ma had just caught me getting down with a chiquita from round the way."

As Kill Dog went on and on Dollar saw first hand how niggaz get to running they mouth off in the spot. This cat was telling all of his business.

"Ral's ass shows up out of nowhere with a mink. I shuts my hoe up with that coat. I ain't even have the money on the spot to give Ral but he looked out. As a matter of fact I just paid his ass a couple three weeks ago. I hit him up with an extra two grand. Hell, ma the mother of my four kids. She special like that. Ral saved my ass."

"Hold up," Dollar stopped Kill Dog before he could continue gabbing. "Ral sold you a coat?"

"Yeah, a mink," Kill Dog said. "He was gon' bring my dude Rob from LA up in here not too long ago to try to cop one. He said dude's who sells them sister works up in here and shit, but them boys had drove up to Chi-Town and put in work and wasn't trying to hang out. But they said the next time they roll through they gon' check out this spot. I told them niggaz they didn't know what they were missing. Don't nobody roll through the Interstate without jumpin' off at The Chocolate Factory......."

Dollar had left Kill Dog standing there talking to himself. One of the biggest mistakes Dollar could ever make was about to go down and he had to stop it.

"Nigga, what the fuck you doing in here?" a dancer shouted as Dollar busted into the dressing room.

"T, it's a mistake. We gotta stop that shit!" Dollar shouted to Tommy.

"Whoa, hold up," Tommy said confused. What's going on?"

"Are you crazy busting up in here like that?" Bear asked Dollar as he snatched him up.

"Man, get your motherfuckin' hands off of me," Dollar said going for his piece.

"Wait!" Tommy yelled. "Come on, Dollar. What's wrong?" Tommy said as she peeled Bear's hands off of Dollar.

Dollar rambled on and on to Tommy about Ral having money because he sold the mink coat to Kill Dog. He told her about why them LA niggaz didn't show up at the club that night they were supposed to rob him in the parking lot. Tommy wasn't fully comprehending everything. All she knew is that a big mistake had been made. It was like a ghetto version of Three's Company. All the wrong conclusions had been jumped to.

"Call Storm's pager," Tommy shouted as she began to tremble.

Dollar searched his persons for his cell phone and it was no where on him.

"Fuck, my phone is in the car," Dollar said.

Dollar and Tommy ran out to Dollar's truck to retrieve his phone. Dollar dug through his pockets and glove box for Storm's number.

"Damn'it, D, hurry the fuck up," Tommy said. By this time she was shaking and tears were running down her face.

"I can't find it," Dollar said.

"Your cell phone...is it stored in your cell phone...numbers called...received calls.....something," Tommy screamed.

"Yeah, yeah," Dollar said remembering that he had stored the number in his phone.

Dollar fumbled through the address book, but couldn't recall what name he stored the number in as.

"Fuck," Dollar said. "It's not under Storm."

"Try M& M," Tommy suggested, and of which Dollar did.

"It's not under that either."

"Hit hoes. You called them hit hoes. Try that."

Just as Tommy suggested, the phone number was stored under Hit Hoes. Dollar hit the quick dial button. The phone rang one time...no answer. The phone rang two times...no answer. The phone rang three times...no answer. The phone rang four times.

"Hello," a seductive voice answered.

"Storm," Dollar shouted.

"No, this is Thunder. Just a moment and I'll get her. Thunder said.

"No, wait a minute," Dollar shouted, but Thunder had already put down the phone. Dollar could hear his heart beat as he waited on the phone.

"This is Storm," she said.

"Baby girl, this is Dollar," he said.

"Hey, Poppa, what's....."

"Have you done that shit yet?" Dollar said cutting Storm off.

"My feelings are hurt that you doubted my skills," Storm said. "Don't worry. That black suit won't go to waste. He's gone."

Dollar removed the phone from his ear. He dropped his head and closed his eyes.

"No, oh no," Tommy whimpered.

Dollar looked over at Tommy and D'ed up. He stuck out his chest, took a deep breath and swallowed. He then put the phone back to his ear.

"You still there?" Storm asked.

"Yeah, I'm here," Dollar replied.

"Yeah, he's gone off that Ecs. Thunder and me bout to finish this shit off. I told you that I would hit you up when the deed was done, so let me do my thang and I'll call you back and......"

"Whoa," Dollar interrupted. "You mean he's not gone gone?"

"Didn't I say not to worry? My girl and me gonna handle this. We ain't amateurs," Storm said.

"No, no," Dollar said. "There's been a change in plans."

"Meaning what?" Storm huffed.

"Meaning I don't need M&M anymore," Dollar said.

There was silence on the phone. Dollar could hear some shuffling and could tell Storm must have been changing to a location where she could speak more freely.

"Look, muthafucka," Storm said. "I done already sucked Opey's little ass dick so if you thinking you getting this money back then you got another thing coming."

"Calm down, Pocohonotis," Dollar said. "You keep that shit and good looking out. We cool?"

"Hell, yeah we cool. We always gon' be cool as long as you don't try to fuck up my money. My daughter's tuition was due so your shit was already spent."

"I hear you and it's cool, ma. Like I already said, you keep that shit. But since you are keeping it why don't you go ahead and see to it that my man has a happy birthday after all. You feel me?" Dollar said.

"That's not a problem," Storm said.

"Alright then, later."

"Hey, Dollar," Storm said.

"Yeah."

"It was a pleasure doing business with you."

Delighted that Dollar was able to stop Storm from finishing Ral off he replied, "The pleasure was mine."

Dollar hung up his cell phone, took a deep breath and planted his head against his steering wheel.

"So it's all good?" Tommy asked, as Dollar sat hunched over the steering wheel.

"If you hadn't of figured out what Storm's fucking number was stored under, then I don't know...," Dollar said becoming emotional. "I don't know what would have happened."

"Jesus," Tommy sighed. "I knew Ral wasn't no rat. I knew it."

Dollar looked over at Tommy who was in a cold sweat. Dollar put his hand on her knee and said, "You did it again."

"What?" Tommy said.

"You saved Ral. Once again, Tommy Gun to the rescue."

Chapter 15

Strictly Business

"Nice place you got here," Hennessey said to Dollar as she walked in his apartment dressed in a navy blue business suit with her butterscotch Coach briefcase in hand.

"Thank you, Miss lady," Dollar replied. "This nice little place cost as much as a mansion it seems. It sucks up my entire paycheck, not to mention the extra fee for parking that's tacked onto my rent."

"What exactly do you do, your job?" Hennessey asked.

"Construction, pretty much," Dollar replied.

Hennessey couldn't help but giggle.

"Construction, huh?" Hennessey said.

"No, I'm serious. I really do construction. I got the work boots to prove it."

"Construction," Hennessey said walking over to Dollar and grabbing hold of his hand. "With nails like these..."

"I wear gloves. You wanna see those too?"

"I'll take your word for it."

"Hey, I'm a hard working brotha. Otherwise I'd be spending more time with you. Not just talking on the phone like we usually do."

"I like talking to you on the phone," Hennessey said. "Besides, you know my job is always sending me out of town to seminars and stuff."

"And I like talking to you too, but I like seeing you in person more."

"Talking to you on the phone up until the wee hours of the night makes me feel like I'm in high school again,"

Hennessey said reminiscing back to those days.

Being hypnotized by the scent of a woman, Dollar lifted Hennessey's hand to his lips and planted a kiss on it. He then proceeded to kiss up her arm until he made his way to her lips. Dollar planted three soft kisses on her lips. Hennessey responded with a deep French kiss. The two kissed for what seemed like an eternity. Dollar ran his hands down Hennessey's back until he reached her bottom. He then squeezed as if she were a package of Charmen.

Hennessey could feel Dollar's nature rising. She had to remember that she was there on business, strictly business. She pulled Dollar's hands from off of her butt and pushed away from him.

"Let me grab the portfolios I worked up for you," Hennessey said as she pulled some folders out of her brief case.

"We have all night to look at those," Dollar said walking up behind Hennessey, pressing himself against her and kissing her on her neck.

It was going to be hard for Hennessey not to fall into lust with Dollar. She had to admit it, he was the finest man she ever had to work with. But business was business. After allowing herself to get a little creamy from the kisses to the tender spot on her neck, Hennessey pulled away from Dollar.

"Well, I really don't have all night and you seemed very serious the other night on the phone about wanting to make some long term investments to provide for a secure future."

"I am serious, but damn, you got a nigga all hot and bothered."

"Come on, Dollar. I'm serious. I have some interesting business opportunities. I really want to help you. I really do. Let me help you."

Hennessey's sudden sincerity showed Dollar that she was all business. She spoke with such passion, as though she had worked hard on putting some things together for him. Dollar excused himself while he went into the bathroom and handled his business. There wasn't any need in letting a woody go to waste.

As Dollar cleaned himself up in the bathroom he asked himself over and over why he thought for one minute Hennessey was going to give him any. *"I told myself I wasn't going to let these broads fuck up my head,"* Dollar said to himself as he headed out of the bathroom to rejoin his guest.

For the next hour or so Hennessey schooled Dollar on some high-risk investments that could either earn him ten times his money or put him in the poor house. That would be the risk he would have to take. Big risk always came along with big money. CDs and Bonds didn't interest Dollar. The payoff wasn't worth the wait.

When Dollar realized that he only had $29,000 in his safe he panicked. He had told himself that he was going to live modest, but those "must have" materialistic possessions got the best of him. Lack of money to Dollar was what lack of crack was to a fiend. It made him nervous and jittery. It also made him anxious. He needed to flip his money. He was willing to take the high-risk investments Hennessey was feeding him. He was willing to risk every dime he had. But doing so meant he had to make a big move to back his shit up. If he was going to put all of his eggs in one basket and turn them over to Hennessey in hopes of her making him a rich man, he needed to keep a golden egg for himself.

As Dollar listened to Hennessey go on and on about the type of investments her bank had made for people and how their investments had paid off, he realized that a bank mans a lot of money for a lot of people. When a person wants candy, where do they go? They go to a candy store. So when a person wants money, where do they go?

By now Dollar wasn't paying much attention to

Hennessey's words. Dollar was fixated on candy...green candy with dead presidents on them. She finally wrapped things up and Dollar offered her a nightcap of which she accepted.

Of course Dollar tried making moves on Hennessey but she refused his advances by stating that she just wanted to *cuddle*.

The two sat sipping on Alize' and watching television.

"So what do you want with me?" Dollar couldn't help but ask Hennessey.

"Excuse me," Hennessey replied.

"I mean, look. I'm just a regular guy. I don't have much to offer," Dollar said.

"I don't want much," Hennessey replied. "Besides, I just like being with you. You're a good guy, Dollar."

"Ahmmm," Dollar laughed in an *if only you knew* sorta tone.

"You don't think you're a good guy?" Hennessey asked, taking a sip from her glass of Alize'. "Then tell me...what are you?"

"I'm just a man, you know," Dollar said looking down at his glass of Alize'. "I mean, an everyday brotha out here trying to make it."

"Trying to make it how?" Hennessey began digging.

The door was opening for Dollar to be able to tell Hennessey about the man he really was. How he had spent time in jail. But that would only make her skeptical of him, maybe even drive her away. Dollar didn't want that. But what kind of future could they possibly have together? It would only be a matter of time before Hennessey found him out. Dollar couldn't see her wanting to have anything to do with a man who robbed people for a living. It wasn't as if robbin' folks was something he was going to do for the rest of his life. He just needed to hit the jackpot and then everything would be good.

Dollar looked over at Hennessey's French manicured

nails and sparkling tennis bracelet and knew that she would never fuck with the real Dollar in a million years. Fuck it, if shit ain't broke, then don't fix it. Telling Hennessey his business was futile at this point. There was still plenty of time for their relationship to move forward. By then, robbery would be a thing of the past for Dollar.

As Dollar looked at Hennessey, he was convinced, now more than ever, that perhaps it was time for a change. Dollar wanted to get closer to Hennessey. It was hard to be real and open with her knowing that there was a side to him that he couldn't share with her. and telling her the truth about him wasn't the way to do it. He would just have to keep her at bay until he got his shit straight.

"It's getting late," Dollar said looking down at his watch. "Don't you have to work tomorrow?"

"Yes I do," Hennessey said sitting her glass down on the living room table and standing up. "Besides, I know when I'm being told to go home."

"You don't have to go home, but you have to get the hell up out of here," Dollar laughed as he stood up with Hennessey.

Dollar walked Hennessey down to her car and made sure she was safe and sound inside.

"Thanks for walking me down," Hennessey said, rolling down the window to her money green convertible Saab.

"Anytime," Dollar replied, as he turned away and headed back up to his apartment.

"Dollar," Hennessey yelled, stopping Dollar in his tracks. "Can I tell you something?"

"Anything."

"I'm kinda diggin' you," Hennessey blushed.

"Oh yeah," Dollar smiled. "Well, I'm kinda...diggin' you too."

Hennessey smiled, blew Dollar a kiss and then drove off. This time Dollar did catch it...and placed it on his lips.

"Now her right there," Dollar said to himself. "She could have my baby. That's baby mama material if I ever saw it."

As Dollar walked back up to his apartment all he could envision was Hennessey's smile. It warmed him. It comforted him, the same way his mother's smile used to comfort him.

Dollar returned to his apartment. By this time it was after eleven and the evening news was on. Dollar walked over to the television to turn it off so that he could get ready for bed. Just then he heard the words from the anchorwoman:

"And now let's go to Barb McNeil for news around the country," the anchorwoman said.

"Hello, I'm Barb McNeil and I'm outside of Orient Prison in Orient, Ohio where convicted felon Ramelle Blake has spent the last 17 years of his life. Well as you know, after years of investigations, the state of Ohio found evidence that confirmed that Blake is, in fact, the Midwest Serial Killer. In less than forty-five minutes Blake will be transferred to Mansfield Correctional Facility where death row awaits him. As you can see behind me, there are many protesters who oppose the death penalty out here on Blake's behalf. No appeal has been filed nor is one expected to be filed, therefore no last minute stay is expected to be granted. Both family members of the victim's and supporters have signed a petition requesting that Blake be put to death as early as next month. If they have it their way, Blake will be transported from MCF (Mansfield Correctional Facility) to Lucasville Correctional Institution where he will be put to death via lethal injection. One of the victim's mother said that the families have been living in hell for years not knowing who was responsible for the death of their daughters. Now that the murder's identity is known, it would be punishing the families even more if the state forces them, via use of their tax dollars, to keep this monster alive any longer. The same mother also stated that she's going to go out and buy a new dress to wear for when she's escorted into the prison to witness Blake's death."

Dollar turned the television off and headed towards his bedroom as he mumbled, "See you in hell, old man."

***

Dollar knew that going back to work for Redd was out of the question. He didn't want to be on pins and needles waiting for the drama to erupt, not with Redd, but with Kera herself. This was all the more reason why Dollar needed to make shit happen. Did he think his big break was going to show up on his doorstep one day? Hell no, he had to go out and just do the damn thang. He couldn't go back to work for Redd and he wouldn't fuck with a fast food joint. That was out of the question. It was time to make that move. Fuck these punk ass stick-ups. Dollar needed to make a big move.

After hours of contemplation's and running game plans through his head, Dollar phoned Tommy and Ral to meet up with him. It was time to share his master plan with them.

***

"You want to rob a fuckin' bank?" Tommy asked Dollar as she squeezed the lemon slice into her ice water.

"Shhhh," Dollar said. "You tryin' to tell the whole fucking world?"

"You've lost your damn mind," Tommy said. "We can't rob no bank."

"Why not?" Ral asked. "A stick up is a stick up."

"You two muthafuckas ain't got nothing to lose," Tommy said. "I got two girls at stake."

"I'm so God damn tired of you using them two girls as your excuse to be soft," Dollar said as he pounded his fist on the picnic table at the DQ. "I'm sorry, T, but it's time you start using them two girls as an excuse to raise up out of this town. What about that bookstore you be talking about? Niggaz in Gary don't read. What you gon' do, open it up next door to Jimmy's Coney Island?"

Dollar always had a way of breaking Tommy down, talking her into doing shit. There was one time when they were kids and Dollar convinced Tommy that she could fly if she swung high enough on the park swing and jumped off. Her arm was in a cast for almost two months.

Tommy couldn't believe Dollar talked her into doing that dumb shit. But this time was different. They weren't twelve-year-old kids. Tommy was grown and robbing a bank just wasn't her MO.

"I can't do it, D," Tommy said, putting her head down sadly. This was the first time she would ever not do something to please Dollar. From the moment she met him, all she ever wanted to do was to please Dollar, but this time she just couldn't.

"Yeah, you pussy alright," Dollar said. Dollar felt some degree of guilt for the way he was talking to Tommy. He hated having to appear to be so callous, but he knew that nice wasn't going to get him anywhere.

"Yo, Dollar, man," Ral said feeling bad for Tommy. He knew how hard it was for Tommy to say no to Dollar.

"Speaking of pussy," Tommy said. "Why don't you let the bitch you fuckin', that Hennessey trick, help you rob the muthafucka. She can be Bonnie and you can be Clyde."

"That ain't even her style. She's on some entirely different shit. She's got far too much class for that," Dollar said. By the expression on Tommy's face Dollar realized that what he had just said hurt Tommy's feelings.

"She's got too much class, huh?" Tommy said.

"Besides, even if she was into this shit, I couldn't convince her of robbing her own shit. That's one of the rules of the game, you don't fuck with your own back yard. Outside of the fence is cool, but not your own backyard."

"So you wanna rob your girl's bank?" Ral asked. "Damn. Won't she recognize you and rat you out, dude?"

"I'ma wear a mask and in addition to that, that's where Tommy comes in," Dollar said, turning to Tommy. "You dress up in some of that dress up shit you got, you know wigs make-up and shit. You pretend to be a customer. Tell her you wanna look into her designing you a financial portfolio. You keep her occupied in back in her office while the shit goes down. If need be, use your piece to keep her back there, but don't hurt her. Just keep her back there out of our way. She'll never suspect a thing. Besides, I just put $20,000 into that bank for investments. Why would I do that knowing I'm about to go rob them?"

Tommy kept shaking her head as if she couldn't believe what she was hearing. Ral was most attentive as he rubbed his index finger under his nose.

"Look, all I'm asking you to do for now is to just at least think about it," Dollar said to Tommy. "This is our big move, T. Remember when I said we wasn't gonna do that robbin' niggaz shit forever? Well this is it, T. This is that big move that's going to put us in retirement."

Dollar looked over to Ral to see where his head was at. "You in, Ral?"

"Hell, yeah," Ral said sniffling.

"It's all on you now, T," Dollar said. "The world is on your shoulders."

***

On Dollar's way home from meeting with Tommy and Ral he decided to stop by the clinic to see what Doc was up to.

The clinic was standing room only. The fact that it was a Monday might have had something to do with it. Folks had been putting off seeing a doctor the entire week before. Come Friday at 5 p.m., once the doctor's office is closed, they realized just how bad off they were. They had to suffer through the entire weekend before seeking relief.

Dollar walked up to the sign in counter and asked if Doc was in.

I'm sorry," The receptionist at the clinic said to Dollar. "He's in with a patient. We're extremely busy today."

"Just let him know that his brother is here to see him," Dollar replied.

The receptionist paused before lashing out at Dollar. "For your information." she said, "His brother is dead which makes your statement very cruel. Now please just sign in and wait your turn like everyone else."

"I'm his brother," Dollar thought to himself. He wanted to scream it loud so that the entire world could hear him. *"I'm not dead. I'm alive.* Instead, Dollar walked away. Fuck it! Doc hadn't even bothered to mention him to anyone. As far as Dollar was convinced, from that point on out, as far as Doc was concerned, he really was dead.

"I don't know what I was thinking," Dollar said to himself. "I don't know why I ever thought shit could be how it was between my brother and me back in the day."

Dollar walked back through the clinic lobby to the exit door. He pushed the door open to leave the clinic knowing that he no intentions of every stepping foot back in there again. Here Dollar had been out of prison all this time and his brother never even bothered to tell anyone about him. He probably had no intentions of ever including Dollar in his life again. Once upon a time, Dollar had asked for this. Be careful what you ask for, you just might get it.

A hand from the person entering the clinic wrapped around the edge of the door as Dollar proceeded to leave out. This hand displayed a very unique tattoo. It was a tattoo of a cross with barbed wire wrapped around it. A hand was grasping the cross as if it barely had an ounce of strength left. Underneath the design were the words "Hold On".

Dollar remembered seeing this before. He knew exactly who it belonged to.

"Well if it ain't Dollar Bill," the man entering the clinic said. "Fancy running into you here. Oh, yeah. I forgot. This is your turf, huh...your home town? What a coincidence bumping' into you here."

Dollar stood still and frozen as the man continued.

"I don't know why anyone would want to live in this shit hole of a town. How that hoe talked me into moving here I'll never guess. I ain't got no plans on making this my permanent home though. I just got some business I need to handle then I'm moving West, Cali or some shit. You know what I'm saying? What you doing up in the clinic? You catch something while you was in the joint? You got the clap or something? I know you probably been running up in everything with a pussy. You know how it is when you get out of the joint. Hell, a muthafucka would fuck a sheep on a farm," the man burst out laughing.

The man stood there laughing as if he and Dollar had been the best of friends.

"My brother works here," Dollar replied.

"Oh yeah. Is that so?" the man said sticking his head around Dollar and peeking inside the waiting area. "If your brother is anything like your father, maybe he can hook me up...you know a tit for a tat. I'd hate to have to wait for all these sick muthafuckas to be seen before I can see the doctor."

"What did you just say?" Dollar asked.

"I said I'd hate to have to wait for all....."

"No, I mean about my father."

"Oh, shit, you know what I mean, I do a little something for him and he does a little something for me...like back when we was all in the joint."

Dollar stared into Wojo's eyes as if he had the capability of dissecting his brain.

"My father," Dollar said, wanting to confirm that he and Wojo were on the same page.

"Yeah, Romeo the ladies lover, or should I say killer," Wojo laughed. "Can you believe they fell for that shit, Romeo, the Midwest Terror?"

Wojo stood in the doorway laughing hysterically. It was an evil wicked laugh. At this point, he was the only one who knew the punch line.

"That old bastard held that shit over my head for years before finding away to put it to use. You know how it is when you first get to the joint, you act like some ol' bitch. I was in for possession with intent to sell. Those funky ass cops were so worried about trying to stick a drug charge on a brotha that they let all the real evidence slip right between their fingers, the rope, the gloves, the blade...all dat shit. A nigga got away with murder, literally. I was bragging to your pops about it, you know, trying to be the big man in the joint. He held that shit over my head for ages. But it's all good though. I ain't mad at him, may he rest in peace," Wojo said as he took his hand and motioned a cross across his chest.

"Then here comes your ass," Wojo said. "His boy was fixin' to spend the rest of his life behind bars, the son he had abandoned as a small child. How could he make it up to you? So, with nothing to lose, he decides he wants to be me, the Midwest Serial Killer. He wants to take credit for my shit so that you could be a free man. Hell, if I was him I would have told the authorities what he knew about me years ago and reaped the benefits myself. But no, he decided to give you freedom instead. That fool made me tell him every grimy detail and he memorized it to a tee. Did he tell you about how I did ole' girl from Kentucky, the part about the hanger? By the time I engraved the details inside your pop's head, hell, he envisioned himself slicing those bitch's throats. I think he started to believe for a minute that he was the Midwest Serial Killer. Well, he's notorious now. He's up there with Bundy and Dahmer. He stole my shine. But, fuck it. We'll just have to take it to our grave, huh? I mean the story made you a free man didn't it? Why would you give a shit about the truth? That would only mean you finishing off your time."

Dollar's stomach was turning 90 miles per hour. He wanted to throw up. He couldn't believe what he was hearing.

Dollar stood in the doorway watching Wojo's dingy off–white teeth open and close as he continued speaking.

"Your father was going to make good with you if it was the last thing he did. Nigga acted like he was God up in the joint or some shit. I guess that makes you Jesus. Who's soul will you sacrifice yourself for to save?"

A woman walked up and brushed through Dollar and Wojo.

"Damn, that's one more muthafucka that's going to be ahead of me," Wojo said as the woman proceeded to the registration desk. "Let me get my ass in here and take care of my business. I'm sure I'll run into you again. Maybe we can do lunch sometime. And hey, I hope you don't hold shit against me from back in the joint. You know how a nigga gotta act hard up in there. It was all show...strictly business."

Wojo chuckled and headed into the clinic. Dollar vomited up everything he had eaten and eventually the lining of his stomach. Dollar stood still, unable to lift his feet, as the world spun around him. He couldn't see straight. He couldn't think straight. All he could envision was a man, his father, being injected with lethal fluids. His life had been taken for a crime of which he had not committed. In all actuality, Romeo had literally given up his life so that his son could have one.

On top of everything, Dollar felt no guilt. In his heart, any man who abandoned his wife and kids deserved the death penalty. Romeo had only gotten what was coming to him.

Chapter 16

Dear Mama

It was late Sunday morning and Dollar lay in his bed flicking channels with the remote control. He had spent a couple of days earlier in the week casing out the bank, the position of the tellers, cameras and the daily routine of the security guards. He had ordered in food and ordered pay per view movies for the past two days. The only thing he got out of the bed to do was use the bathroom. He hadn't even showered.

A small digital envelope was visible on his cell phone signaling to him that he had voicemail messages. He had allowed all calls to go directly to his voicemail. He didn't want to be bothered by anyone.

For some reason Dollar was feeling melancholy... empty inside. Here he was, a free man who was supposed to be spending the rest of his life behind bars, but yet had been spared. He had a roof over his head and food to eat. He had big plans. Soon he would be living more comfortable than ever. Still and yet, there was a major void. Something was missing. A detail had to have been over looked and it was nagging in the pit of Dollar's stomach.

Out of nowhere Dollar raised up in his bed. A sudden wave of energy took over his being. He went to his closet and picked out some garb to sport for the day. He jumped in the shower and hit the road.

As Dollar drove, he took in the city air. With no final destination Dollar just drove while he listened to his best of Al Green CD. Once he had listened to every song on that he popped in his Tupac "Me Against the World" CD. As Dollar listened to the beat of song number nine, the same beat he had just heard Al Green sing to, he knew why he was on the road. He knew what had lifted him up out of that bed and where he needed to be at that very moment.

***

"Dear Mama," Dollar said as he sat on the ground gazing at his mother's headstone.

Choked up, Dollar swallowed hard and maintained his composure.

"I haven't been able to bring myself to come back up here and I know I haven't talked to you in a while. I don't know what to say, mama. I'm your oldest boy."

Dollar put his head between his knees and fought back his tears.

"I made some mistakes and despite my decisions, you taught me well, mama. Me being in jail wasn't no reflection on you, mama. That was all my doing. I was young and just wanted to find a quick route to taking care of you and my little brother. Can you believe he's about to be a doctor? My little brother, a doctor. I still can't believe it. I guess you know me and him ain't tight like we was when we was younger. I know that ain't making you happy. I know I ain't making you happy, mama. I know you looking down on me and ...."

Once again Dollar had to stay strong and fight back tears.

"I'm sorry, mama," Dollar said breaking down. He could no longer hold back his emotions.

"Can you hear me, mama?" Dollar cried. "Do you hear me, mama? I'm sorry. I'm so sorry. I never meant for any of this to happen. I miss you, mama. I love you so much. I wish I could do everything all over again. I would do what you did, mama. I would work at every fast food chain in the city. I would catch the bus, ride a bike, walk even. I would be just like you, mama. Klein and I, we didn't need no daddy. No man was a strong as you, mama...no man."

By this time Dollar was crying and snottin' uncontrollably. His body trembled as he sat on the ground before his mother's grave, pouring his heart out to her, holding a conversation with her that he should have had with her years ago.

"I did wrong, mama," Dollar continued. "But I ain't no killer. I ain't never took another man's life. You didn't raise a perfect son. But you didn't raise no killer either. I just want you to know that. I just want you to have that peace of mind."

Dollar paused and collected himself.

"I guess all you got now is peace. Dear mama, please forgive me for not being strong like you. I'm about to do something that I know you wouldn't be proud of, but I promise you, mama, after that I'm gonna make you proud. I know I've got some nerve asking you to forgive me for a wrong I ain't even made yet, but it's something I just got to do, mama. I've lost everything, you, my brother and Aunti Charlene," Dollar said looking over at his Aunt's headstone.

"All this loss can't be in vain. It just can't be," Dollar sobbed. This time Dollar couldn't control the flow of his tears.

"I miss you, Mama. God I miss you. I miss your smile. Speaking of your smile. I met a woman, Hennessey. You'd like her. She has your smile. She's a good woman, Mama. I can see me with somebody like her. I think.... no I know I need somebody like her. She'll keep me on my toes just like you did, Mama. I wish you were here. Oh, mama."

Dollar kneeled over his mother's grave for almost an hour crying. His once silent shouts were now heard throughout the cemetery grounds. Dollar couldn't hold back his cries, his yells, his wailing. He didn't care who saw a grown man crying.

He had held in so many tears for so long. It was time. It was long overdue.

Just as Dollar had wiped away his last tear he felt a hand on his shoulder. He knew the touch. He needed the touch. So Dollar grabbed the hand tight and began to cry even harder.

"I.....I," Dollar stuttered. "I'm sorry. I'm sorry for everything. I...I...I love you."

Doc had just arrived for his normal Sunday visit to their mother's grave.

"Everything is good. We got each other...again," Doc said as he sat down next to his brother and held him tight.

Chapter 17

The Confession

Dollar banged outside of Tommy's door for at least ten minutes before it cracked open. Tommy stood in the doorway with a white towel wrapped around her hair and another one tubed above her breast.

"Why you knocking like you the police?" Tommy said.

"Why you fronting like you didn't hear me out here?" Dollar replied.

"I was in the shower, duh."

"I been calling you for the last few days," Dollar said. "You ain't got none of my messages? I stopped by the club and you weren't there. Didn't Storm tell you?"

Tommy closed her eyes and prepared to lie to Dollar. Instead of a lie, the truth came out.

"Yeah," Tommy said. "I got your messages. Look, Dollar. This one just doesn't feel right and I'm not down with you trying to pressure me."

"I'm not trying to hear this, Tommy."

"I know. I've been trying to figure out how to tell you," Tommy said.

"Tell me what?" Dollar shouted. "Oh, you bailing?"

"It's not even like that. But I've thought about it like you asked me to and my answer is still the same."

"I guess that explains the "For Sale" sign in your front yard," Dollar said, nodding towards the sign of abandonment. "Fuck you, Tommy!"

"Dollar, please," Tommy said, as Dollar began to walk away.

"Naw, fuck you. I did eight years, for you. I gave you eight years on these muthafuckin streets and this is how you gon' repay me?"

"And I cried for you every day for eight years."

"Nigga, you cried," Dollar said.

"You made that choice," Tommy said. "I showed up at the courthouse prepared to admit my guilt."

"Here we go," Dollar said, down playing Tommy's dramatics.

"You are so fuckin' clueless, Dollar. You're too worried about your own muthafuckin' self to notice anything or anybody around you. You haven't even taken the time to notice me," Tommy said softly, as she approached Dollar.

"I noticed that I was willing to trade in my life for you."

"Why?" Tommy asked.

"What do you mean why?" Dollar said. "You was my partner, my dawg, my boy...you know what I'm saying."

"Well, I didn't want to be all that. I never wanted to be those things to you...being your partner, dawg, boy. I wanted to be your girl," Tommy admitted. For so long she had wanted Dollar to notice the feelings she had for him. She wanted him to stop mistaking her love for him as though she loved him like a brother. She wanted him to just wake up and realize that she loved him like a lover.

"You are my girl," Dollar said reaching out to pat Tommy.

"I mean your ***girl-girl***," Tommy said, trying to overcome the embarrassment of showing her true feelings, which is something she had never been good at.

Dollar was speechless. He just stood there in shock.

Tommy misconstruing Dollar's silence, moved in closer to him. She couldn't have been any closer to Dollar. By now she had stepped out onto the porch, still wrapped in her towel, and was right in Dollar's face. She could feel his heart beat as he could feel hers. As they grew closer together Tommy turned away and went back into her house. She held the door open for Dollar and he stepped in. Tommy then proceeded to her bedroom. She came back out a minute later and handed Dollar a shoebox filled with stacks of envelopes that were held together with rubber bands.

"What's this?" Dollar asked.

"These are letters that I wrote you while you were locked up," Tommy said shoving the shoebox in Dollar's arms. "After the first dozen or so were returned I still kept writing. I just never mailed them. Those letters are a diary. A diary of a woman in love with your black ass."

"Tommy, I don't want to do this," Dollar said, trying to give the box back to Tommy.

"Well you are," Tommy insisted by pushing the box back towards Dollar. "One minute I think you're spending the rest of your life in jail and then one day you just show up on my doorstep ready to hustle. You never even asked how I'd been. I mean we never just spent time together."

"What do you mean? I spend more time with you and Ral than anybody."

"Yeah, me, Ral and a slue of hoes, but what about me? What about just me, Dareese?" Tommy said as her eyes watered. "Tell me why you did it. Tell me why you really did time in prison for me, Dollar. I mean, I really want to know!"

"Tommy, what do you want from me, for me to tell you a bunch of shit that you want to hear like I do these other hoes on the street?" Dollar shouted.

"Say it," Tommy said snatching Dollar's face up by the chin. "Why'd you do it? Just say it. Just say it! Do you know why I would have done it for you? Because I loved you...I love you."

Tommy stood before Dollar crying. The only thing she wanted him to do was to put his arms around her and hold her. He didn't even have to say the words back to her. She just needed him to show his love by comforting her. She had concealed her feelings for Dollar for years. She had acted like *just one of the boys* almost all of her life just to be close to him. The charade was over.

Tommy looked up at Dollar who had tears in his eyes. He had never had a single inkling that Tommy felt this way about him. He stared into Tommy's eyes trying to absorb her hurt. Tommy took Dollar's comforting gesture the wrong way and began to kiss Dollar. He tried to fight her tongue but inhaled it instead. Dollar closed his eyes and kissed Tommy like a preacher had just granted him permission to kiss the bride. Suddenly Dollar opened his eyes and snapped out of the fairy tale and back to reality. He immediately pushed Tommy away.

"Dollar, I don't want to confuse things. I just wanna...." Tommy said as Dollar cut her words short.

"I know what you just wanna. You just wanna trick your way out of your debt to me like you do with those fake ass ballers in the club. This is one debt you can't repay on your back, Tommy. I need you in order for this shit to go down, so you can cut this big act you're putting on," Dollar said throwing down the shoebox filled with the letters.

Dollar saw stars. He didn't know what had hit him. It took a few seconds before he realized that it was Tommy's uppercut that had hit him. When he threw down those letters he might as well have punched Tommy in the stomach.

"Get out," Tommy said swallowing a few tears along with her pride. She was crying so hard that she thought she would become intoxicated from the salt from the tears that had made their way from her eyes to her tongue.

"Thomasena," Dollar said.

"Get the fuck out, Dollar!"

"I'll go," Dollar said licking the blood from his lip. "But I need you, T. Eleven o'clock. I need you there, T. You owe me. Put all this bullshit aside, damn'it you owe me, T."

"You're unbelievable," Tommy said. "Do you think I'm one of these women you manage to wrap around your finger and control? Well I'm not, Dollar. I don't owe you. I don't owe you shit. You made a decision years ago, you live with it."

. Dollar could see the pain in Tommy's eyes as she stood before him opening up her soul. This was so hard for her. It hurt her and he knew it. At that very moment he could see that Tommy loved him with pain.

"I'm not trying to hear this, Tommy," Dollar said going back into hard mode. "You've got a choice to make, your debt to me, or these bullshit feelings you think you have for me."

"I love you. Loving you is my choice."

"Will you shut the fuck up with that shit, Tommy. Don't do this."

"I'm in love with you. I've always been in love with you. You can't tell me you've never felt it," Tommy persisted, unable to control that life altering thing called love.

"Save that bullshit for a nigga who gives a fuck. Save it for one of them tricks down at the club. Save it for someone who loves you back. Cause I don't." Dollar paused. He knew his words cut Tommy like a knife. "I'm doing this shit with or without you, Tommy. You riding?"

Tommy stood frozen. Blood oozed from her ego. She had been shot down at high noon. She was dead and therefore couldn't speak.

"Fine," Dollar said as he stormed out of Tommy's house slamming the door behind him.

Dollar stood on the other side of the closed door. He couldn't believe Tommy tried to drop the love bomb on him. He had always known that Tommy had some weird type of love for him, but the *in love* thang...never that.

Mixing love with money was a definite no-no. Besides, Tommy was like one of the boys and Dollar just couldn't get pass that. Crossing the line of a friendship was surely the end of one. Yeah, Dollar loved Tommy, but not like that. He loved her like a little sister. He loved her like she was blood. He would never cross that line. Once the friendship line is crossed, shit ain't never the same. Tommy meant too much to Dollar for that. Hopefully by thinking such thoughts, Dollar would be able to convince himself of them.

Dollar knew that his rejecting Tommy was killing her softly and that she probably hated his guts. But their love ran deep and he knew that although she was mad at him now, that she would get over it. If he were to cross the line just to appease her emotions he would eventually break her heart. He had to choose the better of the two evils.

So instead of turning around and going back into Tommy's house and satisfying her feelings (which the dawg in Dollar was barking for him to do), he walked away. He walked away with a genuine friendship that he could take to his grave no matter what.

***

Dollar had just treated Hennessey to dinner at the hotel restaurant of which they had their first date. Dollar was clean as hell, suited up with a hat to match. Although he ordinarily didn't get hardcore GQ, it was as if he subconsciously wanted to show Hennessey that he had another side to him that could perhaps be molded.

Hennessey, sportin' a satin like Oscar De Larenta pant and top set, rambled on and on the entire time during dinner about how well Dollar's investments she had made for him were doing. Dollar never heard a word she said. He couldn't stop thinking about his fight with Tommy.

After dinner Hennessey talked Dollar into a trip to the park behind the hotel building.

"Yes, indeedy. Those investments I made for you are looking real good," Hennessey said to Dollar as she pitched a penny into the fountain.

"What was that one for?" Dollar asked not responding to her statement about his investments.

"Huh?" Hennessey said.

"The coin you just threw into the fountain, what did you wish for with it?"

"If I tell you then it might not come true."

Dollar dropped his head and stared off into space.

"Here," Hennessey said placing a penny into Dollar's hand.

"Oh you want me to make a wish too?" Dollar asked.

"No, that's a penny for your thoughts. You probably only said ten words max at dinner and now you're sitting here like you just lost your best friend. Like P. Diddy was lookin' after him and J-Lo's split," Hennessey joked. "What's going on?"

Dollar wanted so badly to spill everything that was on his mind to Hennessey. He wanted to tell her about his bid, and about how he came about being a free man again. He wanted to share with her about Mya's pregnancy and the abortion he was forcing her to have. He wanted her advice on his situation with Tommy. He wanted to tell her about his brother and his mother. He wanted to tell her how he was really starting to have feelings for her.

Hennessey could sense Dollar's hesitation. She knew he wanted to talk. If only she could just get him to.

"I know you think I'm just some stuck up broad who works in a bank who probably ain't never did a day without, but that's not true. Shit ain't always been easy for me. So you can talk to me, Dollar. You'd be surprised that I just might be able to understand and help you out."

Dollar looked at Hennessey sitting there in her $200 Italian shoes and top designer outfit. He thought about how hard his mother had worked during her life and was never able to afford items like that. Dollar began to laugh.

"What?" Hennessey said. "Did I say something funny?"

"Oh, you've had it rough alright. The world can just look at you sitting there and see right away just how hard you've had it. Let me guess," Dollar said as he began to read Hennessey like a book. "You were born into a middle class two parent home. Your mother's pregnancy with you was planned. Her and your father were married at the time and they probably still are to this day. As a little girl you took tap and ballet. Your mother put you in all sorts of beauty pageants of which, by the way, you always placed top three. You won spelling bees and shit throughout grade school and was Captain of the cheerleading squad in high school. You were voted most likely to succeed and even gave the commencement speech at graduation. You turned down your acceptance to Yale and Harvard so that you could go to school close to home. You graduated college, on a full scholarship of course, at the top of your class and never once had to go job hunting because offers came pouring into you. Yeah, what a hard knock life."

"You know what? Fuck you," Hennessey said as she stood up from the bench she was sitting on. "I've tried to be nothing but kind to you and all you want to do is sit here casting these expursions about me."

"Oh my," Dollar said, covering his mouth as if he were the monkey who could speak no evil. "I'm casting expursions. Is that the same thing as casting stones? The next time I want to have a conversation with you I guess I'll have to bring my dictionary, seeming I didn't go to college and all."

Dollar was cracking himself up. This showed by the

way he hunched over in laughter while holding his stomach. Of course only he knew that his mind was so heavy that he was laughing to keep from crying.

"I know what you're doing," Hennessey said. "I see right through you, Dollar. You tryin' to run me off because you're scared."

"Pssttt, scared of what?"

"You're scared that you're gonna fall in love with me," Hennessey paused. "And that I'm gonna fall in love with you back. You don't know how to act about that and it scares you to death. You're scared to let me in there." Hennessey pointed to Dollar's head, mugging him with her index finger. "and there." Hennessey pointed to Dollar's heart. "You're afraid of what I might find. So instead of facing your fears you wanna try to run me off with words. How many other girls have you run off with your words, Dollar? Well, daddy I'm grown and words don't bother me. I ain't going no where."

Hennessey walked over to Dollar and tried to run her hand down his bald head. Dollar pushed her hands away.

"Don't flatter yourself," Dollar said, angry at the truth Hennessey had just spoken. "You think you the only skirt in town? You think you the first chick to ever fall in love with Dollar Bill? Plenty of bitches love me. Love don't scare me. So why don't you take your one woman act and perform it for a brother who gives a damn."

"You win. I'm not going to fight you, Dollar. My job is done here," Hennessey said, walking away.

"What the fuck do you mean your job is done?" Dollar said, running up behind her and grabbing her by the arm. "Was I just some charity case, some thug you bumped into on the streets and decided to be nice to? Is that why you ain't never said hey, Dollar, come over to my place so we can just kick it? You afraid I'm gonna steal your silverware or something? You afraid I'm gon' dirty up your couch if I sit on it?"

Hennessey could see the hurt in Dollar's eyes. There was still a chance that she could get to him-get inside him. She decided to be the bigger person.

"I'm sorry," Hennessey said as she was swallowed up by the look in Dollar's eyes. "I didn't mean it like that. I just want to help you. That's all I've been trying to do. I wish you could see that."

Dollar released Hennessey's arm and just stared off into space.

"Look, I don't know where we took a wrong turn, but can we just start over, please?" Hennessey asked.

Dollar looked at Hennessey and sucked his teeth. He looked at her like she wasn't shit and walked away.

Once again Dollar was running from emotions, not only his own, but a woman's he cared about.

"If only these bitches would just let a nigga get money first, then everything would be cool," Dollar thought to himself. I don't need this bullshit. *Not right now, not when I'm trying to stay focused.*

"Excuse me, sir, but do you have the time?" Hennessey said tapping Dollar on his shoulder.

"What are you doing, Hennessey?" Dollar asked.

"I'm starting over," she replied.

"You're oil and I'm water."

"Opposites attract."

"You're not going to give up are you?"

"Nuh, huh," Hennessey said giving Dollar a sexy smile. "Dollar, you want to be saved. I don't know all of the demons you're running from, but let me be your Kryptonite."

Hennessey kissed Dollar on his lips and said, "Let me save you."

Dollar leaned closer into Hennessey and planted a kiss right on her lips. He allowed his hands to glide down to her butt and he pulled himself against her. Lost in the moment

Hennessey began to kiss Dollar hard.

"Let's go to your place," Dollar said, as he pulled a hand around to Hennessey's breast.

"Huh, what?" Hennessey said in a dazed like manner. "Wait a minute. We just met. We can't do this on our first time meeting."

"Fuck role playing," Dollar said. "I wanna fuck you."

"Umm umm. I can't," Hennessey said drifting back into reality.

"Come on, Miss lady. Stop playing," Dollar said as he pulled Hennessey tighter into him and started kissing on her neck.

Those heated kisses Dollar was branding on Hennessey's neck were setting her pussy on fire. The loud short deep breaths she was taking let Dollar know that she was feeling him. As Dollar grabbed Hennessey's crotch through her pants he could feel the warm moisture.

"Dollar stop. Don't," Hennessey whispered.

"You know you don't want me to stop," Dollar continued.

"Yes I do," Hennessey said snapping fully back into reality.

Dollar stopped and looked at a less passionate and more serious Hennessey.

"Fuck it!" Dollar said under his breath as he turned and walked away.

"Dollar, wait," Hennessey said going after him.

"I don't have time for your good girl-bad boy games. I'm not a fuckin' toy, Hennessey. Why don't you go find some suit you work with and pull this act on him?"

"Dollar, wait!" Hennessey called. "You don't understand. Please don't take this personal. It's not that I don't want to, I just can't...right now."

"No, you don't understand," Dollar shouted as he proceeded towards the hotel and signaled the valet driver to retrieve his car.

Once the driver brought Dollar's car around, Dollar tipped him a $20 bill and got inside and drove off, leaving Hennessey standing behind, alone.

Chapter 18

Get Money...The Final Chapter

Dollar stood outside of the salon watching Mya do some woman's nails for a half-hour before going in. He hadn't talked to her since he had the fight about the baby with her. He knew he needed to holler at her to see where her head was at, but more importantly, he wanted to make sure her tummy hadn't grown any.

When Dollar walked inside the salon there was immediate dead silence and all eyes were on him. "*Bitches always runnin' they mouth, black or white*," Dollar thought as eyes rolled at him and necks snapped. He could tell Mya had confided her situation with them.

"Mya, hey," Dollar said.

Mya pretended as though he wasn't even there and continued putting the finishing touches, a coat of clear nail polish, on the woman's hands she was working on.

"Can I talk to you outside for a minute," Dollar asked.

"She no talk to you," the little Asian woman hurried over to intercept. "You hurt feelings. You go away."

"It's okay, Leila" Mya said to the Asian woman.

"So you doing okay?" Dollar asked.

"I am now. It would have been nice of you to ask me that a few weeks ago. You didn't even call to make sure I was okay," Mya started to become emotional. "Let me finish her up and I'll meet you outside."

"Cool," Dollar said

Dollar headed back outside. Before the door could even close behind him he heard the jeers and chants start up. Dollar stood outside against his car that was illegally parked in front of the salon. He waited for about five-minutes then decided to just leave, he had pretty much found out what he needed to know. Right as he pulled off he could see Mya walking out. She was wearing a form fitting knit dress. There was no tummy bulge. That's all Dollar wanted to make sure of.

After leaving the salon Dollar stopped off and grabbed him a submarine sandwich from a deli before going home. He pulled into his space in the apartment parking garage, turned the car off and then pulled out his cell phone to make a call. This was the hundredth time Dollar had tried getting in touch with Tommy. Her home phone either rang and rang and rang until voicemail picked up, or whoever answered the phone at the club said she was busy. This time wasn't any different.

Dollar hung up his cell phone and got out of the car. He turned on his car alarm, then headed into the building. As he walked down the hall he noticed a figure standing against his door waiting on him.

Once Dollar realized it was Hennessey he proceeded to take out his keys and unlock his apartment door. Dollar had never seen Hennessey in a casual get up, but tonight she was in a nice pair indigo Guess jeans with a matching jacket. The jeans flared at the bottom where the heel of her three-inch black ankle boots could be seen. She was tight to death, which made it extra hard for Dollar to ignore her presence.

"So you don't see me standing here?" Hennessey said. "So it's like that. That's the game we're going to play with each other?"

"As far as I can tell, you like playing games," Dollar said opening his door.

"Come out with me," Hennessey said. "Kind of like a make-up date. I've missed you."

"Not in the mood, got a lot of shit on my mind," Dollar said, with his back still to Hennessey.

Hennessey looked at Dollar and for some reason the sight of him just broke her heart. He was a big man, but there just seemed to be this little hurt boy inside of him. That little hurt boy was calling for her to rescue him.

"Look, baby," Hennessey said walking up behind Dollar placing her head on his back. He smelled of the scent Domain. It made her want to stay there forever, or at least long enough for the scent to rub off on her so that she could go home smelling like him.

"Let me take you out for a drink. No place loud, just this mellow joint I know. Please," Hennessey said pouting her bottom lip.

How could any man turn down such a plead? Dollar stood there for a moment taking in Hennessey's heart beating against his back. Her heartbeat was calm and tranquil, just the opposite of his, which was rowdy and turbulent. Before obliging to Hennessey's request, Dollar turned around and looked into Hennessey's eyes, eyes that perhaps belonged to the one person that could tame his heart.

***

"I be trying to keep my shit straight. I be trying to keep my shit straight, but the world be going round. I said the world be going round y'all", the poet spoke as the audience was mesmerized by his every word.

Dollar sat at the half-empty poetry spot drinking one shot of Henney after the next.

"Slow down," Hennessey, who had pulled her chair up next to Dollar, said to him. "You putting them drinks away tonight. You sure you're alright? Do you wanna talk to me about anything?"

It was almost as if Hennessey was trying too hard to get into Dollar's head. Dollar wished he had never agreed to go out on the make up date with her.

"I'm good," Dollar replied focusing on the poet's words, but not listening to them. His mind was off in a thousand places.

"Sometimes I fall and I be going round. I said I be going round y'all, round with the world y'all. And I get dizzy. I said I be gettin' dizzy and I get off track. And I be callin' yall, but y'all don't answer. Where y'all at? Where my niggaz is at? I'm callin' y'all. Answer me back like y'all be answering the wax. Where my niggaz is at?" the poet continued.

"I'm ready to dip," Dollar said to Hennessey who was enjoying the poetry.

"You sure?" Hennessey asked.

"Did I sta-sta-stutter?" Dollar replied.

Hennessey looked at Dollar as if he was crazy. She could tell his mind was a million miles away so instead of lashing back at him, she decided to try to comfort him.

"Baby, let's go somewhere and talk. Wanna go to the fountain?" Hennessey asked.

"I don't want to talk," Dollar replied. "I got some shit I have to do."

Dollar needed to get home, sober up and start going over his plan again as his big moment, the moment that would define him as a man of the streets, was only a couple days away. This was his meal ticket to easy street for life. With this transaction pending, he couldn't possibly give Hennessey the attention she deserved. He was liable to say some shit that would fuck up any chance of starting something real with her. He needed to take a break from her and then start fresh once his mind was back on track.

Robbing a bank was a major step up from sticking up people. He was taking on a franchise. A franchise that was always prepared for people such as himself. There wasn't no catching a bank slippin'. You just had to go in and do the damn thang.

"What is it you have to do?" Hennessey inquired.

"What the fuck is it with all the questions?" Dollar said loudly which made the poet forget his words. "I said I'm ready to go, so let's go!"

Dollar quickly exited the club with Hennessey right behind him.

"You go ahead. I'm gonna catch a cab home," Dollar said to Hennessey.

"I drove you here so I'll drive you back home. You're in no condition to be trying to get home by yourself."

"I want to be alone," Dollar said.

"But I don't," Hennessey said grabbing Dollar by the arm. He stopped and looked into her passionate eyes. Before Dollar could reject her, she began to French kiss him. Dollar was beginning to get into it before he managed to push Hennessey away.

"Naw, I know what this is about. You just trying to cuddle and shit. You want to kiss all on me and get me all worked up and leave me hangin'. I'm straight on that shit."

"No, you're wrong. Not tonight. I'm ready," Hennessey said, as she grabbed Dollar by the back of his head and pulled him into her. She kissed him hard, tongue all down his throat. She pressed her breast up against him and began to moan. She could feel Dollar's manhood getting hard. After a couple of minutes of kissing, Hennessey stepped back with her hands in Dollars and stared into his eyes.

"So what do you say?" Hennessey asked. "You wanna go to my place?"

"Yeah, but just to talk," Dollar said with a mischievous grin.

Back at Hennessey's condo she lit an inscent and candles. She fixed her and Dollar a glass of wine and excused herself into her bedroom to go slip on something comfortable.

When Hennessey returned, she was wearing a powder blue lace two-piece boy leg lingerie set. She walked into the kitchen and did a shot of Vodka. She then strutted over to the Oriental rug in front of her fireplace and stretched across it. She signaled for Dollar, who was sitting on the couch, to come lay next to her by patting the floor with her hand.

Dollar, who was still buzzing from the Henney he had drank earlier in the night and the glass of wine, made his way next to her.

"You sure you wanna.....," Dollar said as Hennessey cut him off.

"Shhhhhh," Hennessey said putting her index finger over Dollar's lips. She then put her lips against his and began to kiss him. She sucked the taste of the liquor off of Dollar's tongue. She slowly pushed Dollar down and climbed on top of him and began to aid him in the removal of his clothing.

Softly Hennessey kissed Dollar, first on the forehead and then on each eyelid. Once Dollar was fully undressed they each worked on getting Hennessey out of her rags.

Butt naked the two lay there on the floor caressing one another. They would hold one another for a while before Dollar would find himself below Hennessey's belly button. Dollar did not think about it twice, nor did he hesitate before lashing his tongue out at Hennessey's private spot.

Hennessey laid there moaning a silent shout before finding herself in a quiver. If she wasn't mistaken, Dollar had spelled out her full name with his tongue. His first time going down low was undetectable by Hennessey who produced gushes of sweet juices down Dollar's throat.

Looking up at the high beam ceiling as Dollar caressed her, Hennessey knew it was time to give herself completely to

Dollar. She had fought off these feelings for some time, but tonight, she would throw in the towel. There was no turning back. Now, she was in too deep. She closed her eyes and allowed him to enter her world.

Dollar had never been so nervous with a woman in his life, not even with Pam during his first time ever having sex. It was just something about Hennessey that made him feel faultless, that he couldn't touch her the wrong way, caress her the wrong way. He felt like he had already made love to her a thousand times before. She was a perfect fit.

"There's something about you, baby," Dollar whispered in Hennessey's ear as he slowly dipped in and out of her, mesmerized by the sound of her wetness.

"Talk to me," Hennessey whispered. "Tell me what that something is. I like to talk and fuck at the same time."

"Oh shit," Dollar said turned on by Hennessey's words.

"What is it about me?"

"That something about you is everything that you are," Dollar said as he plunged deep inside of her. Dollar passionately stroked his body against Hennessey's as the muscles in his arms flexed. It was as if he was doing push-ups over top of her body.

Tears began to flow down Hennessey's face. She had fought the temptation of giving her body to Dollar for so long and now it was too late to turn things around. She hated the fact that he felt so fuckin' good inside of her. She hated it because it made her want him even more. Hennessey let herself go.

Hennessey wasn't afraid to hump with Dollar as she rocked her hips back and forth, forth and back. The faster Dollar went, the more determined she was to keep up with him.

"Look at me," Hennessey said to Dollar who at the time had his eyes closed. He was taking in every moment of being inside of Hennessey. "Open your eyes and look at me."

Dollar followed Hennessey's orders and began looking into Hennessey's eyes. He wasn't even embarrassed as she witnessed the expressions on his face caused by the pleasurable feeling of being trapped by her walls. Formerly trapped between the walls of a jail cell, Dollar now felt trapped between the walls of paradise. He wanted to bottle up the way he felt at that very moment.

"Go faster," Hennessey ordered.

Dollar began to increase his pace. In and out of her he plunged, not breaking eye contact once.

"Faster," Hennessey ordered.

Dollar pulled his dick out just enough to make sure the condom was in place before he pushed himself deep inside of her. Faster and harder he dove into Hennessey. He was on fire. He never wanted this feeling to end.

The faster Dollar pumped, the wider Hennessey seemed to open up for him. Still staring into one another's eyes, they grinded and pounded like it was the end of the world, like it was the last time they would ever make love. Dollar could feel the blood rushing through his vessel.

"I don't want to cum yet," Dollar said, attempting to ease up.

"Fuck that," Hennessey said as she grabbed hold of Dollars ass cheeks and pulled him hard against her. Hennessey whirled her hips, flexin' her pussy muscle tight around Dollar's penis, which made Dollar lose it.

"Fuck," Dollar said as he began to jerk inside of Hennessey. Sweat dripped off of his forehead onto Hennessey's face. She felt as though she was drowning.

"Oh, God," Hennessey screamed.

"Oh, shit, baby," Dollar said.

"Cum with me," Hennessey said as she began to kiss Dollar. "Cum with me. I'm cumin'. Cum with me."

As the two climaxed together, they felt as though the room was spinning. They had both gotten caught up in the feeling. They were tipsy off of one another.

Dollar and Hennessey laid in position breathing heavily for a few minutes.

"Baby, you felt so good," Dollar said, finally rolling from off top of Hennessey.

"You too," Hennessey responded. Hennessey stared into space as if her mind was a million miles away.

"What's wrong?" Dollar asked. "Did I hurt you or something?"

Hennessey couldn't help but softly chuckle. "No, you were great," she replied.

"Then what is it?" For the first time in a long time, Dollar actually gave a damn about somebody other than himself. "Tell me what's wrong?"

"It's nothing," Hennessey hesitated. "It's nothing at all."

Dollar kissed Hennessey softly on her lips and laid down next to her, wearing what appeared to be a permanent smile.

Hennessey turned away from Dollar and closed her eyes. For the next couple of hours Dollar watched Hennessey sleep. He watched over her like a mother bear does its cub. Something about looking at Hennessey lay there made Dollar want to protect her. He wanted to pick her up and run far away with her to a place where it was just the two of them, to a place where he could say fuck the rest of the world. At the same time he felt safe and protected. It was a feeling he had long needed. At that very moment Dollar knew that his life was about to change.

***

The next day Dollar spent going over the plan with Ral. He sent Ral, with plan in hand, to relay to Tommy. He knew Tommy wasn't trying to hear from him, but he knew she would always have his back. When it came to Dollar Bill, her heart was more forceful than her head. Dollar knew this.

With the big moment in their hustling careers being less than 14 hours away. Dollar was in a zone. He hadn't turned on any lights or the television. At the moment the only sound that could be heard was the sound of Tupac and Scarface coming from his CD player, "Born with less, but ya still precious...." The words echoed through Dollar's head.

Suddenly, the ringing of Dollar's cell phone made him jump.

"Hello," Dollar said.

"I've got great news," Hennessey said with excitement.

"I'm on my way over to share it with you."

"Not tonight, Miss lady," Dollar said, as he laid in the bed in anticipation of the following day's event. In all actuality, he wanted nothing more than to be able to make love to Hennessey again. But he couldn't focus on that right now.

"What do you mean not tonight? This is absolutely, positively the best news ever. I'm going to grab a bottle of Dom and I'm on my way."

"Hennessey, not tonight," Dollar said with authority as silence occupied the phone line. "Look, I'm sorry. I don't mean to yell. It's just that tonight is really bad. I'll call you tomorrow."

"Oh, I get it," Hennessey said. "Now that you got what you wanted, you don't have time for me."

Hennessey's words hurt Dollar. He hated the fact that he had to allow her to think just that even though it was the furthest thing from the truth. He hadn't gotten what he wanted from Hennessey, not by far.

"You know it ain't even like that," Dollar said. "Look, Hennessey, I promise I'll call you tomorrow. Things are going to be different between us, you'll see. I promise."

Dollar hung up. He could hear Hennessey trying to get in one last word, but he closed the flap on his cell phone and closed his eyes. He felt bad, but he would make it up to her. But for now he needed to keep his mind focused and prepare for the next day's events. Although he adored Hennessey and wanted her to be a permanent fixture in his life, Dollar was in gangsta mode. No way was a bitch and her feelings coming before him and his money. Hennessey would be there after tomorrow. Opportunity might not.

Dollar picked up his phone and dialed Tommy's number. The voice mail picked up and Dollar left a message,

"Eleven o'clock tomorrow morning. Eleven o'clock a.m. I need you, T."

***

It was 10:50 a.m. and Dollar was sitting across the street from the bank on a bus stop bench gnawing at his manicured nails. If he wasn't gnawing on his nails he was tugging at the knit hat he had rolled up on top of his head. He was nervous, not at the fact that he was about to rob a bank for major paper, but that he wasn't 100% certain that his back up would show.

Tommy said she wasn't with it, but Dollar knew in his heart Tommy wouldn't let him down. She couldn't. Ral was game, but if he got caught up in some pussy or the pipe, Dollar was screwed.

But his attitude, as always, was fuck it. Many of men had robbed a bank solo. He could pull it off. He had been in the bank a hundred times. He had cased the joint. He knew they only had two security guards and that one took a ten-minute break at 11:15 a.m. At 11:00 a.m. Tommy was to occupy Hennessey's attention while he and Ral handled their business as soon as the security guard left his post.

"I gotta shit," Dollar thought to himself as his stomach rumbled in knots. This was it, though. Dollar wasn't about to turn back. Everything was going to go off without a hitch. He had to keep telling himself that.

"In and out, nobody gets hurt," Dollar thought. *"I'm going in this bitch, get the loot and live like a Don. Fuck it. If push comes to shove, I can do this shit. I don't need them."*

Dollar felt that deep down inside he needed Tommy and Ral. They were his courage, his sidekicks who had always made him feel superior. But then he remembered Romeo's words: *Whenever a cat gets iffy on you, like they wanna bitch out, cut 'em the fuck off. They useless.* Maybe he didn't need them after all. This may very well have been the best advice his father could have given him.

It was 11 o'clock and there was no sight of Tommy or Ral. All of Dollar's money was tied up in that bank. The quick easy change from Redd's place was no more. He had to do the damn thang. He could do it. He could do it alone, after all, he was Dollar Bill. Dollar picked up the gym bag he had with him and headed towards the bank.

***

"Excuse me, sir," Dollar said to the single security guard standing at the bank entrance, underneath the surveillance camera. "Can you tell me where the deposit slips are?"

"Oh sure," the security guard answered.

As the security guard turned to point, Dollar pulled his knit hat down over his face, grabbed the security guard's hand and bent his arm behind his back. He removed the security guard's gun from his holster and put it to his head.

"Nobody fuckin' move," Dollar said at an even tone, not too loud, but loud enough for everybody to know he meant business. "Put your noses on the ground."

No one hesitated to follow their given instructions. With the security guard in hand, Dollar made his way over to one of the tellers. He then handed her the gym bag and ordered her to fill it with money. The teller nervously hit up every drawer in the joint before handing Dollar the overstuffed bag full of money.

"Everybody count to 100 Mississippis," Dollar shouted. "If anybody tries to make a move before then, they're dead."

Just then, Hennessey came running out of her office like she was one of Charlie's Angels.

"Detective Roe," the guard shouted to Hennessey. "Get down. He's got a gun."

"Detective Roe?" Dollar said looking at Hennessey puzzled.

Hennessey trembled as she stood before Dollar, staring him dead in his eyes with her gun in hand.

"Dareese," Hennessey said. "I know that's you. You don't want to do this. Let me help you, please. You don't want to go back to prison."

"Detective! You undercover? You a token?" Dollar shouted as he stood with his gun still aimed at the security guard's head, but looking at Hennessey. "So this is why you always wanted to *help me*. I was just a job. I was strictly business to you." Everything in Dollar wanted to point the gun at Hennessey and blow her fuckin' brains out. Dollar couldn't believe this was happening to him. Dollar couldn't believe he had been caught slippin'. He had been set up.

"Come on, Dareese," Hennessey said. "Let me talk to you for a minute. Just come back into my office so we can talk."

"I'm not going back to no fuckin' office. You talk to me right here and right now...right now damn'it! Why, Hennessey? Why'd you do this to me?" Dollar asked trying to hide the visible hurt in his eyes. "I thought...I thought you and me could...Fuckin' why?"

"Ohio put me on you, to get in good with you. Just in case you slipped, I was supposed to be there when you fell. I'm sorry, Dareese. God, I'm so sorry. You don't know how bad I wanted shit to be different, how many nights I thought about how cool it would be to know you in another life," Hennessey confessed. "But I thought I could help you do right. I thought maybe I could change you."

"*But you did change me,*" Dollar thought to himself. "How in the fuck were you going to change me, Hennessey? Did you really think that love conquers all shit was really going to work?"

Hennessey nodded in the affirmative.

"So when we made lo...," Dollar had to pause. He was so hurt and angry that he couldn't get his words out. "When you slept with me, was that work?" Dollar asked.

Hennessey once again nodded in the affirmative.

"So what if, hypothetically speaking, I did fall in love with you, you know, just say that I was really diggin' you and decided to live in your world. Could we have, you know, been a couple? I just want to know, Hennessey."

Hennessey nodded her head.

"Speak the fuck up!" Dollar shouted. "I can't hear you."

"No, No!" Hennessey answered. "I would have found some way to break it off with you, a job transfer or something. Then I would have gone back to Ohio with my husband and son."

"Husband...son," Dollar said fighting so hard to hold in the tears that the pain of hearing Hennessey's words created. "So that's what all those seminars were, huh...trips back to Ohio to be with your husband and son?"

Dollar couldn't believe it. This isn't how shit was supposed to go down. This isn't what was supposed to happen. Hennessey was going to be that woman that turned Dollar into an honest man, that woman who kept him honest.

"But, I got good news for you, Dareese. Your investment, it shot through the roof. You have enough money to live at the Waldorf Astoria everyday for the rest of your life damn near. That's what I needed to tell you last night," Hennessey said, as her infamous smile spread across her face. "Don't do this. Put the gun down. You're only at an attempted armed robbery charge. You can walk out of here with as little as five years. After that, you can take all of your money and settle down, find a nice girl..."

"Five years," Dollar laughed, interrupting Hennessey's lie. "I'm a fuckin' ex felon who was in for life who got out on a wild card. Do you think all I'm gon' get is five years? Hell they wanted my black ass back in the joint from the moment they let me out. They never had any real intention on ever letting me live my life did they? They've been expecting me to fuck up. You're proof of that. And when I did, I was going right back to jail, huh? Well fuck that, and fuck you, bitch. I ain't going back to jail."

Dollar cocked his gun.

Hennessey just stood there unable to speak, trying to remind herself that this was strictly business and that her relationship with Dollar was for hire. Hennessey had tried so hard not to look deep enough within him to find the good. But she knew underneath his hard exterior was a young man with dreams from the ghetto who got caught up in reality's nightmare.

"Say somethin' God damn'it!" Dollar said as he jerked the gun, scaring the security guard and forcing Hennessey to cock her weapon.

"Oh, it's like that?" Dollar said to her.

"Please, Dareese....," Hennessey pleaded.

"Stop fucking calling me that. My name is Dollar, Dollar Bill muthafuckas. Y'all hear that?" Dollar said to the people in the bank as he removed the knit hat from over his face. "Dollar, Dollar Bill, y'all!"

"Okay, Dollar," Hennessey said in an apologetic tone. "Just think, when you get out, you'll be a rich man. You'll have something to look forward to."

At this point Hennessey's words created an internal inferno in Dollar's body. His eyes bulged with tears as he gripped the gun tighter. He didn't know how much longer he could go on with this alone. He had never expected to be broken down like this. He needed his back up.

"*Where the fuck are my boys?*" is all Dollar could think. The three of them could have handled this shit. It didn't have to be so fucked up. Dollar gazed over at the door hoping to see Tommy and Ral coming through it.

Catching Dollar off guard, fearing for her life and the life of the security guard, Hennessey used her quick and better judgment and began to fire multiple shots at Dollar.

All of a sudden one of the bank customers jumped up from off of the floor and began to fire a gun. The customer appeared to be a man who was dressed in a tan jogging suit with a matching ball cap. Dark sunglasses covered his eyes. The customer fired a shot to the security guard's leg that hunched him over and away from Dollar. He then fired another fatal gunshot to the security guard's head. Quickly, trained and skilled, the customer put one in Hennessey's chest, which took her down, but not to her grave.

The customer then walked over to Dollar and placed his head on Dollar's bloody chest. Dollar had taken a bullet to the chest, stomach and leg. Dollar's heart was beating fast and hard. It was as if his heart was going to jump right out of his chest. Dollar was paralyzed. He couldn't move. His bucked eyes stared straight up as his heart beat like African drums.

"It burns," Dollar said. "Shit, it burns."

"I'm so sorry I was late," Tommy said as she removed the dark sunglasses from her face. "Fuckin' around with that Ral. Went to get him this morning. Son of a bitch overdosed. I couldn't save him this time, D. I went to a pay phone and called 911 then tried to get here as fast as I could. I see I wasn't in time to save you either."

Tommy raised her head and looked at Dollar who couldn't respond. He looked deep into Tommy's eyes, recognizing her, he tried to speak, but no words came out. He wanted to tell her how the bullets felt like heated pokers spearing through his body. He wanted to tell her thank you for showing up and that it was okay that she was late. He wanted to tell her that he loved her too. Right now, with his life flashing before his eyes, he had no pride. Dollar had no ego or persona to hide behind. He loved her. He loved Tommy and he wanted so badly to be able to let her know, but Dollar couldn't speak.

A single tear made its way out of each of Dollar's eyes. Tommy kissed Dollar on his lips that were seeping with blood. It took every ounce of strength in her not to let the tears fall from her eyes. She then grabbed the gym bag full of money that was laying beside Dollar, placed the sunglasses back on her face and exited the bank.

As Tommy walked to her car she could hear sirens approaching. Police cars whizzed by her as she put the key into the ignition and drove off. Everything had turned out as planned after all. Tommy knew that the anonymous tip she had called in to Hennessey from inside the bank lobby only seconds before

Dollar entered, would give her plenty of time to work out *her* plan before the cops arrived. Dollar had taught Tommy to let other muthafuckas hustle and then catch them slippin'. He had trained her well. He just never imagined that he would one day be one of those muthafuckas that she would catch slippin'.

Like the song says, love will make you do right. Love will make you do wrong. Tommy's love for Dollar over the years was proof of that cliché. But in the end, she had to make a choice.

As Tommy drove away from the scene of the crime she removed the baseball cap and let her long hair flow in the wind. Tommy then glanced down at the bag full of money and was sure over $500,000 was stuffed inside of it. That meant that after paying Storm and Thunder for the M&M she had ordered on Ral, she would have plenty left over to pack up her nieces, move to the East Coast, perhaps, and open up her bookstore.

Looking at herself in the rear view mirror, Tommy wondered if she would be able to live with the decision she had made against her comrades. She picked up a stack of the money from the gym bag. She ran it underneath her nose and inhaled deeply. After taking in the scent, that aphrodisiac to muthafuckas from the streets, Tommy exhaled. A smile found it's way to her mouth. It was a smile that was a cross between a seductive grin and a mischievous smirk. It was an "I'm that bitch smile". Yeah, she could live with the decision she had made. She could live with it just fine.

***

Inside the bank Dollar laid on the lobby floor barely holding onto his life. It was true what they say about one's life flashing before their eyes. Dollar thought about his brother and all of the times they had shared, the times they hadn't shared and the times they would now never get to share. "*Which of the dead men pictured on currency wasn't a president*?" was a question that popped into Dollar's head. It was a question that he could have asked his little brother.

Ironically enough, Dollar even thought about his father. He thought about Romeo's last ditch effort to make things right by him and his family. He gave his life for Dollar, to give Dollar back to his family, back to the streets. He wanted Dollar to be able to do for them what he couldn't. Dollar had been too bitter and selfish to appreciate the sacrifice. But now, now that it no longer fuckin' mattered, Dollar understood.

All of the dirt Dollar had done paraded through his mind as he laid near death. Dollar even thought back to his days of being locked-up. Jail was hell and life was hell, but now, with all the fucked up shit Dollar had done, he would truly experience hell. No way would the doors of heaven be open for this gansta, or would they?

Dollar thought of Crissy's words back when he was in the jail infirmary, "God forgives us all." As Dollar took his last breath, he hoped that Crissy was right.

TRIPLE CROWN PUBLICATIONS

ORDER FORM

Triple Crown Publications
P.O. Box 7212
Columbus, OH 43205

NAME ______________________

ADDRESS ______________________

____

CITY ______________________

STATE ______________________

ZIP ______________________

BOOKS AVAILABLE

#QTY	TITLE	PRICE
	GANGSTA	$15.00
	Let That Be The Reason	$15.00
	A Hustler's Wife	$15.00
	The GAME	$15.00
	Black	$15.00
	Dollar Bill	$15.00
	Project Chick	$15.00
	Road Dawgz	$15.00
	Blinded	$15.00

SHIPPING/HANDLING (Via U.S. Priority Mail) **$ 3.50 (per book)**

TOTAL **$**________

FORMS OF ACCEPTED PAYMENTS:
Postage Stamps, Institutional Checks & Money Orders